HIT . . . AND RUN

Charlie raised the small radio transmitter that would set off the explosive charge. The small red LED light gave a very faint glow in the blackness of the alley. Charlie looked back up the alley to make sure nobody and no vehicles had entered, blocking his quick exit.

Charlie pushed the switch down on the handset detonator and the windows blew out of the van with the explosion. Rashad's head was severed completely from his body, and Stinky's right hand and arm were still attached to the duffel bag, but were separated from his body. The whistle, now turned inside out, had embedded itself in the side of his neck, but missed the jugular vein. He immediately started screaming. Down at the corner, Alexander dropped to the ground, covering his head with both arms protectively.

Charlie was already sprinting toward the other end of the alley.

Titles by Don Bendell

CROSSBOW

The Criminal Investigation Detachment Series

CRIMINAL INVESTIGATION DETACHMENT
BROKEN BORDERS
BAMBOO BATTLEGROUND

DETACHMENT DELTA

DETACHMENT
DELTA

DON BENDELL

BERKLEY BOOKS, NEW YORK

THE BERKLEY PUBLISHING GROUP
Published by the Penguin Group
Penguin Group (USA) Inc.
375 Hudson Street, New York, New York 10014, USA
Penguin Group (Canada), 90 Eglinton Avenue East, Suite 700, Toronto, Ontario M4P 2Y3, Canada
(a division of Pearson Penguin Canada Inc.)
Penguin Books Ltd., 80 Strand, London WC2R 0RL, England
Penguin Group Ireland, 25 St. Stephen's Green, Dublin 2, Ireland (a division of Penguin Books Ltd.)
Penguin Group (Australia), 250 Camberwell Road, Camberwell, Victoria 3124, Australia
(a division of Pearson Australia Group Pty. Ltd.)
Penguin Books India Pvt. Ltd., 11 Community Centre, Panchsheel Park, New Delhi–110 017, India
Penguin Group (NZ), 67 Apollo Drive, Rosedale, North Shore 0632, New Zealand
(a division of Pearson New Zealand Ltd.)
Penguin Books (South Africa) (Pty.) Ltd., 24 Sturdee Avenue, Rosebank, Johannesburg 2196,
South Africa

Penguin Books Ltd., Registered Offices: 80 Strand, London WC2R 0RL, England

This is a work of fiction. Names, characters, places, and incidents either are the product of the author's imagination or are used fictitiously, and any resemblance to actual persons, living or dead, business establishments, events, or locales is entirely coincidental. The publisher does not have any control over and does not assume any responsibility for author or third-party websites or their content.

DETACHMENT DELTA

A Berkley Book / published by arrangement with the author

PRINTING HISTORY
Berkley edition / January 2009

Copyright © 2009 by Don Bendell, Inc.
Cover illustration by Edwin Herder. Images by Purestock.
Cover design by Rich Hasselberger.
Interior text design by Kristin del Rosario.

ISBN: 978-0-425-22448-9

BERKLEY®
Berkley Books are published by The Berkley Publishing Group,
a division of Penguin Group (USA) Inc.,
375 Hudson Street, New York, New York 10014.
BERKLEY® is a registered trademark of Penguin Group (USA) Inc.
The "B" design is a trademark of Penguin Group (USA) Inc.

PRINTED IN THE UNITED STATES OF AMERICA

10 9 8 7 6 5 4 3 2 1

Many of the things in my life that I am most proud of occurred because of the influence of hero figures who fascinated me as a child. They, or their characters, set forth ideals for me to try to aspire to that were idealistic and, in most cases, unrealistic, but they gave a young boy a direction to climb—upward. Thank you to each, and this book is dedicated to you or your memory. They are: Jesus Christ, the Ultimate Man ever, and the Son of God, my Savior and Lord; Marion Michael Morrison (John Wayne); Jock O'Mahoney (The Range Rider); Leonard Franklin Slye (Roy Rogers); Michael Ansara (Cochise); Guy Williams (Zorro); Al LaRue (Lash LaRue); Clayton Moore (The Lone Ranger); Jimmy Stewart; Gary Cooper; my uncle Roy Bendell, highly decorated in WWII; Nez Perce Chief Joseph and Lakota (Sioux) Medicine Man and Chief Sitting Bull, both master warriors, orators, and peace-seekers; WWI Medal of Honor recipient Sergeant Alvin York; and my dad, David C. Bendell, who was dedicated to the ideals of scouting and paddled me anytime I said the words "I can't."

Thank you all and may God bless you and your memory.

In respect and admiration,
DON BENDELL

Above all, we must realize that no arsenal, or no weapon in the arsenals of the world, is so formidable as the will and moral courage of free men and women. It is a weapon our adversaries in today's world do not have.

—RONALD REAGAN,
President of the United States of America

FOREWORD

C.A.G., or Combat Applications Group, is the actual term for selection for 1st Special Forces Operational Detachment-Delta (1stSFOD-D), known by most people as Delta Force, or Detachment-Delta, an actual Special Operations unit that, like the fictional 007, has a license to kill. The U.S. Delta Force is the one military unit whose operations and actions are granted complete presidential immunity from the law. Presidential Decision Directive 25 grants Delta Force "freedom from all legal accountability, including exception from the 1878 Posse Comitatus Act"—a statute imposing criminal penalties for anyone using the military for personal gain, domestic law enforcement, or unsanctioned covert operations. Delta Force members are handpicked from the C.A.G.—a classified organization within the Joint Special Operations Command at Fort Bragg, North Carolina. Delta Force soldiers are trained killers—experts in SWAT operations, hostage rescues, raids, assassinations, and execution of enemy forces. They are almost exclusively composed of members of the U.S. Army's elite Special Forces (the Green Berets), although occasionally a few members come from U.S. Navy SEALs, Marine SpecOps command, or Army Rangers. In short, the 1st Special Forces Operational Detachment-Delta is comprised of the world's ultimate warriors.

(Note: Few in the military even know or understand the meaning of C.A.G., and fewer still know the term Combat Applications Group, or that it is the parent group of Delta. C.A.G. is headquartered in a top secret compound at Fort Bragg, North Carolina, and generals, admirals, congressmen, and other government officials cannot even enter it or interview or question the members of its superelite force, who wear civilian clothing, long hair, beards, or whatever is needed to make them blend into society worldwide.)

Authors, historians, reporters, and screenwriters have never been allowed into the compound or allowed access to members of the secret unit. In this novel, in many ways, you will be taken behind the scenes of the real Detachment-Delta. Because of Operational Security (OPSEC) concerns, some actual operations, training methodologies, weapons, and equipment have been purposely altered, although there are no technologies in this book that are truly fictional. Some are very state-of-the-art, and others even reminiscent of James Bond but actually in use by Special Operations operators in the Global War on Terrorism. Some of those operators are in 1st Special Forces Operational Detachment-Delta, the elite of the elite, "the silent group of the quiet professionals."

CHAPTER ONE

Cop Killer

CHARLIE Strongheart looked totally out of place in the restaurant directly across the street from the *Late Show with David Letterman* located in the Ed Sullivan Theater at 1697–1699 Broadway, between West Fifty-third and West Fifty-fourth Streets in midtown Manhattan. The restaurant also had entrances on both side streets and a black-and-white checkerboard tile pattern on the floor. A favorite of many Letterman guests before or after a show appearance, it had standard diner fare. Charlie sat near one of the large picture windows facing the Ed Sullivan Theater. A modern-day traditionalist-looking Lakota (Sioux) man, with ribbon shirt, blue jeans, cowboy boots, beaded belt, and long black braided hair, he was the subject of many stares, especially from several legal secretaries and three female attorneys on their lunch hour, as he was taller than any other man in the room, wider in the shoulders, and had a smaller waistline than most. With a prominent jaw and high cheekbones, he was ruggedly handsome, this especially accented by the deep dimples in both cheeks, and there was an obvious intelligence revealed in his eyes, which were almost black and could stare through a person and seem to see into his very soul. There was a hint of a smile in the corners of his eyes, and if any of the officers of the court who were sneaking occasional glances at him had had a chance they would probably have accompanied him out the door, not realizing that this man was going to expertly execute a New York City cop in a few hours.

A professional assassin, probably one of the best in the world, Charlie noticed everything around him, and he grinned to himself as he saw an obvious hooker leaning against the window, an apparent dealer slipping her what looked like crack cocaine wrapped in plastic, while taking a small roll of bills from her with his other hand. This was done with their hands behind their backs, but toward the large window, where any and all patrons could see the illegal transaction. The red-skinned killer shook his head almost imperceptibly as he thought about how often people treat windows as if they are brick walls. He thought about the times he had seen classy-looking people picking their noses in their automobiles, or singing along with a tune on their car radio with great abandon, as if nobody could see them.

The three attorneys sat at a table laughing and glancing at him from time to time. Their conversation had no legalese as they commented on how good his butt looked when he walked in, how deep his dark eyes looked, and how broad his shoulders were. They started getting more lewd and having fun with one another, but each really did fantasize about him. Little did they know that this was the very night of his dastardly plan.

Charlie finished his meal and headed toward the door with the legal eagles' glances unnoticed, and their fantasies identical but kept to themselves. Then one gasped as a very large street person, his dark ebony skin glistening with sweat and his head literally touching the arch of the doorway, stepped in front of the egressing Indian, blocking his way. The handsome Sioux was much taller than any-body in the restaurant, but this man towered over him.

The street punk stuck out a catcher's mitt–sized hand saying, "Give me some money, Crazy Horse."

Charlie stared up into the tall man's eyes and said softly, "Get a J.O.B."

Charlie started to step around, and the man stepped directly in front of him, a nasty grin on his face, saying, "I don't like to work, Tonto."

Charlie smiled, and his right hand shot out and grabbed the large man by the testicles as he squeezed hard and twisted. The man's face contorted with the twisting, and the women watched openmouthed as his knees bent and a strange sound, almost like a raspy hum, came from his gaping mouth.

Still grinning, Charlie said, "Tell you what, O.J., just go back to the country club and beg for money there."

He let go and walked past the man, who fell on one knee, holding his groin and moaning, as the prettiest attorney chuckled and said to the others, "I have vacation coming up, and I am heading west. Time for me to visit some Indian reservations. I want one of those."

The woman next to her, a paralegal, said, "Can I go on vacation with you?"

Charlie was already a half block away, at his hotel on West Fifty-fourth Street. He went up to his room and lay down, preparing for the night's activities. He slept for one hour, allowing his body clock to awaken him. He got up and started stretching, then went downstairs to the hotel's small workout room. The killer started the treadmill slowly at 3.4 miles per hour, which he walked at for five minutes while watching FOX News mounted on the far wall. Then he cranked it up to 4 miles per hour for ten more minutes, then set it at 5.5 miles per hour and jogged for the next fifteen minutes, starting to work into a sweat. He then began slowing down, which lasted another ten minutes.

When he got off the treadmill, Charlie drank a plastic bottle of water and lay on his back sticking his legs up in the air, crossed at the ankles. Then he placed his hands at his sides, palms down, one inch above the floor. He slowly did a crunch sitting up as far as he could, then lay back down. He crossed his sinewy left arm over his eight-pack abs and slowly did ten more, lay back, crossed his right arm over, and did ten more. Then he pointed both toes and legs together, lifted both feet six inches off the floor, and held them there while he slowly counted to two hundred.

Charlie then ignored the machines and grabbed a chrome barbell off the rack and started doing a series of four sets of ten repetitions for a variety of exercises. He exploded and exhaled as he did each rep, then inhaled and slowly returned the weights to position after each. He lifted for an hour, then cooled down by doing some slow stretches.

He returned to his room, changed into trunks, and went down to the hot tub. There, he let the warmth soak into his muscles, and he let his body go limp.

Returning to his room, he lay down on his bed naked after showering, and he slept for another full hour, awakening feeling refreshed. Next, he sat cross-legged on the bed and opened the sliding door to his balcony, from where he could hear the familiar street sounds of the Big Apple.

Charlie took out a piece of hemp rope, with sage and other items added to it. He lit it and set it on a saucer from the room's coffee setup. Then in the manner of his ancestors, and using an eagle wing from his valise, he fanned the rising smoke into his face and body and got lost in the thoughts of riding his chestnut and white overo paint horse at Pine Ridge Reservation.

Finally, Charlie dressed and went downstairs for dinner. He ate a chef salad and drank iced tea. No beers or wine tonight. He had to be totally clearheaded.

Virginia Hampton was an outstanding labor relations

attorney, a workaholic, and the prettiest and sexiest-looking of the women who had been in the restaurant and fell in lust with Charlie earlier. It was just coincidence now that she was working late on a brief she was preparing and her office was just down the street. She came in to the hotel restaurant wearing a black pin-striped two-piece business outfit with a white silky blouse underneath. When she spotted Charlie, she immediately undid the top two buttons on the blouse, which would reveal a nice hint of her ample cleavage. She could not believe her luck.

His eyes had already caught hers, and because he was the best, he immediately recognized her as one of the hot women in the diner who he felt were talking about him. He saw her undo the buttons, and he started fantasizing about what she must look like under the expensive business outfit. Charlie, however, also knew he had a job he was required to do, and he had not become one of the best hit men in the world by not being tough-minded.

She walked over to his table and looked flush, her face almost as red as her hair, which was the color of a blazing fireplace. The suit could not hide her curves at all. Virginia boldly pulled a chair out and sat down across from Charlie. He hated himself for what he was about to do.

Virginia said, "I apologize for being so bold and brash, but may I join you for supper? Dutch treat, of course."

Charlie smiled, and she nervously placed a napkin across her lap.

The attorney went on, "I have a law office down the street and saw you handle that monster in the restaurant this afternoon, and honestly, it is wonderful to see a real man in this country anymore."

Charlie smiled and put his hand up, which stopped her.

He said softly, "I want to save you a lot of time and effort, ma'am, before this goes any further. I am gay."

Her face really flushed now, and she could feel her ears burning.

Virginia, the great courtroom orator, was at a total loss for words. "I am so sorry, sir. I, a, a, excuse me."

Tears welled up in her eyes, and she almost ran out of the restaurant.

Charlie took a bite of chef salad and shook his head with a smile, whispering to himself, "Charlie, you dumbass Redskin! You could have been lost in that all night."

Then, with the discipline of years and pride in his deadly proficiency, he put the incident out of his mind and started thinking about the events before him this evening. One error, one slip, one mistake, and he could end up very dead. Instead, he planned for one New York City police officer to be the dead man.

"What the heck," Charlie said quietly to himself. "This could be my last meal."

He signaled the waitress over and ordered a warmed-up slice of apple pie a la mode. This was followed by a relaxing cup of hot tea.

Charlie was ready, and he went to his room.

Within an hour, he would be ready to leave and would be looking like anything but a Lakota or Sioux Indian of the Minniconjou tribe.

AN hour passed, and two teenagers wearing iPods came out of the hotel laughing. They were followed a minute later by two different couples in business attire who seemed to have been dining inside. The men were shouting back and forth comments about the New York Stock Exchange, and they were followed by a gray-bearded elderly Orthodex Jew. Gray curls hanging down under his black hat, he carried a suitcase and seemed to be looking for a cab. He was followed seconds later by a very tall bearded 1970s-throwback hippie, replete with long red beard and long hair, a tie-dyed shirt, and faded bell-bottom trousers. He took off down the street at a very rapid pace and was out of sight in seconds. A cab pulled up to the curb, the driver a Middle Easterner, who saw that the fare was an Orthodox Jew and quickly sped away. Another cab pulled up minutes later, and the driver, a young college kid, enthusiastically put the old man's bag in the taxi and helped him into the backseat, handing him his cane.

The Orthodox Jew whispered an address near Bronx Park East, and the young cabbie sped across town, dropping the old man off on a street running off of Lydic near White Plains. The old man, contradictory to what the cabbie had been told, gave him a handsome tip and a blessing, and he pulled the handle up on the heavy suitcase and walked slowly down the street. Within two blocks he turned and entered an old brownstone. He pulled out a key, opened the door to the one basement apartment, and entered. It was well after dark now and not many were on the streets, except for a few coming and going.

Inside the apartment, the rabbi dropped the cane, easily tossed the suitcase on the bed, and stripped off the traditional black suit, hat, and his fake beard and curls.

Charlie was wearing a dark gray body armor suit, and the spandex clearly showed the myriad of muscles and sinews that ran through his perfectly proportioned body. He went into the bathroom, and although it was not prudent for a professional hit man, out of respect to his warrior ancestors he pulled out a makeup kit and, standing in front of the mirror, applied black and red war paint, with black paint covering the upper half of his face with a long red diagonal lightning stripe going through it.

He worked rapidly now; there was no wasted time or energy. Charlie pulled a laptop out of the suitcase and opened it. He brought up a JPEG image of the front door of an apartment, the apartment of his intended target, NYPD Officer James Rashad.

Rashad right then had gleaming beads of sweat running down his well-muscled body. He breathed out hard as he pushed the weights on the Smith Machine upward in his sixth repetition. His partner, Gerome Alexander, sat up on the bench at his own Smith and again wondered in amazement as he stared at the three forty-five-pound plates on each side of Rashad's bar. Gerome was using one forty-five-pounder and one thirty-five-pounder on each side, and felt he was very strong. In fact, he was, but Rashad was massive. James finished the rep, then twisted and hooked the bar on the Smith and sat up, grabbing a bottle of springwater.

The two cops lifted hard and did treadmills every Monday and Wednesday evening, so it was the past two Mondays and Wednesdays that Charlie had come to Rashad's apartment to prepare for this night. He was one of the best in the world in killing, so he left nothing to chance. In the air vent in the hallway Charlie had planted a small video camera, which had a remote hookup to his laptop. A motion detector activated the camera every time a person or pet moved up or down the hallway. He reviewed the recorded video feeds all day long.

Charlie now looked at his laptop and saw that a locksmith had come during the day and replaced the lock. When Charlie had read the bio report on his target, he saw that the man was very security conscious, so he was not at all shocked by this happening. It might make for a slight delay on the assassination, but maybe he would be able to affect his goal anyway. Charlie always had backup plans. He saw Rashad with his workout bag on the video, leaving for the gym, and he was ready to make his move.

Quickly, Charlie packed his small black rucksack and added some additional tools to it. He donned his black vest, with many pockets in it, and his weapons. Wearing night vision goggles, Charlie crawled out the back basement window into the window well and up into the very small fenced backyard. The route to Rashad's apartment was almost routine now, but Charlie would not allow himself to let his guard down. He climbed over the fence into the yard of the couple who were retirees and were sound asleep by nine every night. Having quickly dashed across their tiny yard, he had to stop at the next brownstone and look back to see if the couple's bedroom window was open or if instead the air conditioner was on. When the window was open, their toy poodle kept a close watch on the blacktop parking lot behind the building and would start yapping if he heard or saw Charlie. Tonight was a new moon, so in the shadow of the building he would not be visible, but the little dog could smell or hear him if that bedroom window was open. It was closed.

He made it across the parking lot to the crushed white stone lot at the back of Rashad's long brownstone. Charlie had the key out and knew the schedule of all the tenants, so he knew he would not be spotted in the hallway. He unlocked the door, which was chump change for him after he had digitally photographed the outside of the door during his first nighttime visit, identified the Schlegel lock, and by the second night had a key that would fit and open it.

He made his way down the hallway to the officer's apartment, pulled a stethoscope out, and placed it on the door, listening intently. He then pulled out a small mallet-type hammer and identified the brand-new lock as a Master. Charlie had a key with graduated filing down from base to tip, and he placed it in the lock. He smacked the end of the key with the mallet and it penetrated all the way in, then Charlie pulled slightly and backed it out one notch.

Standard locks are constructed with a series of spring-loaded stacks called pin stacks. Pin stacks are made so that two pins are stacked on top of each other. There is what is called, ironically, the key pin, which is the part that actually touches the key as it goes into the lock. Then there is a spring-boosted driver pin. A proper key makes all the pins line up right, allowing the cylinder to be turned.

Obviously, the wrong key keeps the cylinder from turning, but Charlie used a common and frequently used burglary tool called a "bump key." The bump key is placed one notch out in what is called the keyway. Then you hammer it, and that sends the key deeper into the keyway, and the result is that the smaller teeth of the bump key jiggle all of the pins in the lock, which affects the driver pins. So now the driver pins spring up for a millisecond from the key pins and then the spring inside pushes them back into place. By pulling back almost a notch, you can cause the smaller ridges of the bump key to hold the driver pins from snapping back, and the lock can be turned.

Charlie did this and opened the door on the first try. He looked all around the edges of the door to see if Officer Rashad had put a piece of tape down to see if anyone had entered, as he had done one night, but for some reason not since. Charlie then carefully scoured the floor in the immediate vicinity of the doorway to ensure there had not been a toothpick, coin, or pin placed on top that had now fallen down. There was not.

He immediately made a quick pass through the small apartment to ensure that it was empty. Verifying that, he moved to the cop's bedroom and specifically his valet that he kept there. On the valet was his uniform, IIIA vest with ceramic heart plate, shoes, socks, and underwear, as well as his tactical belt and holster. Rashad carried a Glock Model 17 in .40 caliber.

From research surveillance, Charlie knew there was also a lanyard with a shiny whistle attached, which Rashad wore for luck, even though he had not worked traffic for a couple of years. The original lanyard was made of black plastic strips braided into a diamond-weave pattern, but the plastic had cut into Rashad's neck and frequently left him with red streaks there that looked almost like burns. He wore the whistle now for luck, but the lanyard itself held no significance, so he had switched to a thick lanyard with a harder rubber core and soft cloth cover. It was very comfortable on the neck, and he never had to worry about chafing or scraping.

Charlie now produced from his rucksack an identical lanyard, which had been constructed by experts after seeing extreme close-up digital videos Charlie had made of the entire lanyard and whistle. Charlie compared the new one to the original and you would have been hard-pressed to tell the difference. Even the nylon material covering the outside had the same softness. The only difference was the inside of the new lanyard. The interior of the new lanyard was made of U.S. miltary det cord.

Det cord looks just like old plastic clothesline. Det cord is actually an abbreviation for detonation cord. It was first used during the Vietnam War and has many purposes. The center of it is made of the high explosive pentaerythritol tetranitrate, referred to normally as PETN or Pentrite. It can be set up between various explosive charges to make all detonate simultaneously, as it explodes at a detonation rate of 26,000 to 27,000 feet per second. The rule of thumb to cut a tree in half is to wrap three wraps of det cord around a tree for every foot of the trunk's thickness. It can even be wrapped around steel I beams a few times and when detonated will actually cut a beam in half. It is generally set off by a blasting cap, and Charlie now produced his coup de grace. He pulled a small plastic box out of his vest and opened it. Inside was a microtransmitter attached to the end of a miniature blasting cap with a small amount of composition C4 plastic explosive in the tip of it. The transmitter was so small that Charlie now carefully, with tweezers, inserted it into the airspace of the whistle. Unless Rashad developed a pressing need to blow the whistle, Charlie would get away with the expedient detonator.

Besides being one of the best assassins in the world, he also had some of the best technical experts in the world available to him to help carry out his assignments. This little item was just a minor example of what he could have made in less than twenty-four hours' time. This was an extremely important hit and money was no object.

Charlie put the original lanyard in his pack and carefully made his way toward the door. The entire time had only been minutes and was done in complete darkness while he wore a night vision device. Having taken one last glance around to be sure he had not disrupted anything, he left the apartment, quietly made his way down the hallway, and within minutes, was back in his basement apartment.

CHAPTER TWO

Monkey Wrench in the Gears

HE packed everything up, replaced his elderly Orthodox Jewish man disguise, sterilized the apartment, and made his way to the convenience store two blocks away to call a taxi. The taxi then took him to his next apartment, which he worked out of on the other side of the Bronx, where he followed and kept track of James Rashad and his partner when they worked their patrol shift. He turned on the old TV and waited in the small roach-infested apartment, located above a liquor store owned by an old Korean couple. The two officers would be on shift, go through their briefing, and out on the street within the hour.

IT was two hours later when the two passed by an older, shabbier part of town and a figure in black emerged from an alley shortly after they passed. He moved slowly, carefully, and silently in the shadows as they went down the street. They turned a corner and he dashed down an alley, knowing where Rashad was headed. He pulled his digicam from his pack as he rushed to get ahead of them.

DEA Special Agent Juan Atencio and his partner Felix User, watching from their darkened stakeout apartment with night vision devices, were perplexed as they saw the shadowy figure coming down the alley. Juan tapped NYPD Detective Sergeant Brad Pitt and Detective Dominic Fernella, working the joint operation with the feds, and pointed out the black-clad figure who had just sneaked silently down the alleyway, near an Econoline van. There were officers hiding and watching from several locations, and now some of the eyes were on the unsuspecting master hit man.

Raphael "Stinky" Navarro was a member of the Crips gang, which was quite obvious by his oversized North Carolina jersey and shorts, dark blue kerchief, and blue baseball hat, brim turned off to one side and covering the blue head wrap. He sat in the confines of the white Econoline panel van with darkened windows. He did not know that several snitches had told DEA officers and NYPD narcs that he would be making a major sale tonight. In actuality, he would be delivering to Officer James Rashad what the man demanded from him this night. He had been busted by Rashad one night with one full kilo of pure crank, speed, dextra-amphetamine, but instead of arresting him Rashad turned him into a snitch. For four months Rashad essentially intimidated Stinky into working for him, under threat of arrest. After finding out that his gang of Crips had secured some sophisticated weapons and explosives, James ordered him to secure the package he wanted on this night. It weighed thirty-five pounds and was something James Rashad wanted very badly when he learned about the weapons heist the street punks had pulled off.

The two DEA agents in charge and the two senior detectives had videotaped Stinky earlier when he placed the duffel bag in the van. It was obvious there was some sort of rectangular-shaped container or box in it, and they figured it was a giant stash of drugs.

Gerome Alexander and his senior partner were approaching the corner near the van, and as before, he already knew his place. James had a snitch he would meet with who would roll over on his gang members and other petty criminals. This night the senior black officer had confided in his junior partner that he was picking up a packet of drugs that he could not even look at but had been ordered to secretly turn in to a contact at the DEA, who wanted to fingerprint every inch of the package, which would be inside a duffel bag. James had told Gerome that he had a car coming to get the duffel bag a half hour after the pickup.

Gerome Alexander was an honest cop but a bit of a jerk, who had been a nerd all through high school. Bespectacled and not really looking like someone you would consider a beat cop, he had the highest resisting-arrest bust rate in the precinct, which made the seasoned veterans disrespect him. They knew most of his perps with black eyes and puffed lips had received those after being cuffed. James Rashad, the large, well-muscled black officer, had always treated his partner like a friend though, so he had become close to James even though all the other officers in the precinct found Rashad aloof. He was friendly enough but just not someone who would go have a beer with the others after shift.

They turned the corner and Special Agent Juan Atencio said over the radio, "Two officers coming by. Hope they do not queer this op."

Alexander stopped at the corner and Rashad went directly to the van on the deserted street.

Atencio said, "Holy Crap, Batman! Looks like we might have a dirty cop, unless he is just checking out the van. Two-three and four-six, you two keep cameras rolling and eyes on our man in black in the alley. All units be ready to move in."

James Rashad climbed into the passenger door of the van.

He started speaking with Stinky, saying, "Did you get me the weapon?"

Charlie was listening to this on the transmitter he had placed inside Rashad's radio handset.

Stinky said, "Yeah, brah. It's right here in the duffel bag."

Charlie waited for him to have time to lift up the duffel bag for Rashad to see it, and then he raised the small radio transmitter that would set off the explosive charge. The small red LED light gave a very faint glow in the blackness of the alley. Charlie looked back up the alley to make sure nobody or no vehicles had entered, blocking his quick exit.

Four-six, which was Dom Fernella, looking with a high-power night vision scope, only twenty feet away from Juan, said into his voice-operated mouthpiece, "Damn, one-zero, the guy in black has his thumb on the switch of what could be a detonator of some sort, unless it is a radio."

Juan yelled out in the large room, "Just stay on him!"

Charlie pushed the switch down on the handset detonator and the windows blew out of the van with the explosion. Officer James Rashad's head was severed completely from his body, and Stinky's right hand and arm were still attached to the duffel bag, but were separated from his body. The whistle, now turned inside out, had embedded itself in the side of his neck, but missed the jugular vein. He immediately started screaming. Down at the corner, Alexander dropped to the ground, covering his head with both arms protectively.

Charlie was already sprinting toward the other end of the alley.

Juan Atencio said professionally, "All units close in quickly. Get that son of a bitch in black in the alley. He just blew them up."

Sirens went off as cruisers flew into the alley from both directions, blocking any hope for Charlie's escape.

"Close in on the van but watch for more explosions. Move fast but proceed with caution on the van. Take the officer into custody at the corner. Move! Move!"

Charlie had to make an immediate assessment, and he saw no fire escapes, doors that were not chained or bolted, or basement windows to use to affect his escape. He was already hearing screams to "freeze" or hold his hands up. The handwriting was clearly on the wall. For some reason, there were cops here on a major stakeout, probably because they had heard about the weapon changing hands, and he saw them closing on him and the van. There would be no escape. He would have to give up now and live to fight another day later.

He immediately took off his night vision goggles and rucksack and dropped them on the ground, and unholstered his Springfield Arms .45 XD semiautomatic pistol and set it on the rucksack, along with his large Gerber knife, which had been sheathed on the back of his right hip. He also slipped off the black tactical vest and dropped it on his rucksack, and turned around, placing his hands against the brick wall next to him and spreading his legs apart, to show no possible threat to the approaching officers.

Bubba Dalton was the largest officer in Alexander and Rashad's precinct, and he simply was one of those men who saw the top part of everybody's head. He was so big and solid that whatever he touched would always move. He was also a total racist and a bully, but he knew James Rashad, and the man was a cop in his precinct. Six men were now around the van, guns drawn, and Stinky, neck bleeding and still screaming, was roughly pulled out and Juan Atencio screamed to call for an ambulance.

Detective Sergeant Brad Pitt hollered out, "I know this

officer. His name was James Rashad. His head was blown completely off his body. It's laying on the floorboard!"

By now Charlie was being cuffed, and Bubba Dalton screamed, "You cop killer!"

He grabbed Charlie and slammed him face-first on the hood of the cruiser that had come down the alley from the far end. Then he punched him several times. Charlie spit out blood and grinned at the monster, who got even more enraged and kneed Charlie in the ribs several times.

"Dalton!" Brad Pitt screamed, walking over. "Knock that crap off!"

Bubba yelled, "He is a cop killer, Sergeant! We ought to waste the punk!"

Brad Pitt said, "Yeah, we should but we won't."

Bubba glared at the detective sergeant and then screamed in pain as the now-handcuffed Charlie head-butted him viciously, flattening and breaking his nose. The behemoth cop fell on the ground, and as his knees buckled, Pitt and another officer grabbed Charlie by both upper arms and escorted him to the backseat of the cruiser. Dalton was now rising to his feet, totally enraged, and looking for Charlie.

At the van, Atencio now had the duffel bag in his hand, and it had been unwisely opened by the first man on the scene. He looked inside, and seeing the metal container, he gave out a long, low whistle.

Seeing this from the alley, Pitt yelled, "What is it, Atencio, coke?"

Juan yelled back, "No, it is a damned Stinger missile!"

A murmur went through all the officers.

American soldiers on the ground had concerns in the past about low-flying enemy aircraft because of either bombing, surveillance operations, or inserting and supplying enemy troops. Shooting down these aircraft would be the easiest way to eliminate the threat, so not counting on support from the air or ground vehicles, the army concluded they needed a lightweight, portable weapon that could also be what is called a "fire and forget" weapon, such as the M-72 LAW or light antitank weapon created during the Vietnam War for use on enemy armor and bunkers. It was in essence a disposable bazooka. The Stinger missile is much larger and should be used by two men but can be used by one. The missile and its launcher weigh about thirty-five pounds, and unlike the LAW, the launcher itself is reusable. It is a shoulder-launched weapon, and one person can launch it.

Also the LAW used a pop-up plastic sight, but the Stinger missile is a passive infrared-seeker. If you fire one at a jet or other aircraft, it homes in on the heat signature or jet or engine exhaust and will travel right into the exhaust port of an aircraft and then detonate.

When the seeker locks on, it makes a distinctive noise. The soldier pulls the trigger, and two things happen: (1) a small launcher-type of rocket shoots the missile out of the launch tube, and (2) the launch engine drops away, and the main rocket engine takes over and shoots the Stinger at approximately 1,500 mph.

The missile then flies to the target automatically and explodes. The Stinger missile can hit targets flying as high as 11,500 feet and has a range of five miles. This means, in a general way, that if an airplane is less than two miles high, and it is visible as a shape (rather than a dot), then it is likely that the Stinger can hit it. Stinger missiles are extremely accurate.

"Dom," Brad said, "I want you riding downtown to get this guy booked in and stay with him. I don't trust or like that big jerk Dalton at all. Alexander also has a rep for beating on cuffed prisoners. I want this guy to get the death penalty, and we are not blowing this case and getting chewed out by the DA for screwing up in case prep. Let's get him out of the cruiser now and keep the dips away from him. We will Mirandize him with several witnesses."

Dom said, "Sure, Sarge, but O'Hare already Mirandized the long-haired punk, I think."

"I don't give a rat's ass," Sergeant Pitt responded, running his fingers through his salt-and-pepper hair. He received comments all day long about his name but did not look a thing like the actor.

He went on, "No screwups on this. Let's take care of it. The feds seem to be cooperating good on this case, and I want to comb the crime scene so thoroughly we can find a flea's pubes, if they fall out."

Dom chuckled. "A flea's pubes? Jeesh, Sarge!"

They opened the door to the cruiser and pulled Charlie out. His left eye was almost swollen shut. Bubba Dalton started to lumber forward and Brad raised his hand in a halting gesture. The look he gave the big man stopped him in his tracks.

Brad said, "Dalton, you go help crime tape the area, and I do not want to see your big Lurch ass anymore tonight."

Bubba stormed off, slamming the door shut on a cruiser as he walked by.

Brad Pitt made sure that Dominic and another officer were witnessing and Juan Atencio walked up and politely did not interrupt.

Pitt looked at Charlie, saying, "Sir, you are being booked on suspicion of murder. You have the right to remain silent. If you choose to give up your right to be silent, anything you say can and will be used against you in a court of law. You have the right to have an attorney present during questioning, and if you cannot afford an attorney, the court will appoint one for you. Do you understand these rights as I have explained them to you?"

Charlie said, "Yes, I do. I want an attorney present during questioning."

Sergeant Pitt said, "What is your name, sir? Your license says James Reed, and you had a receipt from an airline ticket saying you are Chuck Wagon."

The Indian chuckled and said, "You can call me Charlie, Detective. That is my real name."

"Do you want to tell me why you murdered a police officer, Charlie?"

"As I said, Detective, I would like an attorney present during questioning, and I would like my phone call ASAP."

"In due time, Charlie," Brad said. "We will get you medical attention at the station, too."

Juan stepped forward, teeth-clenched. "This piece of shit is a cop killer! The hell with his rights. He is gonna tell us what we want to know right now! If he doesn't—"

Charlie said, "You won't do a damned thing, because you guys do not want to blow a case against a cop killer. You must be a fed, or you would not have jumped in like that trying to play good cop, bad cop, with two detectives standing here, and I assume this one is probably a sergeant."

Charlie glanced at Brad, who nodded affirmatively.

The Sioux went on, "So what are you, FBI, ATF, DEA maybe?"

Juan said, "Really smart, aren't you, Charlie? I am DEA Special Agent Juan Atencio and this is NYPD Detective Sergeant Brad Pitt. It will be a lot easier for you if you totally cooperate with us. Yeah, I was trying good cop, bad cop, but you apparently have been around the system. Will you cooperate?"

Charlie said, "I have cuffs on. I don't have much choice. If I discuss anything, it will be with Sergeant Pitt, because we have already established rapport, and I respect the man. He is a professional, and you are going to learn about it anyway when Homeland Security and the FBI hears about the Stinger missile. I doubt you'll find any drugs other than Stinky's personal stash."

Brad said, "So you are an associate of Stinky's? Why did you kill a cop?"

Charlie said, "I want my phone call and an attorney

present during questioning. If you want to keep rapport, Sergeant, respect my rights."

Brad immediately said, "Dom, take him uptown and book him. Charlie, Detective Fernella will see that your rights are protected to a T."

Dominic put his hand on top of Charlie's head to protect him from bumping it, and Juan hollered, getting Charlie to stop as he was crouching into the cruiser, "Charlie! Just tell us this. You used to be a cop or something?"

Charlie grinned and said, "Something," and ducked into the car.

He made his phone call an hour later and was told to sleep and not speak, and wait until morning.

The word had already circulated on the graveyard shift, and men were searching for excuses to come to the precinct to get a look at this ruthless cop killer who had decapitated James Rashad with an explosive device. To a man, everyone figured Charlie was a terrorist with al Qaeda, but they could not figure out his country of origin or how he learned to speak with not so much as an accent of any kind.

When he had showered and had been checked for body lice and other nasty critters, none of the officers present could believe, first, how well built he was, but more so, the obvious bullet holes and jagged scars that seemed to permeate his body.

The officer in charge of getting inmates prepped for holding cells said to the others, "This guy is a hard-ass and punk of major proportions. He has been shot, stabbed, and none of those bullet holes are from a .22, that's for damned sure. I wonder if he is in MS-13 or one of those outfits."

A patrol officer standing by him said, "I say he is a raghead. Al Qaeda, I bet."

Charlie was soon in a holding cell, lying on his bunk and going to sleep. During the arrest he had only been concerned about getting killed by an overzealous cop like

Bubba. Now that he was where there could be witnesses and video, he relaxed. Court did not concern him. He had made his phone call, and all would be taken care of in the morning.

between more, and he even take down their account information, with no response. Gerome Clifford and someone? Herod, the telephone rang, and disturbed a take note. Bob at the one who.

CHAPTER THREE

A Day in Court

"ALL rise!" the bailiff commanded in the packed court-room, and the many people there rose to their feet.

Charlie sat bolt upright, blinking his eyes. A faint light shone through the unbreakable glass on his cell door. He looked around, breathing heavily, smiled at himself, and lay back down. He was almost immediately asleep.

In the morning however, it was no dream, as the real courtroom was indeed packed, and all the officers from the crime scene were there, but so was the chief of police, the police commissioner, and many police captains and lieutenants, even the district attorney himself was there to watch one of his subordinates handle this important case. A number of attorneys, waiting for later cases to start, were present, as well as Officer Gerome Alexander, who had been simply questioned that night, and there was no feeling he was involved in any wrongdoing. He explained that Stinky was one of Rashad's snitches and meeting him like that was quite commonplace when the two were on patrol. He also explained that Stinky had indeed given his partner a number of good leads in the past.

Nobody was there to represent James Rashad's family or friends. Most of the press had been kept out, but several had snuck in posing as family members.

The officers all stared in disbelief, shock, and awe at the legal team that had come in immediately to represent this brazen cop killer. George Rooney, New York City's sharpest criminal defense attorney, was the lead attorney, but he was joined by two associates from his Manhattan firm, and what amazed all in the room was the U.S. Army major who sat next to George in dress greens, wearing many ribbons as well as the brass of the Judge Advocate General's branch. Behind him were four very tall, muscular men who looked like bodyguards in Brooks Brothers suits. This puzzle was getting more complex. They had already gotten permission for Charlie to dress before entering the courtroom, as George easily argued that his client dressed in coveralls instead of a suit would automatically prejudice anybody. The judge, Alicia Silver, was noted for being a tough bird who allowed no foolishness in her courtroom and went overboard being fair to defendants simply so appellate judges would not overturn her decisions. All the cops loved her, because she handed out harsher punishments than any other judge.

One of the attorneys present in the courtroom who wanted to see what happened in this arraignment was Virginia Hampton. She had heard that someone wearing war paint and dressed in black like a modern-day ninja had blown the poor officer's head off with some kind of sophisticated explosive device. She had no idea it was the man she had approached more brazenly than she had ever approached any man in her life. The man who, even after he'd told her he was gay, was still someone she could not help fantasizing about.

The doors opened from the suspect's holding room, and a large jailer walked in followed by Charlie in handcuffs attached to a large leather band around his waist, and also being held by another large jailer. What was amazing to all present, though, was the way Charlie was dressed. He wore a U.S. Army dress green uniform. Several officers who were familiar with army awards and decorations started translating what he wore, and among others, a very shocked Virginia listened intently.

The officer said, "The guy is a master sergeant. Look at those stripes. He has a Special Forces combat patch on his right sleeve, which means he was a Green Beret, and I am not sure about the patch on his left sleeve, but see the sword or dagger upright in the middle of that kind of gold triangle? That is the unit he is in now, and damn, son of a bitch! I think that patch is for Delta Force."

Virginia got a chill down her spine.

She heard the man go on. "Look at his ribbons below the CIB with a star, meaning he served in combat in two wars. He has the DSC, the Distinguished Service Cross, the nation's second highest award for valor. He has got a Silver Star, too. Three Bronze Stars with a V device for Valor, two Purple Hearts, which are for wounds, the Legion of Merit, an air medal. I think that one is the Soldier's Medal for risking his life saving somebody else's in a noncombat situation. He might be a cold-blooded killer, but this guy is a superstud, a major hero. He must be Native American, too, by his looks."

Charlie gave his attorney and the major a very odd handshake with his hands cuffed to his hips on the thick leather belt. Charlie glanced at the big men who looked and acted like bodyguards.

"All rise!" the bailiff commanded and Judge Alicia Silver entered the courtroom and politely smiled at the packed crowd.

She sat down and all followed suit.

Immediately, George Rooney stood up and said, "Your Honor, may we approach?"

She had not even spoken yet, but she nodded and looked

at the assistant DA, who also walked up. She was surprised to see the army major walk up, too.

George Rooney said, "Your Honor, this case presents an incredible set of circumstances that will never happen in our careers again. May we, including not only my respected opponent here but the district attorney himself and the chief of police, meet with you in chambers?"

"Mr. Rooney," she said, "we have not even gotten started and this is only an arraignment. This is highly unusual, but without objection from the prosecution . . ."

The prosecutor smiled and said, "Your Honor, I am curious as hell what Mr. Rooney is up to. We have no objection."

She nodded, and they stepped back.

Judge Silver said, "Defense and the prosecution will meet briefly in chambers. Mr. Smith, they would like you and you, Chief Davidson, too, to join us in chambers if you please, gentlemen."

In the gallery the two men stood, and both said, "Yes, Your Honor," simultaneously. The chief of police and district attorney were both puzzled as to why they were called.

The judge even offered coffee or tea for anyone who wanted some. She poured herself a cup of tea and removed her robe, sitting down in a comfortable dark red diamond-tufted leather high-backed chair.

Taking a sip, she said, "George, will you kindly let us in on this mystery now."

"Yes, Your Honor," he replied. "First, please let me explain. This whole case pertains to national security matters, and we cannot take a chance of anybody in that courtroom blabbing things to the papers. I will be moving that charges against my client be dismissed immediately without prejudice, Your Honor."

He held his hand up, smiling at the prosecutor and stating, "And before my learned opponent or his boss get in a defensive posture, please allow my associate here, Major Ronald Hair of the Judge Advocate General's Corps to explain. Major Hair was rushed here by air force jet from MacDill Air Force Base in Tampa, Florida, and has had no sleep, so please if you will indulge him. I would have lapses in between lapses. Major Hair."

The soldier stepped forward and smiled politely, "Your Honor, our client, Master Sergeant Charlie Strongheart, is a recipient of our nation's second highest award for courage, the Distinguished Service Cross, as well as many other awards, including the Silver Star and multiple Purple Hearts, has been a longtime Green Beret NCO, and is a member of the top secret C.A.G., Combat Applications Group, known to most of the military as 1st Special Forces Operational Detachment-Delta, and more commonly known as Delta Force. Your Honor, we can move for dismissal for a number of reasons, but most notably because Sergeant Strongheart cannot be arrested, by presidential decree."

"What?" the judge said.

Hair reached inside his dress greens, pulled out a small card, and read, "Your Honor, Presidential Decision Directive 25 grants Delta Force members 'freedom from all legal accountability,' including exception from the 1878 Posse Comitatus Act—a statute imposing criminal penalties for anyone using the military for personal gain, domestic law enforcement, or unsanctioned covert operations."

"Incredible!" the district attorney said. "Are you telling me that this guy can come in here and murder, decapitate, a member of our police force, and the president has granted him immunity, and we have to let him walk?"

"Not exactly," Major Hair went on. "That is why we asked for you, Chief, to join us. The man he killed was a known terrorist. James Rashad was a member of the Black Panthers and later joined al Qaeda and has even met Osama bin Laden and al-Zawahiri both in Afghanistan, where he attended an al Qaeda training camp before the war started there. Years ago, he actually changed his name to Ibn Osama Rashad. When he went through the police academy, his entire biography and identification papers were all carefully forged by al Qaeda operators right here in New York City. Chief, we also are bringing you some experts from the Department of Homeland Security to privately assist you so nobody else can sneak into your department like this again."

Major Hair faced the judge again, saying, "Your Honor, Sergeant Strongheart was assigned, as a singleton, a Delta operator working alone, to eliminate James Rashad, before he could carry out his mission, which was to acquire a Stinger missile and fire it at a jet taking off from Kennedy Airport, carrying a number of VIPs, including the mayor of New York City, heading to the national Mayors Conference in a little over a month. The Stinger would have taken out the entire aircraft. Additionally, Your Honor, his instructions were to ensure that the jet was over a major population area, so its destruction would cause additional loss of human life. I have brought documentation which is classified top secret and is for your eyes only as well as the chief of police."

The district attorney said, "What about me?"

Major Hair smiled. "I am sorry, sir. The brass at US SOCOM headquarters have really stretched it by allowing us to reveal so much highly classified, sensitive material to so many right now, but we had to act fast to get a lid on this for national security. They felt that you did not really have a need-to-know to see all the written material we are showing the judge and chief of police. Your Honor, one of those burly men in suits who are with us has the material in a briefcase, if I may summon him in?"

Pouting, the district attorney walked to the coffeemaker and poured a cup.

Judge Silver said, "Please do, Major. Hair, is it?"

"Yes, Your Honor."

He walked out into the courtroom and hooked a finger toward the one of the men holding a large briefcase. One of the other men with him walked forward, too, but was stopped by the bailiff. He never said a word, but pulled a badge and ID out of his suit and showed them to the bailiff, who kind of gulped and nodded to him to proceed.

The two men entered the judge's chambers and walked up to Major Hair.

He said, "The documents go to the judge and the chief here."

The man in the suit said, "Judge, Chief, if you will please look at the documents behind the desk and hold them so nobody else can see them. I am required to tell you that what you are about to read are documents that are classified top secret by the U.S. government and will be automatically downgraded at two-year intervals and will be declassified, unless otherwise noted, at the end of twelve years. Disclosure of anything in these documents to anybody for any reason can result in criminal prosecution in a federal court."

The chief of police pulled a chair over next to the judge, and they started poring over the documents.

The judge stopped and said, "Summon the bailiff."

Major Hair stepped through the door again and caught the bailiff's eye—well, actually everybody's eye in the dark-walled courtroom. He signaled him to the door.

The man walked up to him, while everybody in the courtroom, especially every local and federal law enforcement officer, was now totally puzzled.

The major said, "The judge wants to see you, sir."

"Thank you, Colonel," the bailiff said, walking past him.

Major Hair corrected him, saying, "Major."

"Oh, sorry."

They went into chambers and the bailiff said, "Your Honor?"

The judge said, "Tom, go back into the courtroom and let them all know we will be a half hour anyway, so if anybody needs a restroom break, they will have time. Also, tell the jailers I said to release the prisoner's handcuffs and restraint belt. He is to remain there, but remove all restraints."

"Thank you, Your Honor," George Rooney said, smiling.

Now even the bailiff, who said, "Yes, Your Honor," was puzzled as he walked back into the courtroom.

He relayed the judge's words to the jailers, and they both shrugged their shoulders and removed Charlie's handcuffs.

A murmur went through the courtroom and finally a loud, deep, angry voice in the back bellowed out, "What in the hell are you doing? He is a cop killer! Son of a bitch!"

All eyes turned to Bubba Dalton, red-faced, except for the bandaged nose and black eyes, and shaking with anger and total frustration.

Detective Brad Pitt walked over to him and quietly said, "Dalton, I have already written you up for last night. Now, if you want to get your Andre the Giant–looking ass booted off the police force, keep acting like a loose cannon in public settings. I also spoke to your sergeant. I am not having some out-of-control patrol cop ruining my busts with outrageous behavior. Now, do you have any questions, Officer Dalton?"

Bubba sat down and pouted in much the same manner as the district attorney, except without the coffee.

The DEA agents looked at the NYPD detectives and all just shook their heads.

No sooner had this occurred than the chief of police appeared in the doorway to chambers and summoned NYPD Detectives Brad Pitt and Dominic Fernella and

DEA Agents Juan Atencio and Felix User. They got up and moved quickly to chambers.

At the door, the chief simply said, "The judge wants to speak to you guys."

Dominic spoke as they moved past him, "Sure, Chief."

In the courtroom, Virginia Hampton had already made up her mind she would go to her courtroom and ask that judge for a recess if need be to find out what was going on and what would happen to this Green Beret, whom she'd thought was irresistible before, but twice that in uniform, gay or not. She looked at his broad shoulders from behind and wondered what it would be like to have those massive arms protectively holding her.

In chambers the judge said, "Gentlemen, this court tries to do all we can to support all arresting officers as officers of the court. In most cases, we are in this together in a quest to get those off the street who would murder our citizens, fill them with drugs, and steal from hardworking members of the community. We are always also diligently protecting the rights of the accused, but today I wanted to privately take into consideration the hours of dedicated service you men and your colleagues have put into this case. When I render my decision out there today, I know emotions are running high, but there is way more to this case than meets the eye, and it is a matter of national security. Please trust that we know you are looking for closure, and maybe you will get it now that you have the surviving suspect in custody. I will tell you this, and I do not want one word repeated. Your colleague James Rashad was not worthy of wasting your emotions about losing. I ask that you will simply trust the judgment of the court."

"Your Honor," Sergeant Pitt said, "why don't they appoint you to the Supreme Court? I have never, ma'am, had a judge care enough about what we go through to explain her decision ahead of time in case it would go against us."

She smiled, saying, "Thank your chief. He asked me to explain it to you."

The chief blushed and the men, even the two feds, gave him a smile and a nod of gratitude.

The bailiff said, "All rise," and the judge entered the courtroom.

The rest had previously entered and were seated.

The judge said, "Please be seated except the defendant."

Charlie stood with his attorneys beside him.

The judge said, "I want the bailiff and court officers to physically check every individual in this courtroom before anybody exits. You are to check for recording or video devices, as well as cameras. I am issuing a very strict gag order on these proceedings. Nobody in this room is to mention anything that has gone on or goes on in this courtroom; that means do not discuss it with the press, or any media, your spouse, relatives, friends, coworkers, or anybody. This is a very important matter of national security."

She then looked at Charlie and spoke softly, "Sergeant Strongheart . . . Oh, by the way, I want his name blanked out and replaced with 'anonymous' in all court records, including the transcript. Master Sergeant Strongheart, this court and I myself personally, as the daughter of a Navy SEAL who served two tours in Vietnam, would like to thank you very much for valorous and extremely courageous service to our nation, and even the world in the Global War on Terrorism. I do recognize, sir, the DSC, Silver Star, and Purple Hearts you are wearing, and one alone is worthy of this nation's respect and undying gratitude. No laws have been broken in this case by the defendant, and based upon Presidential Directive 25, the defendant cannot be charged with any crimes anyway, so with consent and no objection of counsels for both the defense and prosecution, this case is dismissed without prejudice and all records of it are to be purged under the supervision of the U.S. Attorney's Office in Manhattan. Court is adjourned."

Charlie smiled warmly at the judge. He then shook hands with Major Hair and George Rooney.

"This is bullshit!" came the scream from the back of the courtroom. "He is a cop killer! Are you all insane?"

The judge rapped her gavel sharply and started to speak, and like a little schoolchild, Charlie meekly raised his hand. Since this was such a mystery, with him at the center, his gesture caught everybody's attention. The judge smiled and nodded recognition to Charlie, who until now had not spoken.

He said, "Your Honor," and he subconsciously touched his swollen black eye. "If it please the court, ma'am, I met this officer last night, and I think I can straighten this out, with your permission, Your Honor?"

The grin he gave the judge reminded her of the same grin she'd seen from her father several times in his life.

She said, "This case has been highly unusual, to say the least, anyway. Go ahead and speak to him, Sergeant. The court will wait."

"Thank you, Your Honor."

Charlie walked back to Bubba with an easy stride, while all eyes were glued on him. He walked up to the apprehensive behemoth of an officer and smiled. Charlie, who was taller than all in the room save Bubba, reached out and up and placed his left hand on the giant jerk's basketball-sized shoulder, and using it for leverage, he jumped up high and pivoted his right hip and shoulder in midair and smashed Bubba in the already broken nose with a vicious elbow. Bubba's eyes rolled back in his head, and he crumpled to the ground in a heap.

Charlie turned and grinned at the judge, saying, "Thank you, Your Honor, I just had to speak in the only language he understands."

Everybody just stared at him, and then Detective Sergeant Brad Pitt walked up to him and shook his hand, laughing his head off, while looking at the unmoving, nasty cop on the floor. Virginia was laughing, too.

The judge, grinning, just shook her head.

She said, "You probably should leave now, Sergeant. Bailiff, get that officer medical attention, and then when he is awake, take him to a holding cell for contempt of court. I will visit this with him later."

CHAPTER FOUR

Making Up

IT was late in the day, when Madeleine Cameron walked into Virginia Hampton's office carrying a bouquet of various colored roses with numerous stems of baby's breath adorning it. Virginia was shocked to say the least.

"Virginia," Madeleine said, "there is a very striking gentleman here to see you, if he can, quote, squeeze in between appointments. He said to tell you that the roses are a peace offering." She then scrunched up her eyebrows, saying, "And he said to tell you that he is not really gay."

Virginia's face blushed, and she giggled like a schoolgirl.

She reached under the desk for her high heels and slipped them on, saying, "Maddie, give me about three minutes, then have him come in. How's my mascara?"

Madeleine grinned. "You look just beautiful as always, Boss."

Virginia headed toward the small bathroom in the corner of her office and winked.

When Charlie entered the room, she had just brushed

her teeth, her clothes, and her hair, and was ready for the challenge. She could not believe how much his shoulders filled out the doorway when he walked in, and what an appearance now, she thought. Charlie wore cowboy boots, tight, slightly faded but very clean jeans, a blue ribbon shirt with white polka dots all over it and small red, white, and blue ribbons streaming down. His long black hair was pulled straight back into a ponytail which actually went down below his shoulder blades.

Earlier, he had cleaned up and moved everything out of the apartments he had rented, leaving the keys in them. Most of his stuff was packed in his hotel suite, and a detail was coming in shortly to pick it up and transport all of it back to Fort Bragg. The detail was composed of two eager young sergeants who'd had to drop out of the Special Forces Q-Course, or Qualification Course, also called Selection, because of leg injuries, and had not earned their Green Berets yet, so now both wore burgundy berets, signifying their active airborne status. They both were trained Military Intelligence NCOs and had top secret security clearances already. They had to seal all of Charlie's boxes with tape and sign for each box with him. At Bragg, they would turn them in to the JFK Special Warfare Center Command sergeant major, who would in turn take them to the top secret C.A.G. compound at Fort Bragg, which previously had been called "the Stockade."

Charlie said, "I hope you like roses. I know roses are corny to some, but there is an old quote that 'roses are the most beautiful thing that God ever created that does not have a soul.'"

She pulled a deep red rose from the vase Madeleine had put them in and smelled it, smiling coyly.

She said, "I love roses, and I love that quote. Who said that originally?"

Charlie smiled and said, "Me."

Her breath caught; then she said, "They are beautiful," and she smelled them again, adding, "Thank you very much, Charlie. All is forgiven."

He smiled, saying, "How about dinner? It is the least I can do for such a mean trick."

"I have to shower and change. It has been a long day," she said. "Where would you like to eat and when?"

Charlie said, "Do you like seafood?"

"I love it," she said, "but it takes me an hour to get home, an hour to get back, plus I have to change and tidy up. Will that be too late? Seafood, hmmm. Where do you want to eat?"

Charlie said, "I was thinking about room service."

Virginia's heart skipped a beat, and she found it hard to breathe.

Collecting herself, she said, "I guess I deserved that. I came on so strong in the restaurant."

"Deserved? Why, did I insult you with that suggestion?"

"No, oh, no," she said, "I just embarrassed myself with my boldness when I approached you."

He laughed and said, "I was cursing my luck. You are truly beautiful and entrancing."

Now she could feel her pulse pounding in her temples, and the air in the room seemed harder to breathe.

Charlie said, "Virginia, I have to go back to Fort Bragg tomorrow morning. We can be painfully honest with each other, or play coy flirting games before I have to leave, and always wonder. Sometimes you just have to let down the protective veneer and open yourself up for possible hurt."

"Then you would just be picking me up," she said. "I would be a one-night stand."

"I am not picking you up," he said. "I picked you out."

She got up and walked around the desk, and approached him hesitantly at first, then stepped forward boldly into his massive arms, but as strong as he was, she was amazed at how soft and careful his first kiss was. It was passionate enough to curl her toes, but unlike so many men, he was not immediately trying to play tonsil hockey. The kiss was simply passionate and firm but on the other hand soft. She worried she would faint.

When they stepped back, she smiled and said, "You are very right."

"What do you mean?"

"You, sir," she said, "are definitely not gay."

He kissed her again, and this kiss removed any and all doubt that might have ever existed.

Virginia reached down and pushed a button on her phone.

"Yes, Ms. Hampton?" Madeleine's voice came back very professionally.

"Maddie," Virginia said, smiling up at Charlie, "I'm leaving early. Clear my calendar for the rest of the day, please."

She went to her closet and rifled through some clothes, selecting an un-attorney-like form-fitting burgundy dress with a slit up the side of the left leg. The excited attorney also selected a pair of black very high heels, grabbed some smoke panty hose, and went to her bathroom to put together a bag of makeup and toiletries. The pair left for Charlie's hotel, and the paralegals and attorneys from her office who were in the restaurant when she first saw Charlie all took notice that she was carrying clothes and a small makeup bag.

At the hotel, Virginia took a long refreshing shower, fixed her hair and makeup, and left the bathroom with a large white towel wrapped around her. She saw that Charlie had apparently gone into the other bathroom, and she could hear water running.

She sat down on the sitting room couch and wondered what would happen. She kept thinking of his kisses, and she was so excited in anticipation of what might be to come. Would he emerge from the bathroom naked, muscles rippling, and scars probably covering his body, or might he be wearing a bathrobe?

The door opened, and she gave a little startled jump. Charlie emerged in a shirt very close to the color of her dress, a blue tie, tight dress blue jeans, and a burgundy leather sport coat with several long beaded pieces of fringe dangling down the side of each arm from the shoulder. He wore expensive cowboy boots and had his hair now in two long ponytails in the manner of the Lakota or Sioux people.

He walked up to her and took her in his arms and kissed slowly below her ears and ran both hands slowly through her just-dried hair and stepped back smiling.

"You smell wonderful, Virginia . . . Mariella Burani Bouquet of Roses?"

"Yes, it is," she cooed, and thought *Where did this man come from?* She asked, "And I love your smell, too. What is that you are wearing? I love it."

"Obsession," he answered. "Listen, I know I mentioned room service, but I really do not want you to think of me or this as a one-night stand. How about dinner downstairs in the restaurant?"

Virginia said, "Sergeant, you are incredible. How did you learn to become such a . . . a . . ."

"Gentleman?" he interrupted.

"Yes," she replied. "I have to tell you, there just aren't many anymore."

Charlie said, "My dad was a raging drunk, but one good thing he used to do was warm my butt if I ever walked through the door in front of a woman or was not respectful to females in any way. He said men are not trained to be gentlemen anymore."

Charlie looked out the window at the lights of Manhattan and said, "My mom was such a lady and so beautiful, what he said made sense, and it was the way I wanted my mom to always be treated, because Dad was so rough to live with. Those lessons kind of stuck with me, I guess."

She said, "You are certainly different from any man I have dated. Any man I have known."

Charlie smiled and handed her her nylons and underwear, which made her blush.

She wanted to drop her towel and let him stare.

Her body was even more voluptuous than he had imagined in his own flirting thoughts. She spent many hours in the gym each week, as well as in a tanning booth.

She said, "If you will give me a few minutes, I will be ready, sir."

They fed each other seafood, and kept feeding each other all through the meal. After they ate, he held her hand and walked her toward the pool room. It was an indoor pool with two hot tubs at the end of the room. Nobody was in the big indoor pool house, which had large trees everywhere around the outside of the room. Easy listening music played from the ceiling sound system, and Charlie swept her into his arms, and they started dancing slowly, rhythmically to the music. The more they danced, the more they pressed their bodies together, and their lips met. The song ended, and they stepped back, staring into each other's eyes and smiling softly.

Charlie wanted this woman. He had been through the grinder as a warrior, and his lust was tenfold because of the events of the past several days.

She thought to herself that this was a relationship that could go nowhere. He was like the ultimate warrior, but would spend most of his adult life off fighting in wars, while the love of his life would be back home waiting, watching the door in anticipation, the TV news, her computer, her telephone.

Virginia was a woman of action herself, and she knew if she gave herself to this man, it would be for the fantasy, the lifelong memory she would always think back to, but it could not turn into a lifelong relationship. They lived in different worlds. She decided it would be worth it.

He walked over to the window to see if the patio looked like a romantic setting, but it did not.

As soon as he walked away, she smiled and whispered to herself, "Well, girl, one night with a cross between Crazy Horse and Harrison Ford would be worth ten thousand nights with some attorney or accountant. Might as well let go, enjoy yourself, and feel guilty later."

He returned, and they danced more.

He said, "I really was not looking for a nicer place to dance, Virginia. I needed to catch my breath and think. You and I live in different worlds, but you have me entranced, totally. I am just being honest. If you and I are together tonight, I want you to understand how seldom I might make it to New York City."

She smiled and said, "I don't want you to think I am a pickup or sleep around, Charlie, but I was thinking, too. I am a big girl, and I believe sometimes in life two people can share and enjoy a common experience that becomes a treasured memory in both their lives."

She stepped into his arms and kissed him and pressed against him.

Charlie said, "Woman, we need to get you upstairs and off your feet. You have had a long day."

"Me?" She gasped.

After the first time they made love, they just lay in bed together, talking well into the night. Virginia was amazed to learn that Charlie was a direct descendant of Sitting Bull of the famous Battle of the Little Big Horn, called by many Custer's Last Stand. Charlie used the Lakota term Battle of the Greasy Grass.

The way he described Montana, and his home at the Pine Ridge Reservation in western South Dakota, and the West itself, made her eager to go there to visit.

"Earlier," he said, twirling a strand of her hair with two

fingers, "you called me Sergeant. I assume you know to never call me that in front of anybody?"

"I figured so," Virginia responded. "Tell me about your work."

Charlie said, "I cannot. You know how you can never betray a trust with one of your clients?"

"Yes, of course."

"I have a top secret security clearance and am in a top secret unit," he explained, "and just like you can never betray a client's trust, I cannot either. It is just that my client is the United States of America and my unit as well."

"I bet you assume because I am a New York City attorney that I am a liberal Democrat," she said.

"I did not really care," he said. "With my job, I am apolitical. I never tell my political views to anybody. I just do what I am told and serve at the pleasure of whoever is the commander in chief."

She said, "Well, just so you know, I am a conservative registered Republican, and I am even actively involved in politics in my precinct in Manhattan."

He grinned and pulled her close to him. "You wanna hold a caucus, Counselor?"

She giggled and said, "Ooh, yes, you have my vote. Let me just go into my private booth."

Chuckling, she slid down under the sheets.

Later, she fell asleep with her head on his massive chest, his arm wrapped around her protectively, just like she had fantasized.

CHARLIE wore the AN, or army/navy, PVS-7 generation 3 U.S. military night vision goggle/binocular system, attached to the front of his K-pot (Kevlar helmet). He was going to be first in the door when they blew it, and his team members were directly behind him. Charlie would go in after the door was blasted and immediately skirt the

right side of the room, while Rico, his partner, who was
hunched over Charlie's back right now, would immediately move to the left, and Spider would take the center of
the room. Their feet would be about eighteen inches apart,
knees slightly bent, leaning forward at the shoulders,
right hand firmly around the pistol grip, with index finger
on the trigger, while the web between the thumb and index finger of the left hand pushed on the upper grip of the
pistol, finger wrapped around the right hand, running
straight forward parallel to the slide in the Springfield
Arms .45 XD, automatic, Charlie's chosen pistol. Normally,
it was loaded with Teflon-coated and serrated Black Talon
rounds, but now it was loaded with simple .45 automatic
wad-cutters.

Charlie saw a figure in the smoke, a pregnant woman
wearing a burqa. Her eyes were opened wide in fear. There
was a hostage taker next to her, and Charlie immediately
squeezed two face shots with the front titanium sight on
the hostage taker's forehead, and the rear sight, as always,
was slightly blurred. *Bang, bang*—both shots hit the jihadist in the forehead, almost simultaneously, but then Charlie
noticed the AK-47 assault rifle pointed directly at him. It
was in the hands of the pregnant Iraqi woman. *Bang, bang.*
His double-tap followed within a millisecond of the first
one. He immediately saw two bullet holes in the forehead
of each life-sized silhouette target.

Now he noticed his teammate Royal seated on a bench
with an al Qaeda member holding another AK-47, a folding stock model, to his head. The hostage taker was very
close to Royal, and Royal was real, no silhouette target.
Bang! Bang! Charlie put two more rounds in quick succession into the terrorist's forehead. The target vibrated from
the bullet shock, and Royal breathed a sigh of relief, although it was much tougher for the shooter than the hostage when each Delta Force teammate took his turn as a
hostage in the House of Horrors live-fire exercises. In the

old compound, called the Stockade, it was called the Shooting House.

Charlie barely noticed all the shooting going on around him, by his other teammates, but now he had Royal by the arm and was bent over taking him out the front door, having cleared his targets, and the entire team had the room secured.

The team made it outside then, and then took a break to have coffee and water, and one die-hard smoker on the team just had to have his cigarette.

Whether it was one of the rooms in the Shooting House or breaching one of the commercial aircraft mock-ups, whenever the Detachment-Delta team members went through a live-fire exercise with real living, breathing persons mixed in with silhouette targets, it was beyond what would be described as an adrenaline high. These men had incredible trust in one another, so they each did not really worry very much sitting in the Shooting House. But when it came to being a shooter, they had to work hard to keep themselves calm so they would not be off-target with a single bullet. Their partners' lives depended on their ability to perform under such stressors.

Charlie had just started to speak to Royal, when the front of the House of Horrors crashed open. The silhouette targets, most of them looking like Islamic terrorists, were still simply targets, but they came forward like a small army with guns blazing. The lead silhouette target-come-to-life was actually James Rashad, and his head was sewed back on, blood seeping, but the threads clearly visible, and he was holding a gun at the head of Virginia, who had a frightened look on her face.

The entire team opened fire with double-taps from their weapons, hitting the jihadists in the face, usually the forehead. Charlie put two shots right between Rashad's eyes, but he shook his head and the expended bullets flew off to the side out of the bullet holes.

"Oh, you want to fight dirty, huh?" he said to Charlie.

With that, the rogue cop stuck his pistol up against Virginia's temple and cocked it.

Charlie yelled, "No!" and sat up breathing heavily, looking all around the hotel room.

Virginia's nude form lay next to him. She was sleeping soundly and was breathing softly. She stirred a little and a smile lit up her face. It must be nice, Charlie thought to himself, as he saw how peacefully and securely she slept.

He remembered various sayings, such as George Orwell's in his 1945 "Notes on Nationalism," in which he wrote "Those who 'abjure' violence can only do so because others are committing violence on their behalf." The quote had been misquoted many times, with credit even being given to Sir Winston Churchill. Most often, Charlie heard it being said, "We sleep safely in our beds because rough men stand ready to visit violence on those who would do us harm." Out of curiosity, he really researched it one time and found the actual quote by Orwell.

THE knock on the door awakened Virginia, and she stretched and smiled, looking at the rose lying next to her face on the pillow. Then she noticed Charlie dressed and moving catlike to the door. He looked through the peephole, glanced at her, and winked, while she pulled the sheet over her, and he opened the door. A waiter walked in pushing a stainless steel catering cart. Charlie thanked him, handed him some money, and the waiter smiled, nodded, and left the room, the door closing with a loud click.

"Hungry?"

"Starved," she said. "What time is it?"

He said, "Daylight."

She laughed and ran into the bathroom, emerging a few minutes later with one of his shirts on, which engulfed her. She sat down opposite him after giving him a soft kiss.

"This is great!" she said, "What did you order?"

He said, "Room service like I promised last night."

"Oh my!" she replied, as he uncovered both dishes, steaming plates with rib steaks smothered in mushrooms, two eggs over easy, hash browns, and wheat toast, along with glasses of orange juice and two pots of hot tea, which he had already learned she liked as he did.

"I won't be offended if you want me to change your order," he said. "Some people are picky about breakfast, and I wanted to surprise you so I guessed."

She came around the table and kissed him again, saying, "You guessed right, Sergeant Strongheart. This is above all my favorite breakfast. You nailed it, pal."

He chuckled at her expression, which struck him funny coming from a female attorney.

Virginia cleared her appointments and stayed with Charlie until he had to leave for his plane.

They wistfully parted, each knowing that this relationship was probably going to be only a treasured memory for both of them.

They both had new adventures to embark upon. Virginia was on an exciting new case, and Charlie actually prayed silently as he left, and told God he would love to have a real love, a woman he could live with the rest of his life, and have children, lots of them. He wondered if there was such a woman anywhere, who could handle his life as an operator in Detachment-Delta and could handle the danger he faced, the long absences, and the secrecy about his work. He had tried betrothal to one woman, and the job killed the relationship, but he could not imagine any other profession. He was born to the job.

As his plane headed southward toward North Carolina, Charlie had no idea what was in store for him when he returned to Fort Bragg, but he new whatever it was, it would make him feel alive.

CHAPTER FIVE

New Operation

CHARLIE drove out Gruber Road at Fort Bragg, past McKellar's Lodge, and finally arrived at the Delta Force compound. He reported in and met with the Old Man and gave him a briefing on the operation in New York City. After a few hours of briefings, Charlie was with his team, doing what they usually did—training.

He found himself on a bench on the outside of an MH6 Little Bird, a light helicopter adapted for Delta Force use. The tops of the trees suddenly swayed, while he and his teammates came up over a stand of pines, and a bus loaded with passengers made its way down a dirt road next to the sandy pine thicket. The Little Bird had flown out in front of the bus and gone into a hover, when suddenly the trunk of a tree exploded and the large pine fell across the bus's path with a loud thump. The Little Bird set down in a cloud of light tan sand, followed by a second Little Bird, as eight Delta operators poured off the seats mounted on both sides of the choppers, with three of them, including Charlie, boarding the bus. A "hostage," Pitbull, who was actually Charlie's team commander, a captain, who was a star full-back on the West Point football team, was flex-cuffed and seated on the second seat, with a dummy terrorist next to him with a gun, and a dummy terrorist behind him holding another gun to his head.

Charlie put a double-tap into the face of the terrorist next to Pitbull, while a teammate double-tapped the forehead of the terrorist behind the hostage. *Boom!* The back door of the bus exploded open and two more teammates came through the emergency exit door and shot up the remaining hostage holders, having to be very careful not to shoot the live bus driver now slumped in faux death over the large black steering wheel. They followed Charlie and his teammate as the two of them grabbed Pitbull by the upper arms and escorted him to the first Little Bird, where he was tossed in. The remaining C.A.G operators had formed a perimeter around the two aircraft and fell back as the remaining team members hopped onto the benches. The pilots cranked up the rotors, and sand swirled out and up from the rotor wash, and the Little Birds lifted up, banked left, and rose over the tree cover, roaring away, leaving a smoking bus, full of shot-up mannequins and one real driver feigning death as he still lay across the steering wheel.

This part of North Carolina was covered with tall, stately evergreens, with interspersed swamps filled with hardwoods. The ground everywhere was sandy with a fine, grainy sand, sometimes almost white. Most of the pines found at Fort Bragg had no lower branches. This was partly from the army very wisely warding off large forest fires by trimming the trunks of the trees at least ten feet off the ground. That way, in a dry year, a fire would be more likely to simply sweep through a forest or thicket burning dry grasses and undergrowth and at the most darkening the trunks of trees, but not igniting the highly flammable and sometimes explosive upper canopy.

The entire team hydrated with water and Gatorade, and

then met in the audio visual room to watch several camera angles of their execution of the mission, after which the self-critique would begin.

Pitbull called Charlie aside after the debriefing, calling him by his nickname, short for Pocahontas. "Poke, the Old Man and the staff want you in the briefing room tomorrow morning at oh-dark-thirty for a heavy-duty briefing."

"'Bout what, Cap?"

"Beats me," the team leader replied. "You know, need-to-know. None of my business, I guess. I just know it is something classified Tango Sierra, NOFORN."

The latter were the phonetic letters for TS (top secret) and the acronym for "no foreigners."

The briefing room was filled with a number of strangers when Charlie entered the next morning. He could tell several were probably retired army officers and in shock when they saw the laxity in the military demeanor of the several Detachment-Delta personnel in the room.

The Old Man and the command sergeant major came in, and Charlie said, "Good morning, Pops. Morning, Weasel."

Pops grinned and nodded. Weasel, the senior noncommissioned officer in 1st SFOD-D, said, "Howdy, Poke."

Just about everybody in Detachment-Delta had a nickname, even the bosses, and there was little or no military formality, because the anonymity was so important. Charlie had even, early on, gotten in trouble for being dressed too noticeably with his obvious modern-day Lakota attire and hairstyle, until he explained that with his dark complexion and jet black hair, he would come under even closer scrutiny by people wondering if he was a Middle Easterner. This made complete sense to the commanding officer, Colonel Peter "Pops" Gresham.

Colonel Gresham had started out as an enlisted man, a grunt, and then made it through the Special Forces qualification course and earned his Green Beret and Special Forces tab as a weapons specialist. He attended language school for Tagalog, which is a native dialect from the Philippines, and worked on an A-Detachment with the 1st Special Forces Group in Okinawa, working his way up to sergeant first class, while also taking night and correspondence classes and getting his bachelor's degree in organizational management, with emphasis on management of human resources.

At the suggestion of the 1st Group commander, he applied for and was accepted to Officer Candidate School and graduated as the honor graduate. He spent a year as a second lieutenant platoon leader with the 82nd Airborne at Fort Bragg, North Carolina, and then was snatched to the USA J. F. Kennedy Special Warfare Center, where he was promoted to first lieutenant and became an aide-de-camp to the commanding general of the center. He soon made captain, and after begging the general for command time, he became a detachment commander of an ODA, or Operational Detachment-A, referred to by many as an "A-team," with the 10th Special Forces Group at Fort Devens, Massachusetts, and then he and the group relocated to Fort Carson, Colorado.

He went through Selection for C.A.G. and was a Detachment-Delta operator for some time, but then, after making it to lieutenant colonel, he ended up becoming deputy commanding officer of the 10th Group. When he finally hit the list for full bird, he was slated to take over either the 10th Group or the 1st Group, and he knew he eventually would have made brigadier and maybe ended up in command of Special Forces, but he made his feelings very clear that he wanted command of 1st Special Forces Operational Detachment-Delta, even if it meant sacrificing a star or two on his lapel. After becoming an operator, Gresham became a true believer that this unit was the elite of the elite and was very much needed, especially since he made his eagle after September 11, 2001.

One day, Poke was speaking to Weasel in his office, and

he said, "Top, I need to speak with the Old Man," just as Colonel Gresham was walking in the door.

"The Old Man?" he joked. "The Old Man? Why not just call me Pops or Grandpa, since I already have one foot in the grave?"

Weasel said, "That sounds great, Colonel, since every swingin' Richard in this unit but you has a nickname. You are Pops from now on!"

So that was how the colonel got his nickname, but Charlie was a different story. One guy tried nicknaming him "Chief" and another "Tonto," and they both got educated.

Charlie was not totally friendly when he explained, "Every white guy in the world, just about, calls just about every red guy in the world either Chief or Tonto, and every white guy thinks he is the first person to think of the nickname."

In Delta and Special Forces, merciless teasing is the name of the game, so Weasel immediately picked up on Charlie's irritation and said, "You know, we are in the army and need to be politically correct, guys, and I can see someone will get punched if you guys call Charlie by such a racially charged name, so from now on, in order to be more sensitive we'll call him Pocahontas."

All the operators, who were actually gathering for beers at the end of the day at the Green Beret Club on Smoke Bomb Hill, just roared with laughter, including Charlie, who laughed at himself and shook his head. It did not take long for that name to be shortened to "Poke."

One of the men in the conference room was Damien Percy Rozanski, a retired major general from the Military Intelligence branch who had spent almost his entire career in staff positions. He was a devout politician and a devout liberal. The current commander in chief was a conservative and so were many officers in the GWOT, regardless of what they showed the public, so Percy, as he was called by his very few close friends, was sneaky and underhanded in many of his dealings. He had political ambitions and clearly saw himself as the future savior of the Democratic Party. He now held a position as an undersecretary of Homeland Security and had a very arrogant attitude toward many in the room and wherever he went. Maybe it was because of his membership in the Mensa Society, or maybe it was because what he saw in the mirror and what the public saw were opposites. When he glanced into the looking glass, he always viewed a Great Dane, but when the public viewed him most saw a sad, old, overweight basset hound.

Kerri Rhodes, the national security advisor to the president, was there.

A very large gentleman, behemoth actually, was there who was an assistant director of the CIA. His name was Bunny Hawkins.

Another participant was Randall Yost, deputy director of the DIA, the Defense Intelligence Agency, and who was a recently retired colonel who'd spent much of his career with the U.S. Army Rangers, until he got enthused about Military Intelligence when he became the S2, the intelligence officer, of his Ranger regiment.

There were several more bureaucrats there, from several government agencies.

Charlie was introduced by Weasel to everybody in the room, and he made his assessments based on eye contact, firmness of handshake, and demeanor. He really liked Bunny Hawkins, Kerri Rhodes, and Randy Yost, but he was totally put off by Rozanski and a few others. This initial assessment of people was very strong.

After people grabbed coffee, tea, and pastries, they were all seated and Weasel went up to the podium.

"Ladies and gentlemen, this briefing is classified top secret and no foreigners regardless of a need-to-know. It will automatically be downgraded at four-year intervals and declassified, unless otherwise attended to, at the end of a twelve-year period. Nothing discussed herein is to be discussed verbally or in writing anywhere outside this room, which is electronically swept daily. Are there any questions on this matter just discussed?"

Without comment, he introduced Pops, who walked out from behind the podium.

Pops said, "How many in this room have not heard of an Iranian named Davood Faraz Dabdeh?"

Charlie wondered what that guy's story was.

CHAPTER SIX

Bad Guy

GISELLE Michelin grew up in the Alsace-Lorraine part of the south of France, the wealthy daughter of a couple who had made their mark in world culinary markets with a very large array of fine French wines and liqueurs. A beauty who graduated from the Sorbonne, she was multilingual, very rich, and loved to play, especially skiing all over the world. On this particular day, she wore a tight one-piece ski suit and was standing at the top of a sunny slope at almost twelve thousand feet in elevation, flashing her eyes at the handsome ski instructor she'd hired at the lodge. The noise of the red, enclosed two-person ski lifts opening and closing was distracting, but it was important to her to bat her eyes at this tall, dark, and handsome foreigner at the top of the mountain. Actually, she was the foreigner in his land, not the other way around, but in her mind, he was the foreigner.

She would hold back on the way down, so his male ego would not be deflated if he learned how good she really was. She had only hired him for his looks and build, and was not concerned about learning to ski. She had been on some of the world's most challenging expert slopes, but she had this thing for ski instructors, especially in foreign lands.

Giselle looked into his dark brown eyes and saw the dark tan of his skin beneath his ski goggles. It took her breath away. Looking out across the snow-filled valley, they headed down the hill, with him following her.

He stared at the movement of her muscles beneath her tight-fitting ski suit, and lust filled his mind. He would have this woman today, he decided. He had her checked out before they even left the lodge to grab their skis and climb into one of the lifts.

There were two lodges at the base of the mountain, and he had the largest suite available, because he was filthy rich, and he was so very, very powerful. It took only a few minutes by the fire in the lodge and then a short meal, and they were headed to his suite.

He held her at the big picture window looking up at the slopes, his muscular arms wrapped protectively around her from behind. He slowly pulled her long hair off her shoulder and kissed her gently on the back of her neck. She felt a tingle running down her spine, and as if she could barely breathe. She lifted one of his hands up to her mouth and started sucking on his index finger. His left hand slid up under her breast and her breath caught. Then he slowly moved it back down. She wanted it to move back toward her breast, which is the way he wanted her to feel.

Suddenly, she felt her suit fall away from her body, and only then realized his hand had stealthily moved away and undone her ski suit. Now her sports bra fell to the floor, and she got goose bumps all over. She wanted to reach up and scratch her breasts, which she always did after removing her bra, but she did not want to move her hands, or anything.

She knew he was doing something behind her and then knew what it was as she felt his hardness against her. He had removed his own clothing. Now his left hand returned and lingered just below her left breast, but then dropped down again. Her breathing became heavier. His left hand now came up on her shoulder, and he slowly spun her around, and their first kiss was soft, very soft. Then their lips came together with a passion, and parted, and his tongue started teasing into her mouth and then withdrawing.

He lay her down on the antique Persian rug in front of the raging fire, and slowly kissed softly down her body until he was where he knew he would send her to the heights of ecstasy. She started cooing and was soon screaming in orgasmic delight, as he alternated teasing her and pleasing her, and the passion kept building.

She wanted their bodies to become one, so badly now.

"*S'il vous plaît?* Please?" she begged. "Get eenside me now. I beg you."

She felt him as he did so, looking into his dark brown eyes and holding on to his very muscular massive arms as he entered and went deep inside her.

They both spoke in English, which each knew quite well.

Finally, he spoke, saying, "Scream!"

This took her by surprise, and she said, *"Qu'est-ce que c'est?"*

He laughed and she saw his large hand come up in the air and whack her viciously across her face. She felt her cheekbone break and could no longer see out of her left eye.

She could not believe what was happening, and now he pumped in and out of her vigorously, injuring her with each thrust. She started screaming, and he laughed loudly. He punched her full power in the face, breaking her nose and pulping her lips. Giselle was barely conscious now.

She awakened slowly and saw him naked in front of the mirror. She reached up and touched her face and wanted to scream again. It was all large swollen areas, and her left eye was swollen completely shut; her nose was shattered, and she felt that half her teeth were missing. Giselle now noticed that her ribs must be broken, as she could barely breathe. She panicked as Davood Faraz Dabdeh walked over to her. He bent over smiling, and stood back as his big leg went up in the air. She saw his heel almost in slow motion as it came down stomping at her face, and she felt all the bones smash as it crashed into her, and then the pain started subsiding, as the life ebbed out of her body. The last thing she heard was Davood picking up the telephone.

"Send up that valet named Muhammad."

Minutes later, a well-built, handsome Iranian twenty-year-old showed up at the door of the suite and was shocked when he saw the dead woman in front of the fireplace. Davood was still nude and still sexually excited.

Speaking in Persian, he said, "She is just a woman. We must get rid of her body later. We will make it look like an auto crash. Women are for procreation. Men are for pleasure. Remove your clothes and come to my bed."

Few people knew about the Dizin, Shemshak, Ab Ali, Darbandsar, and other ski resorts in the mountains north and northwest of Tehran, but this was where Davood posed as a ski instructor and easily met with numerous foreign and domestic agents. He enjoyed skiing, and also met many beautiful women to abuse and men to make love to.

He and the mullahs and oil sheiks behind him felt that Osama bin Laden and al-Zawahiri had really slipped in stature, because they'd lost so many warriors in Iraq and Afghanistan, and Davood Faraz Dabdeh was an up-and-comer. He was born in Iran, but spent much of his life in Saudi Arabia and Afghanistan. He was incredibly wealthy himself from his own family's oil fortunes, and most important he was ambitious and ruthless.

One of his vices was raping and murdering women, and in Iran, under Sharia law, homosexuality could call for death by hanging, stoning, or being cut in half. On Monday, September 24, 2007, during a speech to students and faculty at Columbia University, Iranian President Mahmoud Ahmadinejad declared that there were "no homosexuals in Iran." As crazy as this sounded to every thinking person in the world, this was something he wanted to stringently enforce. Davood, however, was totally immune, because he brought so much to the table for not only Iran, but also that group of fanatical Muslims who desperately wanted the demise of Jews and Christians and who came from not only Iran, but Palestine, Saudi Arabia, Syria, Libya, Afghanistan, and several more countries.

Muhammad had two friends help him take Giselle's body to her rental vehicle. They drove it down the road leading toward Tehran and simply sent it over the side, after setting it ablaze with her behind the front wheel. Then they all jumped in Davood's Cadillac Escalade and rode back to the ski resort. All three young men went home that night with plenty of rials in their pockets.

As he showered, the handsome Iranian terrorist pictured Giselle's wealthy parents hearing about her death and wailing. He started to laugh and wondered how stupid infidels were for giving so much import to women. To him, infidels, all infidels, were completely stupid anyway.

CHAPTER SEVEN

Plan Your Work,
Work Your Plan

CHARLIE Strongheart looked around the conference room, wondering about each man. He knew he was about to be given a mission, and he wondered what role each man would play, and if any would have the naiveté or downright stupidity that might send him to his death. Just then the door opened, and Custer came in the door. He nodded at Weasel and Pops and grinned at Charlie. Charlie winked at him. The large, very beefy man walked over to the coffeepot and poured a huge cup of coffee.

He sat down in the chair next to Charlie and finally said, "Sorry for the disruption, Pops, but I just got paged."

Pops said, "This is a singleton operation and Charlie is the primary, but you will be his backup, Custer. Top, will you come up and give the security lecture again?"

Weasel jumped up. "Airborne!"

He gave the same cautioning words from memory and turned the floor back over to Pops.

Custer was a chief warrant officer on Charlie's team who had opted for Warrant Officer School when both were sergeants first class. He had been a Ranger for a while but wanted more and went through Selection for Special Forces when he was in his late twenties. Like Charlie, he had served on ODAs (Operational Detachment-A, or A-Teams), and he worked on the SCUBA Committee for a while down in Florida, then came to Charlie's team in Detachment-Delta after his C.A.G. selection.

Custer was one of those men who was just always bigger than anybody and everybody, but he never looked fat. His father was a decorated Ranger in Vietnam, his grandfather a decorated Ranger in WWII and Korea. His great-grandfather was a doughboy in WWI, and his family went back in the military all the way to the Revolutionary War. His great-great-grandfather was a corporal with Major Reno in the Battle of the Little Big Horn. Benteen and Reno were two officers who split off from Custer's main column before the battle, which would become famous as Custer's Last Stand. Both of their units had staggering losses, but were not wiped out like Custer was. This Custer's great-great-grandfather had survived the battle.

Because of this background and because Charlie was a descendant of Sitting Bull, the famous Hunkpapa Lakota who was credited as the chief reigning over the Battle of the Little Big Horn, the colonel himself nicknamed CW3 Jace Daniel, as Custer.

Actually, Sitting Bull was a holy man, which had much greater import than being a chief. There were many chiefs who were battlefield commanders in that battle, such as Crazy Horse, Gall, Rain-in-the-Face, but for the most part each tribe, and consequently nation, did not have overall chiefs like the white man has shown, but elders and councils. The feeling was that no man should have a boss telling him how to live. Sitting Bull was like the Billy Graham for the Lakota.

The Lakota or Sioux were a nation; then that Lakota nation was further broken down into various clans, or tribes, such as the Hunkpapa, Oglala, Minniconjou, Teton,

Yankton, Brule or Sicangu, Izipaco, Sihasapa, Ooinunpa, and more. Many white men and others often have misunderstood these distinctions. The names Lakota, Dakota, and Nakota, also called the Sioux, actually mean "friend" or "ally."

Pops told about the ironic backgrounds of Jace Daniel and Charlie Strongheart, as well as their experience and training in the army. He then introduced all the people in the room.

This was followed by an introduction of retired General Rozanski. He had planned to start a PowerPoint presentation on Davood Faraz Dabdeh, but the conference room door opened.

A beautiful, athletic-looking, well-built woman entered the room, and Charlie and Jace gave each other a slight grin. Custer and Poke had never met her and were anxious to learn about her. She apparently would be part of this operation. She spotted them both and walked over very confidently and sat down between them. Without speaking, she turned and shook hands with each of them.

There were actually some women in 1st Special Forces Operational Detachment-Delta, and nobody outside of Detachment-Delta knew about them. They essentially stayed to themselves, trained together, and were called the "Funny Platoon" by the other C.A.G. operators who sometimes worked with them. Most were military intelligence, civil affairs, or psyops specialists of varying expertise, and were used with male Delta operators when there was a need for covert activity and a married couple or boyfriend and girlfriend pair might raise less suspicion. They were also used when it was less conspicuous for a woman to be in a certain area than a man.

She nodded at Pops when he got up and excused himself with the general.

"Folks, I want to introduce you to Sergeant First Class

Fila Jannat. She will be involved in this operation, too. Sergeant Jannat is a decorated combat veteran, an intelligence and language specialist, an expert skydiver, an all-around athlete, and a fully qualified and highly trained member of our unit."

She smiled and nodded at everyone in the room. Fila Jannat was an Iranian name, Charlie thought, and he wondered to himself what her story was.

Fila was born in Tehran to a very strict, traditional Shia Muslim father. Her mother felt sorry for her, as her father was so strict, but she could never show her concern for her daughter to him. The youngster was extremely intelligent and even as a young girl was always the most beautiful female in the room, whether faces were covered or not. Her body was as beautiful as the rest of her, and it developed very early. When she was fourteen years old, Fila was assaulted but not actually raped by her first cousin, and he was caught by her father. She was naked, as he had torn her robe from her, but she had fought the lad off successfully. The young man was severely lectured by Fila's father and his own father, her father's older brother. The boy was even given seven lashes.

Fila's father made his decision about Fila as soon as he learned what had happened. His daughter had disgraced his family and would be stoned to death in an honor killing the next day in the square down the street. He intended to hurl the first stone.

Fila's mother risked her own life and well-being by waking the young lady in the middle of that night. She gave her a handful of rials and told her that her own first cousin, who was a merchant, was traveling to Baghdad and would secrete her there. Her mother had tears in her eyes, but told Fila to leave quickly and make her way to the mother's cousin and hand him the money. She said the man could be trusted and indeed he could.

In Baghad, she got a job in a downtown café and worked hard, saving money, and continued to grow even more beautiful. All was well, until she was spotted by several of Saddam Hussein's top bodyguards one day walking with a coworker. She and the coworker were taken to one of the president's opulent palaces on the Tigris River. The bullies soon learned that she and the young man were Shiites, and Saddam and those who were in his ruling class were all Sunnis. The men laughed while two of them raped her on a sofa, and while her friend wanted to help but watched helplessly. Afterward, she was escorted to the big gates on the giant compound and shoved out into the street. The young man was then sodomized and started crying, so one of the bodyguards put a bullet in his forehead while the others laughed. His body was dumped in the river.

It took two days of hiding and abject fear, but Fila made it back to the café. She sat down with the owner, who was a man who had been trained to run a restaurant while in New York City for four years. He spoke about his positive experiences all the time in America. It was with his assistance that she was finally able to get a one-way ticket.

On her way to America, Fila got into a conversation with the flight attendant. That woman's husband was a Special Forces colonel commanding the 5th Special Forces Group at Fort Campbell, Kentucky. The couple were also very devout Christians. She ended up inviting Fila to their home in Hopkinsville, Kentucky. Fila spoke for hours about her life growing up, and they all became close. They invited her to their church, and she became their foster daughter and ended up converting to Christianity. Before she graduated, she was adopted and became a U.S. citizen.

She had a natural bent for athletics and took to it in high school. Then, there was a little college, but she was so proud to become a citizen, and had such strong feelings against the oppressiveness, especially against innocent children and women, of fundamentalist Muslims like her biological father, that she felt the U.S. Army would help her self-actualize more than anything.

Nobody in any of her training units, starting with Basic and including Jump School, was anywhere close to as gung-ho and intense as Fila.

In recent years she had also joined Brigitte Gabriel's American Congress for Truth and become even more impassioned about educating and putting an end to some of the horrible practices of Islam. Her C.A.G. selection and assignment to the Funny Platoon was the final step for her. She felt she had arrived, and she loved Detachment-Delta and the entire concept of it. Her experience was a lot different from the men's experience, but ultimately, the overall mission was what mattered. The fact that she spoke level 4 Arabic and was totally and completely fluent in Persian made her one of the most invaluable members of Delta Force, man or woman.

Fila acted like just one of the boys between the two men, even juggling three cups of coffee at one point, which Charlie and Custer also did.

At a later point one team would be brought into the operation to act as a standby backup for Charlie and Fila, when the time was right, in case they got into trouble.

During a break in the briefing, Charlie and Jace both started getting acquainted with Fila, and Charlie said, "Hey, my nickname is Pocahontas, but guys call me Poke, and he is called Custer. What kind of nickname did they give you in the platoon?"

Fila's face turned bright red, and she smiled shyly. "Booty," she said.

Custer laughed and said, "Why did they call you that?"

Charlie said, "If you would have looked when she walked in, man, there would not be a question in your mind."

She was embarrassed and slapped Charlie across the

arm, saying, "Hey, Poke, I lift weights and do lots of squats. Okay?"

"I'm not complaining, Boot-Tay," he said, and laughed, as did Custer. "It is working very well. Keep lifting."

Rozanski seemed to be getting to the end of his Power-Point and suddenly spoke directly to Charlie and Fila.

"Sergeants Strongheart and Jannat," he said, "this is where you two come into the overall picture. As we have seen, Davood Faraz Dabdeh is fast becoming the new Osama bin Laden. He is wealthy, well connected, and has the total backing of Iran. He is younger than bin Laden, charismatic, insane, and totally ruthless. The man is attracting all the young disenfranchised Mideastern zanies. You two will infiltrate the country of Iran by means of a high-altitude HALO infiltration with O2 and wearing skis," he said, referring to High Altitude, Low Opening jumping.

Charlie stood and said, "Excuse me, General Rozanski, is it?"

The pudgy man nodded, his face reddening at the interruption.

Charlie was grinning. "General Rozanski, somebody has been watching too many James Bond movies. I do not know about Sergeant Jannat, but I do my skiing on holidays, and we are trained to plan our own methods of infiltration. With all due respect, my boss will give us our mission, and we will all sit down and plan the best method of infiltration, which often is not the popular one of those who do not do our work, a HALO operation."

Rozanski got huffy, saying, "Now, see here, Sergeant, I want to tell you right now—"

Pops jumped up, interrupting, saying first, "Sit down, Charlie."

"Yes, sir!"

Pops went on, "General Rozanski, Sergeant Strongheart is correct. We plan the execution of our own operations, and Sergeant Strongheart and Sergeant Jannat will have the most say-so, as it will be their asses on the line."

Rozanski was not used to being spoken to by a colonel like this, even if he was retired. His roommate from West Point was chief of staff of the U.S. Army, too. He was not afraid to play that card, and had before. He would threaten it now, as that usually handled any problems.

He said, "Well, Colonel, we have spent months upon months and many man-hours putting together this operations order, and we want it followed to the letter to ensure mission success. If you need to get the order from the chief of staff of the army . . ."

"Screw your cousin!" Pops said angrily. "You do not come into this compound, in fact, the chief of staff of the U.S. Army does not come in here, without my blessing. It is not your chair-polishing ass being risked in the most dangerous country in the world for Americans. General, do not come into our compound and try barking orders to my people, especially when you are now a civilian. My operators are the very best in the world at what they do, men and women. We do not lower the bar to allow them into this unit, and we do not lower the bar on our standard of excellence or our operational readiness. Now, if you want to start over, General, and conclude your briefing with the suggested mission, we will coordinate that with the powers that be in MacDill, Langley, DC, or wherever we happen to speak to people, and we will develop our own operational plan for execution of that mission. There is zero compromise on this. Now, would you care, sir, to start over?"

The general stood in a fury, his fists balled, and suddenly a voice shocked him.

"Sit down, General Rozanski," Kerri Rhodes, the national security advisor to the president barked. "As ordered, and with the colonel's knowledge, the commander in chief has been listening to this briefing over my scrambled phone, and he wants me to put him on speaker."

The beautiful White House executive set her cell phone on the briefing table and said, "Go ahead. Mr. President."

The familiar voice came over the expensive cell phone. "Thank you, Kerri. General Rozanski, can you hear me?"

"Yes, Mr. President," Rozanski said meekly.

The chief executive of the Free World went on. "I want to thank you on behalf of the citizens of the United States for your uniformed service to this nation, and your continued service to this nation as a civilian."

Rozanski was shocked. "Well, thank you, Mr. President. It has been my honor."

The President went on. "But I want to make myself perfectly clear, you see the old man they call Pops with the short gray hair and ugly face sitting across from you?"

"Yes, sir."

"Well, you want to name-drop," the CINC snapped, "that ugly old man goes golfing with me every time he is in DC, and we have teed off out by the O-Club there at Bragg a couple times. If you ever invoke your cousin's name to get your way with or ever disrespect that ugly old man again, I will direct him to have Master Sergeant Charlie Strongheart, who is a true American hero and a genuine American badass, stomp you into a puddle of blood and mud. Do I make myself perfectly clear, sir?"

"Yes, Mr. President. I am sorry, sir." Rozanski could barely breathe, he was so upset and embarrassed.

Charlie felt a hand squeeze his thigh, in a reassuring, not a sexy way. He knew it was Fila's. He barely looked over, and they gave each other almost imperceptible smiles. Custer did not miss that and gave Charlie a glance of approval, too.

After a brief few words of encouragement to the assembled group as well as specifically to Poke, Booty, and Custer, the President bid them all adieu.

Weasel stood up and said, "Ladies and gentlemen, before we continue, let's take a ten-minute potty break. Smokers, go outside that door there and smoke 'em if you got 'em."

Charlie, Pops, Custer, Booty, and Weasel met at the pop machine and simultaneously started chuckling.

Pops said, "Good thinking on the break, Top. That'll give him a chance to lock himself in a stall and bawl his eyes out."

Ten minutes later, they reconvened, and Rozanski had apparently composed himself. In actuality, he was infuriated and already doing what he always did, trying to figure out how he would get revenge. For now, though, he would conclude his briefing with the mission and would forget about his long-planned operational phase.

"Ladies and gentlemen, to recap," he said, "Davood Faraz Dabdeh is a brand-new Osama bin Laden in the making, with the complete backing and support of Iran. He is receiving excessive amounts of funding from members of the royal family in Saudi Arabia, as well as funding sources in Syria and Palestine. We cannot afford to have him around much longer, because each day his security heightens and his popularity soars. Most importantly, he has the full support and backing of the most radical mullahs. Your mission, Sergeants Strongheart and Jannat, is to infiltrate the country of Iran, breach his considerable security, and facilitate his demise in a malicious manner. You are then to exfiltrate from the country of Iran without being detected. It is of major import that nothing connects this operation to the United States of America."

Custer raised his hand, smiling. "General, you said 'facilitate his demise in a malicious manner.' That isn't your expression, is it?"

Rozanski started grinning himself, and said, "No, Mr. Daniel. That is not my expression. I think I would have used the word 'assassinate' or 'execute' or something. One of our executives came up with that."

There was a relieved chuckle in the room and Fila chimed in, "How about 'pop a cap in his jihadist ass'?"

The room burst out in laughter, and even Rozanski laughed, maybe a little too hard.

Weasel added, "Well at least it's better than 'terminate with extreme prejudice.'"

Charlie stood and said, "It seems this might be an operation more suited to a singleton, than both of us going in. No offense to Sergeant Jannat at all, but why must she risk her life on this operation?"

Pops interrupted. "We will discuss her exact role in our mission planning, but the feeling is that you could pose as a couple, and she speaks Persian as her original language and also speaks Arabic at a level 4 fluency. She knows all the habits and nuances in Iran and Iraq, too, if you would have to E and E there. She grew up in Iran and then moved to Iraq before coming to the United States. On top of that, she is a C.A.G.-qualified operator, and is a good backup to take out Dabdeh in case you get killed or wounded."

"Yes, sir," Charlie replied. "Fine with me if you have confidence in her."

Pops stood and said in a conciliatory voice, "General Rozanski, we really appreciate the hard work you and your staff put into the J2 and J3 on this assignment. We can accomplish this mission and will begin planning immediately."

More participants were introduced and all aspects of the operation were covered by various experts.

At the end of day, Pops said to the Delta operators, "Can I buy you all a beer at the Green Beret Club?"

All agreed and met less than a half hour later on Smoke Bomb Hill, driving up over the curb and parking under pine trees across the street, as the place was always so packed. They went inside, ordered drinks, and got out of the main room, filled with civilian-garbed Special Forces retirees, as well as those still on active duty and wearing duty uniforms. The small group went out onto the adjacent enclosed porch and got a table in the corner, avoiding some of the loud chatter from within. On seeing the ages of the group and their manner of dress, long hair, and facial hair, everyone else there figured these were Delta Force operators. Several in the room knew they were, as some had served with each person. They ignored the Delta group, knowing they would want to be left alone.

After two or three beers Weasel would always start to become philosophical, much to everyone's delight. He grew up not far from Billings, Montana, the son of a third-generation cattle rancher. He loved the American Indian growing up and read many books on the subject. Whenever he had a little too much to drink, he would always try to impress Charlie with what he considered Native American folklore and philosophy.

His opportunity came when Booty said, "I could not believe what a jerk that retired general was. What was his name, Rozanski?"

Weasel took a long sip of beer and grinned, saying, "Yes, but you never let that interfere with accomplishing the mission. Since Poke and Custer both are here, I want to tell you a little story.

"There once was a young man who was a member of the Cheyenne nation. His father was a great leader in his tribe and was the leader of his family's band, a leader in both war and in peace. When the buffalo disappeared, he was the man all turned to for words of wisdom, for he understood the buffalo and the seasons, even grazing patterns.

"Walking among the lodges, he would feel all eyes on him waiting, hoping for some word of comfort to let them know the buffalo would come, and with them would come the hides needed for the approaching winter months, and the food for their bellies, the tools made of bones, and the fun sitting around a fire at night wiping greasy fingers onto the arms and legs to comfort the skin treated so harshly at times by Father Sun."

Here he paused to take a long drink from his beer and begin the next glass provided by Pops.

Weasel went on, looking out as if he were Chief Gall surveying a field of battle on the grassy plains of Montana, "Sensing the fear and apprehension, Fights the Bear would stop within the tribal circle and many would gather round. He would pause and survey the crowd, so his words would have greater effect when he spoke.

"Finally, he would say, 'Hear me, my people, for my words have iron. Mother Earth is feeding her children, the bison, in the valley of the Greasy Grass, then they will move this way and will soon feed in our valley, maybe seven suns (days), maybe ten. The bear lives in my belly, too, but we have many rabbits here to eat, and berries, and fish in the river, and soon *tatanka* (buffalo or bison) will come here and our bellies will be full, our dogs will have bones, our lodges will be warm. Do not fear.'

"People would go about their way, feeling relieved and better and hopeful for the future, and his little son, Red Moccasins, would stare up at his dad with wonder and admiration, but without a cursory glance at his little boy, Fights the Bear would walk on to the games lodge for a game of chance with his friends. His oldest son, the apple of his eye, Angry Horse, had tried to count coup in the season when the snows melt, and he fought the mighty bear, but a grizzly weighing over one half a ton broke his neck and killed the young man. Privately, Fights the Bear wept.

"When Red Moccasin's older brother died, it seemed to him like his father, the father of the youngest son, had died, too. He no longer looked at the little boy. He did not teach him how to hunt or fish or trap. But Red Moccasins was a young man of great wisdom who would also someday alleviate the fears of his tribe. He knew that his father, although he acted like he did not know him, actually loved him so much he feared he might lose another son if he loved too much. Red Mocassins knew that Fights the Bear was like all others and was also afraid. He was afraid of loss. Red Moccasins tried to speak to his father about this, but the old man would not listen. His heart was cold. So Red Moccasins decided to love his father for what he was, and grow up to be a better man, and he grew to be a mighty and wise chief and a great warrior and a leader among the dog soldiers and the strong-hearts."

Charlie grabbed a napkin and pretended to be crying and wiping away tears.

He said, "Kind of brings tears to your eyes, doesn't it?"

The group started laughing and Weasel just stared at him, finally saying, "Stick it up your red ass, Poke."

He took a swallow of beer, and Custer said, "Now, there is some wise philosophy."

Everybody laughed even harder.

This evening was now turning into a going away party, maybe a farewell party, as everybody drank more rounds.

Getting serious, but winking at Booty, Pops, and Custer, Charlie said, "Weasel, that was a great story. I have one for you now to tell your grandchildren."

Weasel looked up from his beer and said, "Huh?"

Charlie said, "There was a magnificent, mature bald eagle, sinewy and graceful in flight, a gentle quiet bundle of muscled power at rest. There was wisdom in those sharp eyes that could see a rabbit stirring miles away on the prairie. Young eaglets came to him to learn how to become an eagle, but most were not willing to listen to all, and one by one they would perish.

"The life of an eagle is harsh and tough, and only the

strongest survive. Some would listen and learn and live longer, but very few would do all that he would suggest. Very few got to the point where their head feathers and tail feathers were pure white like his. Many would perish while still covered with down, and some even armored with a coat of brown feathers. A few, a very few, would make it long enough to grow some brown and white feathers. He hurt for those who did not make it, but knew that was the way of nature, and of life itself.

"One day, he was teaching one of his young protégés, a handsome young bird named Egbert. This was a bird who had actually become garbed in the fine plumage of brown and white speckled feathers, but had not earned that pure white crown."

While Weasel sat transfixed by the story, his eyes a little glazed, Charlie quickly turned his head and grinned at Booty, whispering, "Egbert?"

He continued, "Out over the prairie, the elder eagle spotted a wicked storm brewing and headed their way. He knew, from his own survival and lessons learned at the side of his father, what a real eagle has to do to survive such a plight.

"He looked at Egbert and said, 'If you want to become an eagle that this country uses for its national symbol, a bird of great wisdom and power, if you truly want to soar, you must follow me when this storm arrives and do whatever I tell you.'

"The winds of the storm were increasing, and lightning flashes crashed into objects far out on the prairie, now getting drenched like a giant sponge. The front of the storm was approaching like a giant tidal wave, and Egbert trembled in fear. He spotted a small overhang on the cliff face and thought it might produce shelter from the storm. He would get drenched but maybe he would survive.

"In a panic, Egbert bolted for the overhang and the old eagle screamed, 'Egbert, that will not work! Follow me!'

"The storm was almost upon them and the thunder made frightening sounds. Shivering, Egbert huddled under the overhang and watched in more fear as the mighty eagle flew directly into the path of the storm and entered the black clouds, leaving Egbert to get drenched and shiver in fear and panic, but scared enough to decide not to move. He would show that old eagle.

"There was a loud crash and a blinding light as the lightning bolt tore through Egbert's body, which was now tossed off the cliff by the powerful winds, to simply become just one more piece of muddy ruins on the canyon floor below. He was not dead though. He was in frightful pain, but before he crashed onto the rocks at the cliff base, he remembered how many times the wise old eagle had helped him learn and grow before. With his last strength, he started flapping his wings harder than ever before. Still scared, he looked up at the black skies all around him, but he closed his beak tightly, determined to survive. He would think of everything that old eagle ever taught him. Right before he hit the ground, a big swirl of wind caught under his wings and lifted him up. Worn out and still frightened, he smiled and said, 'Oh.'

"In the meantime, the wise old eagle sought out the most powerful winds in the storm and used their fury to lift him up higher and higher, until he emerged into the sunlight thousands of feet up, high above the killer storm below. He felt very badly for Egbert, but knew the best way to keep teaching eaglets how to be mighty eagles was to first always be one himself. Even stronger than before from the struggle, the wise old eagle soared above the storm, watching the ferocious winds below as he dried out in the sunlight and swirled in the warm blue skies, his majestic wings reaching out and brushing the cheek of God. He heard a noise and saw Egbert approaching.

"Flying by his old mentor, Egbert smiled, saying, 'I'm sorry I did not trust you.'

"The old eagle grinned. 'That is how we get scars. When they heal, you will be even stronger.'

"On the horizon, they spotted a sun-drenched snow-capped range and decided to soar over and admire its beauty. That, Weasel, is the end of the story."

Everybody looked at Weasel and grinned as he, seemingly oblivious to them, wiped away a tear from his eye and said, "I love you, Poke."

Everybody laughed and Pops said, "I think we had last call already. Come on, Top, I'm driving you home."

Weasel looked up slowly and said, "That was a wonderful story, Boss. Did you hear it?"

Pops laughed and said, "Sure did, Top. Let's saddle up."

"Yes, sir."

CHAPTER EIGHT

Best Laid Plans
of Mice and Men

CHARLIE opened his eyes and looked out the window at the very first rays of morning sun piercing through the glass above his head. He closed his eyes, half awake and half asleep, remembering back to an incident in training that really put Charlie's name and face in everybody's mind for some time.

Charlie had, like many men in Special Forces, a varied background in the martial arts, starting in childhood. He held black belt ranking in freestyle karate, had studied Brazilian jujitsu long enough to earn a brown belt, and had trained for two years in Muay Thai kickboxing. He had also been a star middle linebacker in high school, making all conference his junior year and all state his senior year.

At the time, he was a sergeant first class with the 3rd Special Forces Group at Fort Bragg and had just returned from Afghanistan. He was volunteered for an assignment to the JFK Special Warfare Center, where he was to help out as an "aggressor" for Special Forces trainees going through Small Unit Tactics and Training exercises.

An Operational Detachment-A consisting of twelve

trainees was to search a group of buildings that were set up for this exercise. The buildings contained hidden aggressors armed with industrial-strength red-paint guns. The trainees also had paint guns and were to breach doors, enter buildings, and kill, or preferably capture, aggressors hiding therein. To that end, the team commander, a young captain, carried a couple pairs of flex cuffs to restrain captives with.

The customary breach was to set up an explosive and blow the door to the room. Any aggressors within would hide in the next room while the door was blown, and then jump into the room and try to shoot the Americans as they entered.

The job of each trainee or each aggressor who got shot was to drop in place and die in a rapid and grotesque manner. The Tacs (Special Forces–qualified training sergeants), who are like drill sergeants on steroids, were assembled and watching the trainees go through this exercise.

The plan was for four men to blow the door, and then breach the room and search for any aggressors, killing or taking them prisoner. The men approached the door, while the rest of the team covered the outside watching for potential escapees. The assault team used a small C4 charge to breach the door, as they hid behind a Kevlar shield.

Instead of hiding in the next room, Charlie stood in the middle of the room and braced himself for the explosive impact. He knew that the first trainee would come into the room and move to his right, his eyes sweeping the whole right side; the second would move in and go to the left, his eyes sweeping the left; the third would come in with his eyes sweeping the center of the room; and the fourth would stay back close to the door, covering all.

The door blew and Charlie shook it off, aiming at where he thought the center mass on the first trainee would be coming through the door. Sure enough the first trainee appeared in the doorway and Charlie watched the fake blood splatter all over the center of the man's Kevlar. Shocked, he looked down and then fell, feigning death right in the doorway to the room.

The second man was right on his heels and had to jump over him, getting blasted by two red paintballs in the center of his chest before his feet hit the floor. When they did, he fell backward on top of the first faux dead trainee. The third man jumped over his dead partners and Charlie had him center-mass coming over the pile. He squeezed and *Click! Click!* He looked down and saw his rifle was jammed. Charlie's eyes went up and everything went into slow motion. He saw a grin start on the face of the third trainee, and his eyes open slightly, while also seeing his trigger finger tighten, and Charlie drop-stepped with his left foot spinning sideways. The man's paintball splattered on the wall behind Charlie, and he immediately drop-stepped with his right foot and drew his chest back, as a second paintball also slammed into the wall. The trainee knew he had to take more careful aim. Charlie threw his weapon up in the air for a distraction and took two long fast steps and hit the trainee with a diving tackle, his shoulder catching the young man in the center of his midsection, as Charlie heard the wind leaving him in a rush. They flew backward out into the dirt in front of the building, and the trainee, now under Charlie, scrambled to get free and struggled to breathe right, getting panicky.

The team commander yelled, "Take him prisoner! Do not shoot! Do not shoot!"

The rest of the team ran up and all jumped Charlie at once, and laughing at them and taunting them, he leg-swept the trainees, put a few in wrist locks as they would try to grab his arms, and really frustrated them with his powerful resistance.

Imitating the *Saturday Night Live* send-ups of Arnold Schwarzenegger, while getting strangled, punched, kicked, and pulled on, Charlie said, "Come on, guys. Are you a bunch of girlie men who cunnot evun cuff one scrawny boy?"

One trainee finally got frustrated and put his left knee on the side of Charlie's neck and punched him full power in the face.

Charlie laughed, spit out blood, and said, "Ees that all the harder you can punch, you girlie man? You punch like a pussy boy!"

It was more than fifteen minutes before Charlie was finally cuffed and pulled to his feet. His lips were swollen and bleeding and his right eye was swelling shut.

He looked at the trainee who'd punched him and spit blood into the man's face. In a fury, the trainee lunged at Charlie, whose right foot came up with a vicious side-kick that caught the man on the chin coming in. His head snapped back with an imprint of Charlie's boot on his jaw. He fell backward unconscious.

One of the trainees started to attend to him and a Tac yelled, "Leave him be!"

While the others stayed behind to wait on him and police up brass and their litter, two men held Charlie's upper arms and walked him toward a waiting truck. He moved his feet very slowly, which made it even more difficult for both men, who were sweating profusely because of the hot North Carolina day and horrendous humidity.

The one on his left was fed up and said, "Start walking faster!"

Charlie lied, "I can't. Your buddies flex-cuffed my ankles together."

The trainee said, "I don't give a damn. Walk faster, or we'll drag you."

Charlie chuckled, then grinned and said, "Fine."

He went limp, and they had to grab him with both hands, get a better grip, and start dragging his feet through the dirt.

The other trainee glared at the first and said, "Way to go, genius."

By the time they got to the truck, the others were following, and these two were sweating like stuck pigs in a barbecue shack. They stood Charlie upright, and each grabbed a side of the tailgate to let it down to put their prisoner within.

Charlie backed up slowly and then took off at a dead run, into the woods, his hands still flex-cuffed in front of him. Seeing this from a distance, all the Tacs started laughing and shaking their heads in disbelief. The two men could not catch him, as he was so fast.

After ten minutes of running through the woods, Charlie felt something slam into his ribs, and he flew sideways. One of the trainees had also been an outstanding football player, a free safety, and he loved to tackle. He had run through the woods from his position, as several friends also had, hoping to cut Charlie off. This time several men held his arms and escorted him back to the truck. Half the team crawled in and then Charlie was placed in the middle, as the rest filled in.

Soon, the men were all laughing and talking about their success at capturing Charlie. He kept his mouth shut and feigned nodding off, as the truck slowly wound its way down the one-lane white sandy road in the woods at Fort Bragg, out toward the drop zones, named for WWII drop zones and battles sites, such as St. Mere Eglise, Sicily, and Normandy. Peeking out, Charlie saw that the entire team was engrossed and all speaking with one another and thinking about getting back to garrison, so they ignored him sitting on the floor between their boots.

Charlie looked out the tailgate at the narrow sandy road passing by, grinned to himself, and launched himself over the tailgate headfirst in a powerful dive, somersaulting in midair. He hit the ground on the balls of his feet, but the momentum took him backward, so he simply did a PLF, or parachute landing fall, and ended up relatively unhurt. The SUV following behind the truck loaded with Tacs had to skid to a stop to avoid hitting him. The Tacs all roared with laughter as he raced into the woods, and they saw the trainees trying to get the truck stopped. They bailed out and ran into the woods in pursuit, but Charlie was long gone.

They searched for a half an hour while the Tacs berated and ridiculed them for being made a fool of by one man, who'd escaped not once but twice.

It was closing in on dark, and they had further training the next day, so the head Tac sergeant got a bullhorn from the vehicle and yelled in the direction Charlie had run, "Sergeant Strongheart, this is administrative! You escaped and the exercise is over. Come on in."

Less than one hundred feet into the woods the trainees and Tacs saw movement high up in one of the trees. Sure enough Charlie had climbed the tree and hid there while all the trainees had run below and past the trunk. He approached the Tacs and one cut his flex cuffs with a knife.

All of them started shaking hands with him and patting him on the back. Two handed him plastic bottles of water, and he rode back in their SUV. His eye was already swollen all the way shut.

The next day, almost every man on the team wrote a peer report sharply criticizing the jerk who placed his knee on Charlie's neck and punched him in the face.

He was kicked out of the Special Forces Qualification Program the very next day, and his jacket stated, "Not suitable character for Special Forces operational environment."

Less than one month later, he was in the 3rd Armored Cavalry Regiment with orders for Iraq.

Charlie went home and stayed in bed for two days. He felt like a giant toothache. At the time, he was engaged, and the guys on his team teased him unmercifully over his black eye, which he did not explain. They talked about how she caught him in bed with another man and beat him up. Within a few days, however, the story about Charlie's exploits started circulating on Smoke Bomb Hill and his legend started to grow.

He really loved his fiancée, but she just did not get it with Special Forces. He would come home from something like this, and suddenly not show up for a week with no warning. The young lady was just not cut out to be a Special Forces wife, which really takes an incredible breed of woman.

His eyes snapped open, and he realized he was in a strange place. He looked all around and the room he was in was a bedroom, but it was feminine. There were black-and-white Holstein cows everywhere. There was a clock with the black-and-white patch pattern, a comforter, black-and-white stuffed animal cows all over the dressers and headboard, Holstein curtains, and even a throw rug on the floor with the pattern to it.

There was a light tapping on the door, and it opened. A smiling, radiant-looking Fila walked in. She was already dressed and showered and was holding a large glass of freshly squeezed orange juice.

Charlie was embarrassed and said sheepishly, "Morning, Booty."

She laughed and said, "Here, drink this. Don't worry, Charlie. Nothing happened. We all got blown away last night, and I called us a cab, and I brought you here to my place. This is my spare bedroom."

Charlie took a long sip of orange juice and said, "Thanks. That is good."

"Liquid sunshine."

"It sure is," he said. "You like cows, don't you?"

She laughed, saying, "No, not really, but my little sister does. She visits me a lot, and she collects them, so I decorated this room for her. I was adopted by a Special Forces colonel, you know. He used to command 5th Group at Fort Campbell. She was his youngest daughter. In middle school already."

Pointing, Fila said, "There is a bathroom in there. Help yourself. There's not an extra toothbrush, but there is toothpaste and plenty of washrags you can use. If you want to take a shower, everything you need is in there."

Charlie said, "No, thanks. I'll just brush and clean up. I need to shower and put on some clean clothes at home. I'll be right with you."

A few minutes later, Charlie appeared in the doorway to the kitchen and smelled breakfast and fresh coffee.

She had the small table set, and a steaming breakfast sitting on the table. There was French toast, bacon, and grits with butter on them.

Charlie sat down, saying, "Grits? You're from Iran, and you make grits?"

She chuckled.

"Mom was from South Carolina," she said. "Grits, black-eyed peas, turnip greens, barbecue, hush puppies, you name it. Oh."

She ran to the oven and pulled out some hush puppies and carefully transferred them into a wicker basket covered with a white cloth napkin. She brought them over to Charlie, grabbing a jar of honey and some butter on the way.

"Hush puppies," she said. "That is real butter, but I have some margarine somewhere if you'd rather have it."

"No, thanks," he said. "This is great! I only eat butter. Margarine is one chemical away from plastic. Did you know that?"

"Yes," she said, sitting down and grabbing her fork. "I only eat butter, too. Margarine was originally invented to fatten up turkeys, but it started killing them. They had a big supply, so they added yellow color to it and started marketing it as a butter substitute."

"Amazing!" he said. "This is great, by the way. You are a super cook. I knew that about margarine, too. I won't ever touch the stuff. Nice house you have here. Where are we?"

She said, "We are out off of 401 South towards Raeford."

"Still in Fatalburg?" he asked, using the local expression for Fayetteville, North Carolina, the main city by Fort Bragg.

"Oh sure. It's not very far to Post from here. Where is your place?"

"I actually live off of 401 North," he replied, "near Pine Forest High School."

"Oh yeah. My dad has friends that live at College Lakes, and I have visited them," she said. "We aren't far, in fact, from Seventy-First High School."

Charlie said, "Okay, I know where we are then. I need to call a cab so I can get home and get ready for work."

He looked at his watch, a Black Hawk Special Ops watch with a ballistic Velcro band. It was good even underwater down to a depth of 330 feet.

It was 7:30 A.M.

"What time did you get up and start making this great breakfast . . . oh-dark-thirty?" he asked, gulping some hot coffee.

"Thanks," Fila said. "Nope. Just a little bit ago. You are not calling a cab. I'll take you to your place, and we don't need to rush. Pops knew I was bringing you here last night, and he said for you and me to hang out for a couple days and get to know each other since we will be working so close."

Charlie said, "Speaking of that, how will you feel about shooting Muslims?"

She laughed and said, "Charlie, nobody hates the jihad-ists more than a Muslim woman who is converted to Chris-tianity. I knew you would worry about that, buddy, and you can put it out of your mind."

Charlie laughed at himself.

She said, "I spent my childhood in Iran, part of my teenaged years in Iraq, and am a nationalized American. Do you suppose they might have checked me out from ass-hole to elbows before letting me into C.A.G. Selection?"

Again, Charlie laughed at himself and said, "Sorry, Fila. My life is going to depend totally on you."

"You don't have to explain," she replied, "I understand totally. In fact, since we have to depend on each other to-tally, I know how we can start spending time today getting to know each other a lot better."

CHARLIE sat in a chair and looked around the plywood-wall room. Behind him, placed on a folding table, was the upper half of a terrorist mannequin with a folding stock AK-47 in his hands. Around his head and neck was wrapped a red and white checked kaffiyeh held in place on his head by an *agal,* a rope circlet. Wearing ear protectors, Charlie sat still in his folding chair, checking once more to ensure there was a clear line of fire between the manne-quin and the door without him being in that line of fire. Charlie wore a black-and-white checked kaffiyeh and an *agal* himself.

Suddenly, with a loud bang, the handles blew off the double hollow pine doors, and a woman entered wearing a black burqa with black netting covering her face. In her hand was a small polymer plastic Glock Model 19 9-millimeter automatic. She ran through the door, moving to her right while placing two rapid-fire rounds into the terrorist's face. Then she put another double-tap into the center of his torso. Then, she purposely dropped her Glock on the floor, and almost instantly, a second Glock Model 19 appeared in her left hand from under the folds of her burqa. Two more quick rounds went into his forehead, and two more went into his chest, right over the heart.

She ran to Charlie, yelling, "Hands out!"

He stuck his hands straight out, wrists side by side, so that they would simulate him being handcuffed. Now a large Yarborough knife appeared in her right hand, and it sliced through the air between his wrists as if cutting flex cuffs. Without looking, she placed him behind her with one hand while handing him the Yarborough knife. She led the way out the door, picking up her first Glock and handing it behind her to Charlie. Again, without looking, she took the knife back from him at the same time, and it disappeared just as quickly under the folds of the black head-to-toe Muslim garment. She led him out the doorway of the House of Horrors.

Outside, she pulled the hot cotton garment off and Charlie gave her a high five. Underneath the burqa, she had worn digital tactical trousers and two Blackwater CQC carbon-fiber composite holsters, carried on standard tactical thigh rigs, plus she had a wide array of Blackwater magazine carriers around her waistline. On the back of her right thigh was the scalpel-sharp Yarborough knife sheath.

Charlie handed her a bottle of water and opened one himself and started chugging. It was a hot and humid day, and it was especially suffocating in the Shooting House with their adrenaline pumping, and especially with her wearing a full burqa over her other clothes.

He smiled at her and winked, saying, "Sergeant Jannat, I will have no problem going into Injun country with you as a partner."

With Charlie being full-blooded Lakota, this remark really struck her funny bone, and Fila started chuckling, which turned into laughter. Infectious as it was, Charlie started to laugh, too, not knowing why.

He got a puzzled look and said, "Why are we laughing?"

She pointed at him and said, "Injun country!"

Charlie chuckled now and said, "What's wrong with that, Booty? That is what everybody in SF says for enemy territory."

She laughed even harder.

Charlie smiled, saying, "I take back what I said about you covering my behind."

She laughed even harder.

Seventh Special Forces Group was having a special luncheon at McKellar's Lodge, which was very close to the Detachment-Delta entrance, so they both had lunch with some old friends there and then went back to the range.

When they left, one of the younger sergeants at their table said, "So who was that guy, an SF retiree and his wife?"

One of the master sergeants sitting nearby said, "Naw, that's Charlie Strongheart. He's C.A.G."

Another one said, "Wal, purty boys, I worked with her. She's an intel sergeant herself. She was 'tached to us at the Third Herd for a bit in the Sandbox. She went to C.A.G., too, I heerd. If any women deserved to, it was Ole Fila Jannat. They is a clangin' noise when she walks."

"They have women in Delta Force?" the E6 asked.

The first master sergeant said, "Shh. We'll have to kill ya, man. Nobody's supposed to know. They are in what's that called?"

"The Funny Platoon," the Southerner master sergeant replied.

The staff sergeant spoke again. "A clangin' noise. That woman was downright beautiful. She is tough?"

The E8 replied, "What d'ya s'pose I weigh, son?"

"Two-fifty?"

"Naw, two-sixty-two," he said. "And I was one of the three wounded guys she carried ta safety under heavy gunfire in Sadr City. She got brass ones awright. Thet's why she got a Silver Star, too."

"Damn!" the staff sergeant said.

The other master sergeant said, "That old Charlie Strongheart is a handful himself. He has seen the elephant. If they got those two partnered up, somebody is gonna be in a world of caca."

The Southern sergeant said, "Wal, ya did notice them boobs and that butt, gents. They are prob'bly jest datin'. I had me a partnuh thet looked like thet, we'd be under the sheets firin' RPGs."

Driving back, Charlie said, "How did you get your hands on a Yarborough knife?"

She got a sad look and said, "I dated a guy from Third Group I had served with in Iraq. He left me his Yarborough when he died."

Charlie said, "Sorry. He must have thought a lot of you to leave his Yarborough knife."

Major General William P. Yarborough was the man who encouraged his Special Forces operators to wear green berets on their heads and then tried to get the Pentagon to approve it as official headgear for his special breed of men. Yarborough, who invented the army's Jump Wings in World War II, where he personally earned four gold stars for his own set of wings, for combat jumps he made, was the commanding general of the USA JFK Special Warfare Center at Fort Bragg when President Kennedy did indeed declare the green beret as the distinctive headgear for the U.S. Army Special Forces and referred to it in 1962, saying, "The green beret is again becoming a symbol of excellence, a badge of courage, a mark of distinction in the fight for freedom." General Yarborough was also an innovator of many things, such as creating the now legendary Special Forces medic, who had training better than most EMTs and physician's assistants.

He is considered by most in Special Forces to be the "father of the modern-day Green Berets."

For some time now, any young man who graduates from the grueling Special Forces Qualification Course switches on the parade ground from a burgundy to a green beret. But the following day, wearing a class A uniform and his new Special Forces tab, when he walks across the stage, usually in the Fayetteville, North Carolina, Civic Auditorium, the man is handed a diploma and a numbered and personalized Yarborough knife. Designed by Bill Harsey and manufactured by Chris Reeve Knives to be both a tool and a weapon, the Yarborough was the winning design from a field of nearly one hundred different contenders.

It's made from CPM S30V steel, an alloy that has greater strength than most blades, as well as superior edge-holding ability, and it is coated with KG GunKote, a baked-on nonreflective corrosion-resistant finish. The handle of the knife is actually canvas Micarta, chosen for its toughness, chemical resistance, and wet-grip capabilities.

Most people never put the Yarborough anywhere but a display case, but Fila loved hers and used it always in the field. It just never would seem to slip in her grip, even if she was not wearing Kevlar gloves, which she usually did, and even when it was wet.

CHAPTER NINE

Getting Closer

CHARLIE said, "Hey, how about we pop some silhouettes outdoors, go to our places, clean up, and I take you out for a really nice dinner tonight?"

"Poke," she teased, "are you asking me out on a date?"

Charlie thought for a second and said, "No, we are partners. If you were a guy, I would ask you the same thing."

"Would you take a guy to the same restaurant where you are planning on taking me?"

Again, the tall Indian thought, and then said, "Naw, if you were a guy partner, I would invite you but maybe take you to Texas Road House or Hooters."

She chuckled and said, "So, are you asking me out on a date?"

"I guess I am," he replied. "Pick you up at seven?"

"I'll be ready."

"Nice restaurant," he said. "I'll wear a suit or sport coat with slacks."

It was exactly seven o'clock when Fila's doorbell rang, and she opened it. Just having a man do that and not honk the horn was refreshing compared to many of her dates.

She was doubly surprised when she opened the door and saw Charlie in a dark blue pin-striped Brooks Brothers suit tailored with a European cut. He wore a cream-colored shirt with French cuffs and a silk striped maroon tie with dark blue and cream stripes. On his feet were shiny black Gucci loafers with strips of bamboo attached to the tassel on them. He held in his hand a bouquet of white roses as well as baby's breath and ferns.

He handed them to her and she cooed, smelling them, saying, "Thanks, Charlie. I love roses."

"I picked them out of my yard," he said proudly.

"Ooh, white for passion," she said. "Out of your yard?"

He said, "I raise a few flowers. Keeps the place looking nice. Have you eaten at the Vineyard?"

"Oh yes," she said, genuinely enthused. "That is the best eating in Fayetteville. I love the piano music, too."

Charlie looked at her, and it took his breath just about. This woman could make any man forget any woman. Her shiny black designer dress clung to her body like the finest silk, which it was. It was low-cut and her cleavage was like a sign to Charlie, shouting "Please Stare!" But he would not allow himself to, as much as he wanted to. The dress was slit up the back, and he noticed her tanned, shapely legs. Fila wore beautiful shiny black stiletto high-heeled shoes with tiny straps that wrapped around her ankles and looked very sexy to him. She had on long dangly earrings that had little crosses at the end of each, and there was a small diamond in the center of each cross. Around her neck was a nice necklace with a large matching cross and a larger diamond in the center of it. She wore several classy-looking dress rings on one thumb and her hand, and he noticed she wore two small toe rings, and an ankle bracelet on her left leg, which matched the earrings and necklace.

Her hair hung halfway down her back and was very shiny and beautiful.

Charlie said, "I have to tell you, Fila. If you ever dress

like this on our assignment, I am worried you will get me killed. How could I ever take my eyes off of you, you are so beautiful?"

She blushed and smiled seductively without even meaning to. She stood on her tiptoes and kissed him softly on the cheek. He felt his heart beat harder.

The Vineyard was on South McPherson Church Road, one of the main business streets in Fayetteville, and was considered by many to be the finest cuisine and atmosphere in the military town.

It was really a classy place with great atmosphere. They had a pianist indoors, but you could also eat outside on the patio. The service was excellent. The waitress they had was very attentive and brought out their appetizers and salads in a very timely fashion. She also checked on them throughout the meal. The couple decided to order one steak meal and one seafood meal and share. So Charlie got a filet mignon smothered in sautéed mushrooms, and it was good enough and tender enough to melt in his mouth, and was cooked medium rare. Fila ordered wasabi grilled tuna, which was very scrumptious. They shared throughout the meal and each chose to have only one glass of wine, because of tying it on at the Green Beret Club the previous night.

After dinner both declined dessert, but drank lots of coffee while they talked about anything and everything.

He finally smiled and said, "I just have to ask. That dress is so beautiful."

"Thank you," she interrupted.

"So, you know how we all think 24/7," he said. "I have to ask. Where do you have your Glock 19 hidden?"

She grinned and said, "Come here."

He slid over into the chair next to her from his seat across the table.

"Slide your hand up the inside of my left thigh," she commanded softly.

His heart pounded in his ears and the side of his temples. Charlie had not had a woman have this effect on him in years. Ever, he thought. He looked around and slowly slid his hand up the inside of her leg. Halfway up her thigh it bumped against the bottom of her molded polymer plastic thigh holster.

He chuckled and moved back.

"So," she countered, "what are you carrying?"

Charlie said, "I usually carry a Springfield Arms .45 XD Tactical, but tonight, because of you, I am carrying a Glock 19 with Corbon copper-jacketed hollow points."

She pretended to speak like a teen and said, "Ooh, Charlie. Me too! We have so much in common!"

He laughed.

She then said, "That's nice, but what else?"

He chuckled.

"Okay," he said, "of course I carry a backup. In my front pocket, I always carry—"

Charlie stopped as Fila raised her hand, laughing.

She said, "Did you notice my little black makeup purse I have been carrying tonight?"

He nodded.

She said, "I bet you are going to tell me you are carrying the same exact gun in your front pocket, a Kel-Tec P3AT.380. I never leave home without it."

Charlie laughed, and said, "One round in the pipe and six in the mag. I can even carry it when I am wearing shorts."

Fila started laughing again. He asked why.

She said, "Nice first date. You and I talk about guns."

"I don't know about you, sweetheart," he said, "but the more I learn about you, the safer I feel going on a dumb-ass suicide mission into the middle of Iran."

"Charlie," she said, "I already felt safe with you the first time I saw you in the conference room."

Now he got embarrassed, and said, "Why do you say that?"

She replied, "When I heard about you, I of course started asking around. I heard how you needed intelligence really badly on the Taliban, and you went out by yourself at night in the Khyber Pass wearing night vision and waited along the road used by the Taliban, al Qaeda, and major drug smugglers. You waited all night, until you found one straggler behind one patrol of Taliban, snuck up behind him, knocked him out with your gun, and carried him over your shoulders, with flex cuffs on his hands and legs, for over a mile, to where you had your dirt bike hidden. Then, you carried him on that, coasting down an old mountain road, and had to hide several times. Finally, when you could see where your team and the warlord were headquartered across the valley, you cranked up the bike and rode across that valley floor, taking occasional volleys from hidden Taliban and a few RPGs shot at you. Is that story true?"

"No," he replied, "absolutely not. They were firing mortars at me, not RPGs. Hey, we needed intel right then."

She shook her head and then said, "But that is not why I felt safe. I read about your ancestors and figured what pride you must have grown up with."

Charlie said, "My old man was a twenty-four-hour-per-day drunk. That is why I don't often do what I did last night and pour the booze on."

She said, "Charlie, lots of Native Americans have alcohol problems. It is still a race of powerful warriors. I want to ask you a question."

"What?" he answered, grinning.

"Do you have big scars on your pectoral muscles?"

This embarrassed him even more than her asking about his Taliban adventure.

"Yes," he said. "Boy, you do research. Don't you?"

"I knew you had gone through the Sun Dance ceremony just like your famous ancestor."

Sitting Bull went through a Sun Dance ceremony, which actually entailed his arms each being sliced fifty times from each wrist to each shoulder. Blood dripped from both arms, and he hung in the sun all day, both pectoral muscles on his chest pierced by eagle talons, and then awls were stuck through the two holes over each nipple and these were tied to leather thongs which went up over a cross pole, and he was raised up hanging by his flesh until the flesh tore away. During the second day Sitting Bull fainted from excessive blood loss, but received a vision about his victory over the whites in a coming battle. In his vision he saw the *wasicun* (white men) "falling into our camp like grasshoppers falling out of the sky." The Sun Dance was totally condemned by missionaries and Indian agents.

On June 16, 1876, General George Armstrong Custer came to the Black Hills area, with 1,300 men broken into three commands, the main headed by Lieutenant Colonel Custer, another by Major Reno, and a third by Major Benteen. Custer was actually a brevet general in the Civil War, but then retained his true rank in the cavalry of lieutenant colonel. This was only three days after Sitting Bull had endured the Sun Dance ceremony and lost so much blood. Sitting Bull was too weak to fight, but Crazy Horse was the real war chief. He had to go into battle in the older chief's stead.

On June 25, 1876, the battalion of George Armstrong Custer ended up in a very lopsided fight. This time there were over 3,000 Sioux, Cheyenne, and Arapaho warriors fighting against Custer's 250 troopers. His command, all of Custer's men, were dead in an hour's time. Some of Benteen's and Reno's commands survived, but they were decimated, too.

The next day, Sitting Bull moved his camp down the river to get totally away from the stinking, bloating corpses and to consider a plan, as he knew the *wasicun* leaders would now want his blood. He eventually fled, leading his people into Canada.

Fila leaned across the table and said, "You take great pride in being a Native American."

He grinned, saying, "I hate that term. It sounds so politically correct. Being very serious, I am very proud to be descended from Sitting Bull. I am very proud to be a modern-day dog soldier of the Lakota Nation, and I am equally proud to be an American warrior."

She said, "Charlie, we are not drinking tonight, and Weasel is not here. I love the poetry of the way I have read some of your people speak and what you said last night. Please tell me something poetic and wonderful and inspirational like the story you told about the eagles."

He thought for a minute and grinned, then said, "My grandfather told me this story many times.

"There was a young Lakota boy named Dancing Hare, and his first cousin and best friend was named Boy Who Climbs Trees. Dancing Hare and Boy Who Climbs Trees were both very adventurous and both were students at the Mission School. While attending the school, Dancing Hare became very excited about the white man he met who was called a missionary. He liked what the man spoke about, and what the missionary said made perfect sense to him. After some months, Dancing Hare became a Christian, and his cousin and best friend, Boy Who Climbs Trees, remained true to his tribal beliefs and was indeed a true follower of Wakan Tanka, the Great Mystery.

"The religion of choice did not matter to each boy, and they respected each other's differences and opinions. What they really enjoyed more than anything was adventure. They could not wait to grow and hunt game for the family circles and fight in battles and count coup. Both hoped someday to become dog soldiers, the best of the best warriors in their tribe.

"There was one major difference, though, and that was Dancing Hare always believed in winning and would never admit defeat. Once when wrestling with Fights the Badger, he would not give in when put in a painful hold and actually had two of his fingers broken, but he would not quit and he would not cry. Boy Who Climbs Trees, however, would give in easily in games and wanted to give up and do something else if he started losing.

"One day, the two boys decided to hunt coyotes far away from the safety of the tribal circle of teepees, their neighborhood. While they moved through a wooded draw, Dancing Hare heard a strange noise and held up his hand. Then they saw them, a band of Pawnees, wearing war paint and carrying many weapons. The boys were afraid and knew they must hide in a safe place, but where?

"Boy Who Climbs Trees said, 'We will be killed or captured!'

"Dancing Hare said, 'No, we will not. Do not give up so easily,' but while he ran, he prayed harder than ever before.

"Finally, he spotted a cave ahead and ran into it, followed by his whimpering friend. Dancing Hare discovered another cave entrance. It was actually shaped like a horseshoe with two holes opening in the side of a draw. They hid inside and saw the Pawnee war party far off studying their tracks, which they'd tried to hide.

"Then they saw a mighty bear startled by all the commotion run out of the trees and straight toward them. It headed right at the cave and Boy Who Climbs Trees yelled, 'Run! He will eat us!'

"Dancing Hare said, 'No, stay put and do not move. If you run, the Pawnees will surely catch you.'"

Charlie also fascinated her with his dramatic hand gestures as he told the story.

He continued, "The bear ran into the cave and turned to face in the direction of the danger behind him. He lay down. At the same time, Boy Who Climbs Trees, crying, ran as fast as he could out the other cave entrance. Dancing Hare saw him get captured almost immediately by the band of Pawnees. They looked at the cave entrance, but the leader said they should not bother the mighty bear they saw run into it, or they might be killed. They rode off with their captive, tied and bound.

"All good Lakotas bathed often and would keep their hair and skin shiny with bear grease made from bear fat. This smell kept the mighty grizzly calm in the cave, and he did not smell Dancing Hare and did not look around and see Dancing Hare. A few minutes after the Pawnees rode away, the grizzly emerged and ambled away towards the trees.

"Hours later, scared but safe, Dancing Hare trotted towards his village but looked up at the sky and smiled. He knew then that what many like his cousin Boy Who Climbs Trees would see as nothing but a bad thing, could turn out actually to be an answer to a prayer, but dressed as something scary. The rest of his life, he would always look for the good news hiding inside the bad news. Now he would summon the dog soldiers to go and rescue his cousin.

"That was the day that Dancing Hare was saved by the bear who came there by prayer."

"That was terrible," she said, laughing. "What happened to Boy Who Climbs Trees?"

"Probably got killed," said Charlie. "I don't know."

She slapped his arm and said, "I'm just teasing. I love the story. I wish I could have seen you go through the Sun Dance ceremony. I bet you were very brave."

"Naw, I was pretty much of a wimp."

She said, "Do they do it the same way as they did in your ancestor's day?"

"No, they don't," Charlie said. "They cut the pecs with a scalpel and swab the skin with alcohol first. The awls they put through the slits are sterilized, too. Let's forget that. I want to hear about you."

After the dinner, Fila wanted to see his home, so they went there. She was enthused to see it was so clean, and commented on it.

He laughed, saying, "I have a housekeeper, Mabel, who keeps this place straightened up pretty good. Her husband is on his fifth tour in the Sandbox."

"SF?" she said.

"Nope." He laughed. "A big, overweight, gray-haired old leg truck driver that they cannot keep out of the big trucks no matter what rank he is."

She laughed, picturing the man and loving his enthusiasm for his work.

Fila was drawn to the bright light and colors in the dark corner of Charlie's living room. The house was very masculine, and he had a nice collection of Western art. There was American Indian memorabilia displayed throughout the small house that was fascinating to her. In the dark corner was a giant aquarium with fish of vibrant colors she had never seen before—shiny blue and black fish, a bright yellow and blue, barber pole–looking fish that seemed like they could be shrimp, a sea horse—and beautiful coral and vegetation. There was also what looked to her like a giant octopus with many tentacles and a small fish swimming right in the middle of it.

"This is amazing," she said. "I have never seen an aquarium this large in a home before, and the fish are beautiful."

He said, "It gives me a lot of tranquility. It is a hundred-gallon saltwater aquarium. That is called a blue tang, that is an angel fish, those are coral shrimp, that is of course a sea horse, and this is called a clown anenome. That is a clown fish, and the anenome is poison to all the other fish that come around it. The clown lives in it basically."

She just stared into the water and felt his presence behind her. Her breath caught a little. Gently, he touched her shoulders and slowly turned her around. His right hand came up, and softly, the back of his hand rubbed along her cheek, and she almost purred.

Even more gently, he caressed both cheeks and pulled her slowly forward. He bent down and kissed her full on the lips, but even more softly than he had touched her cheeks. The kiss got more passionate, but he was playful now with the kissing and totally different than all the men she had dated before, who, by this time, would have been trying to get their tongue down her throat. Her heart pounded. She had never had feelings like this before, for any man.

He said, "Let me show you my bathroom. It is down the hall, second to the last door on the right."

She was appreciative, as she went to take care of her personal needs, check her makeup, and give herself a quiet pep talk.

Charlie went out his back door with a pair of scissors in his hand and returned with a large deep red rose. He carried it in his left hand and started breaking thorns off of the stem.

She came out of the bathroom, saw him down the hallway, and smiled, then turned and walked into his family room. He joined her on the couch. They kissed passionately again, and he leaned back.

He said, "We have got a problem. We are partners, and we are going into a very dangerous situation."

She said, "I agree totally. We have to be able to rely on each other and be mission-oriented, but there's another problem."

Charlie said, "Coming off as husband and wife and not two operators pretending to be husband and wife."

"Exactly," she replied. "So what do we do?"

"Let's sleep on it. I have a guest bedroom with everything you need down the hall where that sliver of light's coming out," he said. "Because you are my partner, I will always be totally honest with you, Fila. From all I have seen of you so far, I will have no problem pretending you are my wife."

She blushed and kissed him softly, then headed toward the bedroom and in a husky voice said, "Good night, Charlie."

He smiled, saying, "Night," but he wanted to punch something.

"Why didn't she reciprocate?" he wondered. He felt she was attracted to him by the way they kissed, but why hadn't she at least said, "I could stomach posing as your wife"?

CHARLIE was upset at what he was seeing. He watched while Fila prepared for bed, amid horrendous thunder and lightning flashes outside. The scene was very tense and very scary, and the lights flashed on and off on several occasions. Fila started getting really nervous and checked in the closet, under the canopy bed, behind the curtains, and there she found one window unlocked and quickly locked it. Several things were amiss in her bedroom, which seemed to scare her even more. Finally, after making a thorough search, she seemed satisfied that her room was secure. She nervously laughed at herself, removed her gown, and got under the covers, lying on her side.

As she reached over to turn off the bedside lamp, she rolled on her back and finally looked up at the ceiling of the canopy bed. She was speechless, as she looked straight up into the smiling evil face of a killer, spread-eagled and holding himself on the frame of the canopy roof by firm hand- and footholds. It was Officer James Rashad, whom Charlie had killed, but he was alive now somehow. Large knife in hand, he dropped onto the now-screaming beautiful Fila and plunged the knife into her body over and over in a passionate rage.

Then there was silence, as Rashad, breathing heavily,

slumped over her lifeless, bloody body, sitting astraddle
the victim. There was total silence now except for the heavy,
labored breathing of Rashad, as Charlie could not scream.

Suddenly, from off-camera, a voice yelled, "Cut," and
the very bloody Fila sat up immediately and, laughing,
slapped Rashad on the arm and said that he bumped her
ribs with his knee when he dropped, and it really hurt. He
laughed and apologized, then teased her, playfully tickling
her. Charlie was suddenly there and walked up from
off-camera and yelled, "Print!" shaking hands with both
actors, and then gave her a kiss and looked all around at a
large film crew, lights, and entire set.

Another voice from off-camera now yelled, "Cut!" and
Pops, wearing a director's beret and ascot, walked into the
scene and started talking to Charlie and the two actors, as
in a broader view Charlie now saw that the first crew and
he were also part of the movie and Pops and his bigger
crew were obviously the real director and crew. He told
Charlie that he should have yelled, "Print!" right after yelling, "Cut!" It now became very clear to Charlie that Pops
was directing a film about Charlie directing a suspenseful
movie.

James Rashad came over to Charlie, and they shook
hands.

Charlie said, "Hey, you are an American. I am really
sorry I had to kill you, man."

"Oh, that's okay, Charlie," Rashad said. "You saw I was
going to kill the woman you love. But I was just acting. I
wasn't going to kill her."

Charlie got angry and said, "Yes, you were. You had a
Stinger, you son of a bitch. You were going to kill plenty of
women and children."

Rashad started laughing and Charlie sat up, looking all
around. It was morning.

He got up, moaning from his daily aches and pains,
hobbled into his bathroom, and said to himself, "Damned

nightmares! Wonder if antiwar protestors have nightmares about being beat to death by flowers and cardboard signs."

Fila was up and drinking coffee. They ate and showered, and she wore one of his shirts over a pair of women's jogging shorts that had somehow appeared in his apartment. He gave no explanation of how they got there, and she did not ask. He took her to her house, where she changed, and they headed to Bragg.

CHAPTER TEN

Getting Serious

HE called Pops before they showered and was just getting a call back on his cell. He hung up and smiled at her.

Charlie said, "We're going to the compound. Pops and Weasel have been busy."

"What's up?"

He replied, "They would not let us load out of Simmons Army Airfield at Bragg, because you are a female, and there aren't supposed to be any female HALO jumpers in the army. We've got the use of St. Mere Eglise Drop Zone 'cause there aren't any drops there today, but Pops worked it out on an aircraft and even a jump master for just you and me, girl."

"Great, but what is the deal? What did he work out?"

He said, "Let me surprise you, okay?"

They arrived at the compound and immediately went to the tarmac where two Little Birds were parked.

Charlie introduced Fila to a tall, slender black guy with dreadlocks and a graying beard.

"Booty, this is Dick 'Coon' Turner," Charlie said as

they shook hands. "Coon, this is my partner, Booty. She is C.A.G."

"Hey, nice to meet you, Booty," Coon said. "I see how you got your nickname."

She grinned and flipped his bearded chin with her index finger and said, "Yeah, and I see how you got your nickname, too, Holmes."

"Touché," he said, with a deep-voiced chuckle.

Fila said, "We're going to HALO out of Little Birds?"

Coon said, "Yes, ma'am, the MH-6J model there has a ceiling somewhere a little above fourteen grand. Pops does not want you two jumping O2 today, so we are to drop you at ten thousand feet. The chief is going to start warming up that Little Bird over there."

Coon waved and a chief warrant officer in a flight suit came jogging from one of the buildings. They all waved at him, and he waved back. He had flown Charlie on many training missions as well as flying Fila on several different ones. The man always had a smile on his face.

Charlie and Fila escorted Coon to a small hangar-type building close to the House of Horrors, and they went inside and changed into jumping suits. Both were given ram-air chutes, and they headed toward the tarmac, where Coon would give them his official jump master briefing.

The Little Bird was warming up behind them. The MH-6 Little Bird was the only light assault helicopter in the army inventory, and the MH-6J was a newer version that was used by Detachment-Delta. The Little Bird provided assault helicopter support to not only Delta, but also other Special Operations forces, and could be armed with a combination of guns and rockets. It had a range of 288 miles.

Charlie asked Fila if she was familiar with the military square ram-air chute. She chuckled.

You use the square ram-air canopies for HALO free-fall jumping, not normally for static line. With a round or parabellum chute, you can jump with more ammo and equipment, but you hit the ground harder, and the chute is not nearly as maneuverable. The ram-air is more like having a set of wings on. You can steer it wherever you want it to go just about, but you can't jump with quite as much weight. Of course, you manually deploy the parachute by ripcord on the free-fall jumps instead of it being opened by a fifteen-foot static line attached to the plane or helicopter as in most military jumps. They knew they had to think about the extra weight, but Charlie was thinking about Fila's chuckle.

"What are you chuckling about?" he asked.

Fila grinned at him. "What unit are we in?"

He said, "First Special Forces Operational Detachment-Delta."

She nodded and added, "That means I am a member of it, too, just like you. And do we not always color outside the lines?"

He said, "You are HALO-qualified, not just a civilian skydiver?"

She said, "My 201 file cannot officially reflect it, but nowhere in the army regs does it say females cannot become HALO/HAHO-qualified. It says you must be a member of a Special Operations unit to attend the school."

Charlie said, "Did you go to school at Yuma Proving Grounds?"

"Nope, more in-house for us," she said. "Instructors in Arizona did not have a need-to-know."

"Us?" he said, surprised. "So more than just you got HALO-qualified? Cool."

"Look at our mission and our options. The SOCOM regs," she said, referring to Special Operations Command, "say that SOCOM can provide a waiver for candidates for certain special circumstances. It was meant for medical waivers, but we are specops."

Charlie said, "How many official jumps you get in training?"

She smiled. "Fourteen, probably just like you did at Yuma Proving Grounds."

"Wow!" Charlie said. "No wonder they call you ladies the Funny Platoon. A lot of funny business going on we did not know about."

The two boarded the Little Bird twenty minutes later and took the short flight to St. Mere Eglise. Coon rode shotgun in the front. He spoke on the radio to Custer, who was on the drop zone with a green smoke grenade popped, and he placed a bright orange air panel out for them to use as a target. Charlie and Fila watched out each side of the chopper and gave each other hand signals about separating away from each other on their exit. Coon had already been giving them jump commands.

"Check equipment!" he hollered.

Both checked their harnesses, quick releases, the dummy bags they carried for ballast and bulk, as they would jump that way into Iran. They gave a quick check of each other's chute.

"Get in the door!" Coon yelled and gave them both a smile and okay sign. They sat in the door with their feet on the skids ready to launch themselves out away from the craft.

Coon looked at the smoke and panel, the pilot gave him a nod, and he yelled, "Go!"

They both dove away from the Little Bird and went into a stable body position almost immediately. Charlie tracked closer to her, and they dropped, occasionally looking at each other and smiling. They had agreed to open higher on the first jump of the day, so they would open at three thousand feet, to ensure they were on the same page. The rest of the jumps they would open between two thousand and one thousand feet. Both wore altimeters anyway, which are required by the army and automatically open parachutes at a thousand feet just in case something bad happens.

The pair repacked their chutes and jumped again and again and once more. After they got back to the compound, they offered to buy lunch for Coon and the chopper jockey. The warrant officer had other plans, but Coon accompanied them to the main NCO club, where the three enjoyed a nice leisurely lunch, then Charlie and Fila returned to the compound. They asked to meet with Weasel, and the two joined him in his office.

"Top," Charlie said, "we wondered if we could hole up somewhere with the latest intelligence reports on Iran?"

"Sorry, Poke, but the S2 and S3 team are busy working on the intelligence forecasts and then possible operational scenarios to present tomorrow. All the material is being used right now by the team in the briefing room. We have an all-day planning meeting tomorrow, and I think the CG of SOCOM will be here for at least part of it," the command sergeant major said.

Fila said, "What about other reports?"

Weasel said, "Good idea, Booty. Hang on."

He pushed his intercom button and a female voice said, "Yes, Sergeant Major?"

He said, "Mary, get me the S2 sergeant major of the Third Herd on the phone."

"Wilco."

A minute later the intercom buzzed and Mary's voice came on. "Line one, Weasel."

"Thanks."

He picked up the phone and said, "Howdy, Art. How's the wife?

"She did! Sorry, I didn't hear," Weasel said, after a pause, winking at Charlie and Fila. "Your brother?"

There was another pause. Weasel tried to suppress a laugh. "Both your brothers? At the same time? So, did you shoot them?"

Pause.

"Why not?" Weasel said. "I would have blown their disloyal asses away. Well, anyway, sorry. Listen, I have two operators that need to study the Top Secret Area Study on Iran. Can you help them out?"

Another pause.

"Oh yeah," Weasel said, "they both have TS clearances. One has a TS Crypto Gamma clearance and both have a definite need-to-know."

Another short pause.

"Thanks, pal," the sergeant major said. "I will send an email with their IDs, and you can ID them when they arrive there. Sorry about the old lady and your brothers. Don't pay her a penny of alimony. Tell your brothers to pay it."

He got off the phone and chuckled, saying, "Don't even ask. You two go to the 3rd Group headquarters and find the S2 office. I think it's on the second floor. Ask for the 2 Shop sergeant major, show him your driver's licenses, and military IDs, then he will direct you to the S2 shop area studies vault and office. They will give you the TS Area Study for Iran, updated daily, and a desk to study at."

They studied all afternoon, but what made them take note was not the passages about Iran's executive or legislative branch, but what they read about Iran's political parties and political leaders. Under "Political Parties and Leaders," *The CIA World Fact Book—Iran* read:

> *Formal political parties are a relatively new phenomenon in Iran and most conservatives still prefer to work through political pressure groups rather than parties, and often political parties or coalitions are formed prior to elections and disbanded soon thereafter; a loose pro-reform coalition called the 2nd Khordad Front, which includes political parties as well as less formal groups and organizations, achieved considerable success at elections to the sixth Majles in early 2000; groups in the coalition include: Islamic Iran Participation Front (IIPF), Executives of Construction Party (Kargozaran), Solidarity*

Party, Islamic Labor Party, Mardom Salari, Mojahedin of the Islamic Revolution Organization (MIRO), and Militant Clerics Society (Ruhaniyun); the coalition participated in the seventh Majles elections in early 2004; following his defeat in the 2005 presidential elections, former MCS Secretary General and sixth Majles Speaker Mehdi Karubi formed the National Trust Party; a new conservative group, Islamic Iran Developers Coalition (Abadgaran), took a leading position in the new Majles after winning a majority of the seats in February 2004; following the 2004 Majles elections, traditional and hardline conservatives have attempted to close ranks under the United Front of Principlists; the IIPF has repeatedly complained that the overwhelming majority of its candidates have been unfairly disqualified from the 2008 elections.

Then under "Political Pressure Groups and Leaders," the book read:

The Islamic Republic Party (IRP) was Iran's sole political party until its dissolution in 1987; Iran now has a variety of groups engaged in political activity; some are oriented along political lines or based on an identity group; others are more akin to professional political parties seeking members and recommending candidates for office; some are active participants in the Revolution's political life while others reject the state; political pressure groups conduct most of Iran's political activities; groups that generally support the Islamic Republic include Ansar-e Hizballah, Followers of the Line of the Imam and the Leader, Islamic Coalition Party (Motalefeh), Islamic Engineers Society, and Tehran Militant Clergy Association (Ruhaniyat); active pro-reform student groups include the Office of Strengthening Unity (OSU); opposition groups include Freedom Movement of Iran, the National Front, Marz-e Por Gohar, Baluchistan People's Party (BPP),

*and various ethnic and Monarchist organizations; armed
political groups that have been repressed by the government include Democratic Party of Iranian Kurdistan
(KDPI), Komala, Mujahidin-e Khalq Organization (MEK
or MKO), People's Fedayeen, Jundallah, and the People's
Free Life Party of Kurdistan (PJAK).*

Charlie said, "Did you notice there is no mention of
Davood Faraz Dabdeh or his organization?"

Fila said, "What is the name of it? I am not even sure I
know."

"J.J.," Charlie replied, "El Jalil Jahangir."

The Great Conquerors of the World," she responded.
"Well, at least the jerk knows how to think big."

She opened the yellow-covered folder of a top secret
document and said, "Look. Here is why it is not mentioned
in *The CIA World Fact Book.*"

Charlie read the document, a CIA interagency circular,
which read:

*According to five current humintel and electronic sources,
with high credibility factors, the Jalil Jahangir is an
Iranian-backed and centered burgeoning global-oriented
terrorist organization, previously listed by this Agency as
an al Qaeda-sponsored terrorist cell but which has now
blossomed into a terrorist network having grown in such
proportions to be regarded as a growing worldwide threat
with an extremely high interdictory-necessitation quo-
tient.*

*El Jalil Jahangir, meaning, the Great Conquerors of
the World, was started and is headed by Iranian entrepre-
neur Davood Faraz Dabdeh, who has been openly critical of Osama bin Laden and Ayman al-Zawahiri as
"shrinking lions cowering in dens of fear instead of ag-
gressively continuing the global jihad." Dabdeh has
called upon his followers to recruit the "many sons of*

Muhammad to my side to further Dar el Islam through aggressive mujahidin actions at the four winds and conquer with glory the lands of the infidel and the unclean. In this noble effort we will take the heads of the unclean and toss them into viper's pits for the pleasure of Allah who reigns victorious. Any measure we choose in this great cause is blessed by Allah."

Davood Faraz Dabdeh has received hundreds of millions, if not billions, in funding and support from fundamentalist members of the Saudi Royal Family (SRF), as well as the Iranian government, certain members of Hamas, and Egyptian and Syrian benefactors. Our current fiscal estimates place his net worth in excess of $780,000,000(USD). His youthful enthusiasm, funding, and the blessing of many Iranian mullahs have brought countless followers into his fold and are making him a greater attraction than the rapidly dying al Qaeda movement.

His termination with extreme prejudice, but without martyrdom, is of significant import to the free world community. It is in the estimate of this Agency that an operational plan to bring termination of this target has gone far beyond critical prioritization, but is of immediate determination. With each passing week, the Jalil Jahangir membership rolls are accumulating at a 7 percent monthly rate of increase. Newer recruitment tools are being added weekly as well, and as the organization continues to balloon into greater numbers, the estimated rate of recruitment will increase disproportionately.

This Agency has made seven studies, included as addendum 1 through 7 herein, on Davood Faraz Dabdeh's extensive security network and proactive defensive methodologies. It is this Agency's estimation that standard target acquisition and elimination stratagems are unwarranted and would be ineffective in the accomplishment of the proposed mission. It is the strong encouragement of this Agency to rapidly perform a Target Destruction Estimate and Operational Plan with immediate haste for the sake of national and even global security.

For organizational and fiscal recruitment, Davood Faraz Dabdeh sometimes operates as a ski instructor, races offshore boats, and often poses as a merchant, or an oil line or operational inspector for the purpose of meeting those with oil monies in covert innocent "bump-ins."

He is reputed to be a sadist, rapist, and brutal murderer and torturer in the manner of Uday Saddam Hussein al-Tikriti, the late eldest son of the late Iraqi dictator Saddam Hussein. He also is reputed to favor homosexuality as his preferred sexual lifestyle, although exposure in fundamentalist Iranian circles could possibly bring disfavor.

Dabdeh is also noted for his tremendous distrust of all around him, thus he defers to few and is considered very ineffective at delegating authority and often carries out some of the most menial of tasks on his own behalf. He owns a palace near Tehran and has luxury suites as well in several locations, including a resort villa outside of Iranian security coverage in the vicinity of Cannes, France.

In his occasional quest to race offshore boats, he frequently cruises various cities where such offshore races are held in a large luxury yacht referred to as el MehrdAd meaning "The Gift of the Sun."

Subject is further reportedly lactose-intolerant and is thought by some to suffer from classic bipolar disorder and possible schizophrenia. A Level 2–rated humintel source reports that he possesses only one testicle.

Charlie said, "Did you read where he has one testicle and is schizo?"

Fila said, "I sure did."

Charlie said, "That proves it then."

"Proves what?"

"He's half nuts!" Charlie pronounced.

Fila laughed so loud that it made several NCOs working on daily updates of classified Area Studies jump half out of their seats.

"Why didn't the CIA have him or his group listed in their *CIA World Fact Book*?" she asked when she stopped laughing.

Charlie said, "Simple. They do not want to acknowledge him and give him more power."

"Really?"

He walked over to a refrigerator and got them both plastic bottles of water and opened hers.

Charlie said, "My main martial arts instructor was a cool guy. Really cool. He was a grandmaster, and he deserved that title. So a close friend introduced this kung fu guy who had won some national championships, but only within his style in both weapons kata and sparring. Since the friend introduced them and spoke so highly of the kung fu guy, my instructor flew the guy in, put him up, fed him, and let him do a clinic for us on wushu. You know, kung fu.

"Two of my instructor's black belts, a husband and wife, were kind of wimpy and soft when it came to sparring or grappling. So they got real intrigued with this kung fu guy's weapons forms. He spotted this, so behind my instructor's back, they privately went out for coffee together."

"He stole them away from your instructor?" Fila said.

"Yes," Charlie replied. "To make that part of the story short. Secret phone calls, manipulations, and he ended up moving to our town and opened a school with them. He had them call all of my grandmaster's students and say my grandmaster had a felony record. All kinds of vile stuff. They never stole any other students and went out of business in five months. The kung fu guy left town in disgrace."

She laughed.

Charlie said, "What's so funny?"

She said, "What does this have to do with the CIA?"

"Sorry, I guess I'm writing a book," he responded with a chuckle. "Some years passed and a guy called who the grandmaster knew was a student of the kung fu guy in another state. He figured the kung fu instructor was sitting right there with the guy waiting for a good laugh, after pushing the grandmaster's buttons."

He swallowed some water and went on. "So the kung fu guy was named Sifu Smith. Original, huh? So the other guy said, 'Hey I have had some problem with Sifu Smith and would love to see him go to jail.'"

Charlie laughed thinking about it.

"'Sifu Smith? Who is that?' the grandmaster said.

"I was sitting right there and started quietly laughing.

"The guy said, 'You know, Sifu Smith. He was a competitor of yours.'

"The grandmaster said, 'Sifu Smith, huh? Name doesn't ring a bell. If he was called Sifu, he obviously was kung fu. Oh yeah, I think there was a guy who did a clinic here once and opened a school for a month or two and went out of business. Was that the guy's name, Smith? Guess I forgot.'

"The other guy was frustrated and said, 'Yeah, but I want to sue the bastard. You want to help me?'

"'No,' my instructor said real firmly. 'Why would I do that? I don't know the guy. He probably isn't even in the martial arts anymore. I cannot even remember what he looks like.'

"The other guy said, 'Yeah fine, see you.'

"The grandmaster explained that he totally stole the man's power, and you have seen the ego in some martial artists. He did not even acknowledge the guy. It must have totally crushed the flake."

"I love it!" she said. "So by not publicly mentioning Davood Dabdeh or mentioning his group, even though it is growing like crazy, the CIA steals some of the horsepower from his revved-up engine?"

"Great disinformation program on their part," the La-kota warrior said.

She came back. "But wouldn't it make Dabdeh think that he is pulling off a major operation? He might think he is recruiting tons of people and building this giant jihadist network, but the CIA are not even on to him?"

"No way, baby," Charlie said. "The guy is not that dumb. It will destroy his little ego anyway, and probably make him more determined to make the organization even bigger."

"We have to close up shop, folks," a good-looking Military Intelligence captain said, approaching their desk. "We have to replace the TS folder you have been looking at."

"Sure thing, Captain," Charlie responded.

They took the folder over to the desk by the large vault filled with Top Secret Area Studies on all the countries in Africa and most of the ones in the Mideast. They had to log it back in with the young sergeant sitting by the vault door, who wore a loaded .45 automatic.

They thanked the captain and several sergeants for their assistance and left.

"Well, Fila, tomorrow we have the briefings and Oplan development starting," the big sergeant said, referring to the operational plan. "We only have this evening left to continue getting acquainted like the Old Man ordered. How about dinner at my house? I'll grill us some steaks."

"Instead . . ." she said. "It was hot today and we made those four HALO jumps. I sure could use a nice tall, cold beer. How about the GB Club?"

"Sounds great to me," he said.

They stopped there and each had a cold beer, then went on to Charlie's place, where he fired up his deluxe grill. After a great dinner, they talked awhile and then took a walk outside holding hands.

CHAPTER ELEVEN

Unplanned Rehearsal

THEY were two blocks from Charlie's house, walking along enjoying the smells of fresh-mowed lawns and the fragrances of some well-manicured yards filled with blooming flowers. He kept asking about her past in both Iran and Iraq.

They came to a small building that said "BBQ" on the outside, nothing else, but several cars were parked outside. They went inside, and Fila was surprised at the number of people in there ordering dinners to go with barbecue, hush puppies, cole slaw, and other Southern treats.

They came up to the counter and a large, smiling ruddy-faced woman came up to Charlie and spoke with a thick Southern accent. "Why, Charlie, I swanee! I haven't seen you in a dog's age. Want some hot barbecue today?"

"No," he said and smiled. "My friend Fila here has not had the opportunity to taste a piece of one of your home-made pies or your carrot cake. Fila, this is Rose. Rose, Fila."

They both nodded and lipped, "Hi."

Then Rose gave a big laugh and said, "The way she has been looking at you, Buddy-Ro, Ah'd say ya oughta get a piece a carrot cake and split it."

She winked at Fila, who blushed deeply.

He said, "Sound like a plan, girlie?"

"Sounds like a plan, Stud Muffin," she shot back without missing a beat.

Rose went to her cake dish to pull out a thick, rich-looking carrot cake, and she said, "Bettah hang onta that one, Charlie. Ah like her. Woman's got some gumption. Ya heah?"

Charlie held the chair for Fila to sit at the tiny corner table, and he sat down opposite her. Rose brought a piece of cake over, set it between them, and handed them two forks.

"How ya like your coffee, Fila?"

"Black, please."

"Comin' up."

She returned with two steaming cups of coffee and Fila took a bite of the cake. She swallowed it and said, "This is delicious! Really delicious, Rose!"

Rose said, "Wal thank ya. I have a trick that makes mine bettah than all the othahs."

"What's that?" Fila asked.

Charlie said, "Oh, I didn't want you to ask."

Rose laughed and said, "Real carrots. Everybody else uses orange Crayolas. How you like them apples?"

Sporting a big smile, Fila said, "You are a marvelous cook. I mean fantastic, but you suck as a comedienne."

Charlie laughed and pointed at Rose, and she smacked his hand with a towel she carried. "Oh pshaw."

She went back behind the counter.

With his back to the corner, Charlie glanced at every customer who walked in the door. He was used to always sitting back to the wall, facing possible dangers. This was very common for all specops types and police officers. Fila felt comfortable, though, knowing he was there to spot any danger behind her.

On about their third bite of the delicious cake, which they were eating using only one fork that was held in his hand, with him feeding her and then taking a bite himself, trouble came.

Charlie's eyes opened as he looked to the door, and he whispered, "Trouble."

"Don't nobody move. I'll pop a cap in yo asses if ya do!" a young black punk in oversized shorts yelled.

He was also wearing a red Cardinals baseball hat and an oversized red tank top. He held what looked like a .380 semiautomatic pistol in his hand, which he now pointed at Rose, who looked like she was going to have a heart attack.

Just past him was another large white youth, who also wore the colors of the Bloods, with a red scarf under his cocked and tilted red baseball cap.

Charlie looked at both of them but whispered through closed lips, "I got Big Mouth. You take White Bread."

"I'm locked and loaded. Say when."

"Gimme all the money you got in that drawer, bitch, and move!" the leader said.

Two middle-aged women stood at the counter waiting for a take-out order and looked like they were ready for a heart attack, too. A yuppie-looking man walked in wearing a suit and immediately had a sawed-off twelve-gauge shotgun shoved in his face, and his hands went skyward.

Charlie quickly whispered, "One, two, three! Now!" and in one fluid motion, Fila spun and rose, and he moved out one step away from her.

Both were leaning forward, knees slightly bent, their left hands coming up in front of their chests as if they were saying prayers, and this slapped the butt of their Glock 19 9-millimeters and extended the guns forward, their right hands cradling the grips.

Charlie yelled, "Do not move, punks! Freeze or die!"

Both gang members looked at him and Fila pointing guns at them, and their demeanor showed they knew what they were doing.

The black kid stuck his jaw out, saying, "You want me to shoot this old bitch, Player?"

Charlie said, "I don't know her. Who cares? I just know if you do, I can castrate a flea with this nine at a hundred meters, so I will not kill you. I will put a bullet in your spine and paralyze you. You both have till the count of three to lay the weapons down or die. One."

Both punks got panicky looks on their faces and swung their guns at the same time toward Charlie and Fila, and the woman at the counter and Rose screamed. At the same time, Charlie and Fila each fired twice in rapid succession and both gang members fell to the floor just like that, crumpling like rag dolls. Each had two holes in his forehead.

Charlie yelled at Rose, "Call 9-1-1 now!"

He ran out the door, gun in hand, while Fila checked the pulse on both gang members. They were quite dead. She then ran out behind Charlie, to see the driver of the car and one more gang member in the backseat.

Charlie said, "Driver! Both hands on the wheel, engine off, and throw the keys. Now or die. No arguing! Backseat, both hands out the window, crawl out the window, and lay facedown, spread-eagled. Fila, cover me!"

He heard her say, "Got it! Go!"

Charlie moved around the car to the driver's door, while the still-shocked customers inside watched out the window and neighbors were now running up, but staying back a safe distance.

"Both hands out the window!" Charlie commanded.

He approached the man, saw that Fila was covering him and the passenger very well, and slipped his Glock in his pocket, grabbed the driver's two thumbs together in a viselike grip, knocked his hat off, grabbed him by his dreadlocks, then hauled him out the driver's window and face-first onto the ground. Charlie then lifted him, marched him quickly around to the other side of the car, and laid him down about ten feet from his friend.

Now the crowd of neighbors started cheering and applauding as cruisers drove up, screeching to a halt.

The first officer out pointed his weapon at Charlie and started to tell him to drop his weapon, but a man from the crowd ran out holding up a police badge and yelling, "Aesop, Narcotics! They are one of us! The man and woman are good guys!" The officer nodded at Charlie and Fila.

Charlie said, "One at the back of the car was backseat, one in the front was the driver. They have not been searched."

Fila yelled out, "Two holdup men inside are both dead!"

The crowd started cheering again.

Charlie said to Fila, "Call Weasel. Then call Pops."

He held his weapon on the two gangbangers from the car until other cruisers arrived and took over. Charlie holstered his weapon, and Aesop came up from the crowd and shook hands very enthusiastically with both him and Fila. Soon, the first sergeant to roll up came up and shook hands with both of them also.

Within twenty minutes, a helicopter could be heard and a Little Bird landed right in the middle of the street, and Pops emerged, wearing Bermuda shorts, a Hawaiian shirt, and sandals. He went up to the Fayetteville police lieutenant now in charge, showed him his identification, and spoke to him.

He then ran over to Charlie and Fila and said, "You two okay?"

Aesop was still there and said, "Hey, I know you, Colonel. You two aren't cops." He looked at Charlie, saying,

"You must be C.A.G. I did twenty-two years in Group, many of them at Bragg with 7th and SWC." He was referring to the Special Warfare Center.

Charlie explained, "He is a Fayetteville detective."

Pops stuck out his hand, saying, "They both are C.A.G."

"Damn," Aesop said. "The Funny Platoon, huh? I didn't know it was real. Heard it was rumor." Sticking out his hand to Fila, which she shook, he said, "Didn't mean to diss you, ma'am. I didn't know you were Delta, too. Don't know what to call you. Don't know your rank."

Fila grinned and said, "Don't need to call me ma'am, Officer. I work for a living."

Charlie and Aesop started laughing, and Pops groaned.

Aesop said, "Nice to meet you, Sergeant. I'm a retired E9 myself. Nice meeting you, too, sir."

Charlie grinned, saying, "No need to call me sir, Sergeant Major, I work for a living."

Pops groaned again, while the other three laughed.

Saying "Do not call me sir, I work for a living" was a cliché among Special Forces NCOs and had been that way for decades.

Rose was now outside, with several officers around her and visibly shook up. She ran up to Charlie, throwing her arms around his neck.

"Oh, Charlie," she said, "You and, and oh, I am so shaky and ready to faint, I can't think of your name, sweetie. Oh! Fila, thank you both so much. You saved my life. You saved everybody's. That officer over there told me these were the gang members they think killed that convenience store clerk down on Hays Street last week, after they took all her money. I was so scared!"

She grabbed Charlie and kissed him on the cheek and then did the same to Fila, and gave her a big hug, too.

Charlie held her protectively and said, "Rose, this is Pops, a friend of ours."

She shook hands with Pops and said, "Are you a detective, too? All this time, I didn't know Charlie was a cop, let alone this sweet thang he brought in today."

"No," Pops said, "I'm just a friend. They are really great detectives, but they work undercover so please do not talk about them to the press."

"Lord have mercy," she replied. "Ahm gonna thank the Good Lord every day we have such brave officers protecting us. Of cause Ah'll keep mah mouth shut."

The lieutenant came out of the café and Rose was escorted away. He shook hands with Aesop and said, "Sergeant Aesop, hello."

"How ya doing, Lieutenant Hogan?"

He stuck out his hand to Charlie and Fila, saying, "This community owes you two a lot. These punks had killed before. We are sure. Two rounds each dead center in the forehead."

Pops said, "Thanks, Lieutenant. Now we won't be able to fit their heads through the door." To them, he said, "The lieutenant said you two can give a quick statement and get out of here, before the news media shows up. Which is what I am going to do." Pops shook hands all the way around and said to his charges, "Good job! We'll talk in the morning."

He headed at a fast walk toward the Little Bird, swung his two fingers in a fast circle overhead, and the chopper started revving up. As soon as he hopped in, the rotors revved rapidly, and it lifted off, banked, and disappeared over the tall trees.

The lieutenant said, "Everybody told us the same thing. You two are heroes. I heard you live close. Do you want an officer to take you home and take your statements there?"

Charlie looked at Fila, who nodded, and he said, "Lieutenant, we would love it, but one request?"

"What's that?"

Charlie said, "Can we each get a piece of carrot cake to take with us?"

Aesop yelled, "No problem," as he headed toward the café door pulling his badge out. The lieutenant signaled an officer by the door to cooperate with him. Aesop whispered to Rose, and she escorted him. They emerged with a small cake box a minute later, and Aesop thanked her and carried it to Charlie.

Aesop said, "Rose said to give you two the whole cake, you lucky turkeys. Man, I love her pastries."

They thanked him, shook hands with him and the lieutenant, and headed toward a cruiser with a Fayetteville PD sergeant.

The lieutenant's voice stopped them at the cruiser. "Hey, both of you! My wife and I will keep you in our prayers! God bless you both for what you do for this country."

Charlie smiled and waved, and Fila said, "God bless you, too, and thank you for your service to the community!"

As they got into the cruiser, all the assembled crowd spotted them and started clapping again.

They got home and went into the house. Charlie poured each of them a snifter of brandy. They drank quickly. The sergeant took an offered cup of hot coffee.

Charlie and Fila drank bottles of water while they gave their statements. In a half hour, the sergeant shook hands with them at the door and thank-yous were again exchanged.

As soon as the cruiser pulled out of the driveway, Fila turned to Charlie, tears welling up in her eyes, and he held his arms out. She started crying and ran into his arms.

"Charlie, that is the first person I have ever killed," she sobbed.

He said, "I know, honey. I know. You did not hesitate at all. You showed me I would want you on my team anywhere, anytime."

"You were wonderful," she said. "You were so calm and took charge and made it work out for everybody."

He replied, "We need some carrot cake."

She stopped crying and smiled, nodding her head, wiping her tears. She said, "Why don't we both take quick showers? After what happened, I was drenched in sweat. You cut us each a piece of carrot cake, pour us each some coffee, and we eat them after?"

Charlie smiled, "Sounds like a plan to me. See ya in a few."

They each went to one of the two bathrooms. Charlie climbed into the shower, and now he was alone, he sobbed hard, letting the water pour on his face. He thought about the young punks and how wasted their lives were. He thought about all those who hammered his red brothers into thinking about what victims they were until many thought their lives were hopeless. He thought about how many people in the lives of the dead gangsters, from parents to teachers to news media, had told them they were victims of prejudice, corporate greed, and so many other victimization excuses, and how alive they might have been if just someone would have told them they were strong or smart and had opportunity if they were willing to work for it. He thought about how they probably had been in and out of jail, not learning about consequences for their actions. He cried and let the water drain the negative away. He knew the action he had taken had saved lives, and he was so thankful for all the training he had received in the U.S. Army Special Forces. By the time he finished rinsing off, he had his shoulders back and his chest out a little with pride.

He started drying off and heard Fila speak loud from the bedroom. "Hey, Poke! I got your dessert, and it is ready for you."

Charlie splashed on a little Obsession and dabbed on deodorant, brushed his teeth, looked in the mirror, and smiled at himself, then opened the door.

There was some light but not much, and his incense

burner on the dresser was lit and so was the large candle, and the ones on his nightstand and headboard. He looked at her and smiled. Fila lay on the bed with her long shiny black hair spilling across one shoulder.

She was smiling at him and said, "Ready for dessert, darling?"

The sight of her tanned naked body took his breath away. Her body was near perfect, to match the rest of her, and it was obvious that she worked out very hard. He saw low on her right side below the rib cage a very obvious bullet-wound scar with a larger exit wound on the back right side. This made her even more attractive to him.

Removing his clothing, he slowly walked forward, smiling, and now it was her turn to marvel at *his* magnificent physique. He was indeed all man.

He sat down on the bed, and pulled a rose out of the vase on his dresser and softly ran it all over her neck, face, and shoulders, and teased her sensitive areas without really touching them. He then started peeling off rose petals, one at a time, and dropping them on her tummy, breasts, and all over. As each would land, he would softly kiss wherever it landed. He took his time, and she was elated. This went on for twenty minutes. Never had she experienced ecstasy like this, and what was amazing to her was that he had not even touched her breasts yet, or her more private areas, but now his lips were all over the breasts where the fragrant petals landed. Ten minutes later, his lips were almost down to the bottom petals. He just started to kiss there, and she grabbed his shoulders and sat bolt upright.

"Charlie!" she said suddenly. "Stop! Please stop! I am sorry. I am so sorry!"

He immediately sat up and took her hands and said, "I'm sorry, Fila. Did I move too fast? Did I do something wrong?"

She now took his face in her hands and tears started dropping down her cheeks. He was very concerned now.

"You did nothing wrong." She explained, "You have been wonderful. It is not you. It is me."

She continued crying, and he pulled her gently against his massive chest and held her. She sobbed for five minutes straight. He jumped up and ran to his bathroom, returning with a box of tissues. She thanked him and started dabbing tears away.

He said, "It is so hard to deal with killing someone. I have nightmares—"

"No, Charlie, it's not that," she interrupted. "I was going to be stoned to death when I was a girl, because my cousin tried to rape me and got my clothes off, but I fought him off."

"And they were going to stone you for *not* getting raped?"

"Exactly," she said, "and it was my father who instigated it. An honor killing, they call it. Then later, as a teenager, I was actually raped in Baghdad."

He stroked her hair, saying, "I'm so sorry, Fila."

She said, "I have not been able to have sex of any kind with any man since. I tried several times but just could not. Nobody ever made me want someone like I wanted you just now. You had me going far beyond anything any man had ever accomplished, but when it came to the moment of truth I panicked."

Charlie said, "Look. We have to pose in Iran as husband and wife, but we do not have to do anything. We can sleep behind closed doors, but I want you to feel you can trust me. You do not have to worry, Fila. I would never hurt you, and I will never let any man hurt you again."

She hugged him tightly.

Then he said, "Why don't we lie down under the covers, and I will just hold you? Nothing else. You just stay with me tonight."

"Charlie!" she said.

Part of her was scared to give trust to this man, but an

even bigger part wanted him to become one with her. She was falling in love, but how could she let anybody touch her ever again? She decided she would conquer her fear and allow herself to let her guard down.

Fila crawled under the blankets and sheets and his giant arms embraced her. She felt so safe with her head on his massive pectoral muscle, and she sobbed little sobs, until she finally fell asleep. The last thing she remembered was Charlie softly stroking her hair.

FILA awakened with a start and looked around. Charlie was asleep next to her, holding her protectively. She looked at his face and wished his eyes were open. They were what made him the most attractive. They showed somehow intelligence and humor. She drifted back to sleep.

Fila opened her eyes and looked at the alarm clock radio on the nightstand. It was 5:15 A.M. and the alarm would go off in fifteen minutes. Charlie lay nude next to her. She watched him in his sleep and thought about what a great man he was.

Fila knew that, although she was a rape victim and that would carry a life sentence, this man had shown her love— pure, complete love. It was a totally different scenario, and she felt so relieved she could now imagine even trusting a man.

She drifted off.

Charlie had another nightmare and this one made him sit up suddenly. Eyes barely even open, he immediately grabbed the hand that had just grabbed his throat. He looked into the eyes of Fila, who had been startled by him sitting up and immediately grabbed him by the windpipe, but she was now wincing from the wristlock he'd placed on her hand. They both let go of each other and started laughing at themselves.

"Nightmare?" she asked.

"Yeah, but you were in it," he replied defensively, without realizing what he was saying.

"Gee, thanks a lot!" she said, slamming him in the face with a pillow.

Now he was really embarrassed.

"Wait, I didn't mean it like that," he protested.

They both started laughing.

They returned to the bedroom from quick trips to the bathrooms, still nude, and plopped down on the bed.

She suddenly got serious and said, "Charlie, I feel so guilty about last night. I want you to make love to me."

He leaned over and kissed her, saying, "I'll make love to you when you feel giddy, not guilty. Come on, let's get dressed. More exciting briefings today."

"You know, that's a good idea, but Charlie, I mean it," she said. "I want you to make love to me."

He grabbed her hand and pulled her out of bed and into his arms and hugged her, saying, "Look, we will be posing as husband and wife, and it would help if we acted like we were 24/7. That is simple survival. I also know you are trying to do the right thing for my sake. I appreciate it, Fila. When it is time for you and me to make love, you won't have to ask me. We will both know. I do not want you to make love to me for the wrong reasons, even if they are noble."

"Are you sure?" she asked.

Charlie said, "Can't wait to get in and see that Rozanski again. The man has had a charisma bypass."

"A charisma bypass?" she said, laughing hysterically.

He chuckled now and added, "Yeah, he went to the Osama bin Laden Charm School."

They both laughed going out the door.

CHAPTER TWELVE

Peak Planning

THE briefing started with the S2 (Intelligence) personnel offering their latest reports and assessment. Davood Faraz Dabdeh had excellent security around him twenty-four hours per day, seven days a week.

One of the things that Charlie and Fila had discussed was how they would dress.

One of the Intelligence briefers stated: "Currently in Iran, the Islamic dress code is still pretty strictly observed all over the country. That code requires women to cover their hair, necks, and arms. Modern women in Iran today, wear a manteau or overcoat, which is almost like a standard uniform. The manteaus are constructed with long sleeves and usually come below the knee. Checking back on our area studies of Iran, we have seen that the length of this long overcoat changes with the times. For a while, we guess trying to be fashionable like our women in America, they tried something different. Really long ones were in fashion, but then just a few years ago, women tried to get away with very short coats, as well."

He ad-libbed then. "You can imagine how that went over with the mullahs. Anyway, to cover their hair usually a scarf or a shawl is acceptable. What they do is fold the two opposite corners of a scarf to get a triangle and then simply tie the scarf around their heads. Modern women will wear trousers, even blue jeans, or dark stockings under the manteau.

"For men, short sleeves and Western clothing can get your ass kicked by the government."

Everybody laughed, and he went on. "As a rule in Iran, shorts, T-shirts, and ties are not worn out in public by men. You will find that many Iranian men and women really like to dress very Western in private settings and for special events. When dealing with government agencies, schools, embassies, and the like, you obey the rules, period, or it will be like Pops finding you having a beer party with a bunch of marines."

Everybody laughed again, and one of the men in the room, who apparently was a marine, grinning, said, "Hey, all you army types want a leatherneck to whip your collective asses?"

"Naw, there ain't any *Life* magazine photographers around to take your picture, so it would be against your SOP," Weasel said, meaning standard operating procedure.

Pops stood up and said, "Charlie, what did you two come up with as far as your dress code and cover?"

Charlie had been wearing a cowboy hat all morning so far, but he now stood up and pulled it off. Weasel shook his head as if he really felt bad for him. Charlie's long black hair had been cut off, by Fila, and she had given him a buzz cut with an expensive razor kit he had at his house. His long hair had been tied and kept in a giant ponytail to be donated for cancer patients.

Charlie said, "A lot of Iranian men would love to wear Western hairstyles, but that would be like wearing a sign screaming 'Notice me!' Fila and I knew my long, long hair was out of the question, so we are donating it to make a nice wig or two for somebody with cancer that has lost their hair. I have started today growing a beard, but my race usually is not noted for facial hair, so we talked about me wearing a fake beard or mustache."

Pops stood up and said, "Top, do we have any resource people in Hollywood that are top-notch makeup artists?"

Weasel said, "Aye, aye, Boss. We gotta good one who used to be in the 10th Group and served in Bosnia, and he also had a tour in the Gulf War. They know how to make stuff that works and don't come off when you are in a room full of al Qaeda or whatever this guy's people call themselves. I think that is the way ta go. Sorry, Poke. You are Lakota and should have been able to keep your scalp."

Charlie grinned and pointed his thumb at Fila, saying, "Thanks, Weasel, but, see, this woman is not even my real Iranian wife, but has been around American women so much, she already runs my life and does what the hell she wants."

Fila said, "You remember that."

He grinned.

During the ten-minute break after the first hour, they went to the break room and Fila said, "This is my first big op. I cannot believe how much planning goes into this."

Charlie responded, "Honey, we are just getting started. Most people have no clue how much Delta plans and rehearses before a shot is even fired. Remember when Weasel said 'NMDO' the other day to Pops?"

"Yeah," she replied, "What does that mean?"

"It means No More Desert Ones," Charlie said, referring to the tragic rescue mission Operation Eagle Claw by Detachment-Delta and others on April 11, 1980, under President Jimmy Carter, when a number of Delta Force operators and others were killed when a navy helicopter with a marine pilot and an air force jet collided in the desert after aborting the mission to rescue the American hostages taken in the embassy in Iran.

He added, "You notice it is being planned by us, here, and not in the Pentagon, where every general and admiral has to fight to get their boys and equipment into the plan. And you noticed already Pops is asking our opinions on this, because our asses are on the line. I am so glad he is our boss."

"Oh, me, too," she agreed. "We better get back to the conference room."

They walked into the room and were in shock. There was the vice president of the United States. All in the room jumped to their feet and started clapping when the two walked in. They looked at each other in shock. The veep walked up to them, and both snapped to attention, accompanied by the lovely national security advisor, Kerri Rhodes. Pops walked up next to the veep and handed him two Soldiers Medals.

The vice president said, "Master Sergeant Charles Strongheart and Sergeant First Class Fila Jannat, less than twenty-four hours ago, you two risked your lives saving the lives of a number of civilians in Fayetteville, North Carolina, in a noncombat situation. I happened to be giving a speech yesterday at Central Piedmont Community College in Charlotte, and the President this morning directed me to come here to honor you two on his behalf and on behalf of the citizens of the United States of America. Your good colonel here will have some writing genius word the documents for presentation later, so it will not compromise the clandestine nature of your real work and your identities. I understand the news describes the heroes who killed the gang members, who had already killed before, as two off-duty police detectives, but we all know who the heroes are. It is with great honor and pride that I pin the nation's highest noncombat valor award, the Soldiers Medal, to each of you. Congratulations and thank you."

Everybody enthusiastically applauded, and Pops and Weasel shook hands with them. Pops winked and said, "I told you two we would address this today. Congratulations."

Weasel came up to Charlie and said, "Poke, I want to tell you something. You know I love and revere the history of your people. I am telling you right now, your great-great, whatever it was, Grandfather Sitting Bull himself, is sitting up there with the Great Mystery looking down on you right now with a big smile on his face. Bet he is tapping Jesus on the arm, and saying, 'That is my grandson.' Bet he is. Congratulations."

Kerri Rhodes congratulated and shook hands with both of them, and Fila noticed how long the beautiful major player from Washington held Charlie's hand. She felt her face reddening a little. After she let go of his hand, Charlie glanced over at Fila with a slight look of guilt on his face.

Good, Fila thought to herself. *He ought to feel guilty. That is good for him.*

"All right, everybody," Pops said, walking over to the table carrying a large box, which he set on it.

Weasel ran to the door and took a bag from a Delta member there. He set it down and unloaded its contents—plastic plates and forks. Pops opened the box, and it contained a large carrot cake baked by Rose.

Pops said, "This was baked this morning by the woman who Poke and Booty saved. Grab a cup of coffee and let's dig in. Mr. Vice President, how do you like your coffee, sir?"

The next hour was spent eating cake and talking to the vice president. After he left, they started back into the planning. The method of infiltration became the next issue. Immediately, HALO was brought up. Then somebody else in the room brought up HALO/SCUBA. Rozanski, who had been keeping mum, was obviously pleased.

Pops again looked at Charlie and Fila, and said, "How do you two feel about going in by HALO?"

Charlie said, "Well, sir, we did four HALO jumps yesterday and landed within fifty feet and ten seconds of each other each time. We talked about using Stealth wings in fact."

One of the others asked about Stealth wings, so Weasel explained them. "Some wings made of high polymer plastic have been developed which were used by a special CID specops unit stateside, and they have been tested by the British SAS. The operators are dropped from high altitude with these wings on and they can track for one hundred and thirty miles or so vertically. In other words, covert insertions can be effected without radar detection. The operator then deploys their regular ram-air chute to land, and the wings fold up alongside their body."

Rozanski said, "So what do they do with the wings after they land? Leave them for the enemy to find?"

Weasel grinned, saying, "That is why God invented thermite grenades, General."

Thermite grenades have long been used by Special Forces to burn down into bunkers, safes, to destroy operational orders, bridge supports, dams, and destroy classified documents in a safe, as they burn much hotter than an arc welder and cannot be extinguished by water.

Charlie went on. "We feel that with the tough talk about Iran, they remember shock and awe in Iraq, and Booty and I felt that they will have eyes on the skies 24/7 countrywide, just watching for us or an Israeli strike. For that same reason, we feel they have probably got their radar stepped up significantly. We looked at some of Dabdeh's activities such as offshore racing, his villa in France, and his yacht. Regardless of his tight security, it seems he will be much more vulnerable outside the confines of Iran."

"Excuse me, Sergeant Strongheart," Kerri Rhodes chimed in. "The one thing that is very important to the commander in chief is that this hit is made in Iran, because of the psychological effect of their being incapable of saving a high-profile player in their own country."

Pops said, "That settles that. We now know it must happen in Iran and no other location, so that brings us back to infiltration. What about horses through the mountains?"

"We discussed that, sir," Fila added. "Too much cross-border activity with the Iraq War in one sector and al Qaeda/Taliban and drug smugglers in the other. Rules out dirt bikes and ATVs, too."

Weasel said, "How about SCUBA through the Caspian Sea, Persian Gulf, or Gulf of Oman?"

"Good question, Top," Charlie said. "We briefly discussed that, too. I am SCUBA-qualified, but Sergeant Jannat is not and is not experienced enough in SCUBA to risk it. Also, there's the issue of how much we can carry diving and, most importantly, the paranoia of Tehran. They have to be watching the shores like eagles, waiting for the Navy SEALS being led by GI Jane herself, Demi Moore. We ruled it out, too."

"Did you two come up with a method of infiltration that you feel will work?" Pops asked.

"Yes, sir, we did," Charlie said. "We felt we could enter the country in a Mercedes with plenty of money for bribes. They will watch the skies, seas, and mountains for Rambo to show up. We feel going in their front door as a well-to-do couple with oil money can get us quietly across the border. Bribes are a way of life and those taking them keep their mouths shut or else. We also can be somebody Dabdeh wants to meet with, maybe an oil official and his wife."

Pops looked at the others in the room, and wondered why the hell he was even allowing so many in on the planning of an operation. This was against the standard operating procedure, but his hand had really been forced on this one by the powers that be. So often it seemed that the army had become so politically correct, and general officers and

DOD (Department of Defense) bureaucrats wanted to stick their noses into the very clandestine inner workings of 1st Special Forces Operational Detachment-Delta.

Most times, Pops thought about how much easier it must have been for Colonel Charlie Beckwith, Delta creator, as he had commanders "upstairs" with mission success and Opsec (operational security) in mind, so nobody ever got into what used to be called the "Stockade," the former U.S. Army Fort Bragg stockade, which had been converted into the Delta Force headquarters compound. The Stockade gave way to the Compound, and the famous Shooting House was replaced by the more modern House of Horrors.

In actuality, no expense was spared for Detachment-Delta operators. They had a wide variety of weapons and aircraft at their disposal, as well as the latest in military technology such as "Smart Dust," which is comprised of thousands of small particles that are actually microchip transmitters and which are sprinkled on vehicles and even clothing belonging to members of al Qaeda, Hamas, and other terrorist groups. The particles look like harmless large pieces of sand or industrial dust, but each one transmits a radio beeping signal which can be used to follow whatever they are on by UAV (unmanned aerial vehicle) or drone flying high above and out of sight and hearing, or the signal can be picked up by other vehicles with a receiver. Many terrorists have become martyrs in the Global War on Terrorism or led U.S. specops forces to terrorist leaders inadvertently because of Smart Dust.

The technology behind Smart Dust is similar to that of stuff like smart cards (EZ Pass, etc.) and the tiny little grain-sized tracking devices people have injected into their pets. Smart Dust, however, is even more revolutionary in that it is small enough to be disguised as dirt, the kind someone might pick up on shoes or clothing. Actually, each little MEM (memory) or bit of Smart Dust is given a unique serial number that, when hit with an "interrogation signal" from either troops on the ground or aircraft overhead, like the UAV already mentioned, broadcasts a signal back. Several very advanced forms of Smart Dust are in use in Iraq and Afghanistan, almost exclusively by 1st Special Forces Operational Detachment-Delta. It was actually Smart Dust that played a very significant role in the locating of and ultimate death of Iraqi al Qaeda leader Abu Musab al-Zarqawi. In this case, an agent recruited by Detachment-Delta was able to sprinkle some Smart Dust on Zarqawi's clothing, and then he was simply tracked down with great precision. Iraqis and Afghanis have long feared what they refer to as "magic dust." Most Iraqi, Afghani, and Iranian terrorists have a tendency to exaggerate American capabilities, especially regarding technology, so Davood constantly had his clothes and vehicles cleaned.

"According to our research, Davood Faraz Dabdeh travels continuously," Charlie said. "I suggest that at each location he appears we sprinkle his vehicles with Smart Dust, on a continuing basis so we can track him. Even when he washes the vehicles down, you know that some MEMs will stay in a few cracks and hiding places."

Rozanski felt the whole Smart Dust thing was just too *Star Wars* for his feelings, so after a long silence and pouting period, he finally spoke up again. "How can this Smart Dust be delivered regularly without detection?"

"Rotor UAVs," Fila replied.

"What is that?"

Pops opened his briefcase and pulled out a written paper and tossed it down in front of Rozanski.

He said, "Does anybody else need to know what that is?"

One other did not know what it was but did not want to admit it. Fila glanced over at Kerri Rhodes to see if she raised her hand, then she got embarrassed about even looking.

Rozanski started reading about just one group of rotor-type unmanned aerial vehicles, also called "rotorcraft." This group, constructed by Tactical Aerial Vehicles or TAG, featured a variety of military-type rotorcrcaft, including one which could fly at 102 miles per hour, had a gross tactical weight over 1,400 pounds, carried over a 550-pound payload, and had a flight ceiling well over 10,000 feet.

The retired general said, "Colonel, does Delta Force use this aircraft?"

Pops grinned and said, "No, we don't, General, but it gives you an idea of one of the types of delivery vehicles we can use. We have one that is more like a Stealth and can fly under silent mode and is barely heard even getting down close to the ground in altitude. We can fly these in from ships and even small boats on the bodies of water bordering Iran, or from the mountains, or even from several spots out in the desert, then fly them back for refueling and maintenance."

"What kind of rotary UAV does Delta Force use?" the general queried.

"Now, General Rozanski," Pops replied, "that is not really important. You do not really have a need-to-know, but knowing that one of them will be our delivery vehicle for Smart Dust is enough."

Well, that settled that, Charlie's grin told Fila. Pops was going with their suggested means of keeping up-to-date surveillance on the ruthless terrorist. Through the studies of his habits, Charlie and Fila had become concerned because Dabdeh was so security conscious, he was to the point of being paranoid. They felt that, with bribe money and their wits, they could cross several of the border areas into Iran without too much trouble, but once there, they still had the challenge of arranging a meet with Davood Faraz Dabdeh. That was going to be the real challenge.

On top of that, besides meeting with him and killing

him, they also had the challenge of getting past his many layers of security to both get to him and kill him and get out of Iran without death or capture. Their fingerprints and DNA could possibly be used to identify them as members of the U.S. military, which would prove very embarrassing for Washington, to say the least. Even worse, it would become a very effective propaganda tool for Tehran to use worldwide against the United States. Charlie and Fila both could envision headlines speaking about secret Delta Force commandos killed in an elaborate infiltration and assassination plot in Iran, which was effectively uncovered by the Elite Republican Guard forces.

Charlie explained all this and said they really had to plan and figure out how to attract Dabdeh into their trap, plus figure out an effective plan not only for execution but exfiltration from the country.

Charlie and Fila were facing a very complex problem. Specifically, 1st Special Forces Operational Detachment-Delta and the army specops community stated, regarding direct action missions:

> *Short-duration strikes and other small-scale offensive actions conducted as a special operation in hostile, denied, or politically sensitive environments and which employ specialized military capabilities to seize, destroy, capture, exploit, recover, or damage designated targets. Direct action differs from conventional offensive actions in the level of physical and political risk, operational techniques, and the degree of discriminate and precise use of force to achieve specific objectives.*

All specops units engaging in a direct action mission, when proceeding to the mission or infiltrating the enemy ground while dressed in civilian attire, were required to wear U.S. military unit patches on their civilian clothing and to have the patch covered by black tape. This tape had to be yanked off before actually engaging hostile forces. But Charlie and Fila knew that if they were captured, Iran couldn't care less about the protective tenets of the Geneva Convention. They would wear no patches or anything to identify them as Americans. They both knew that if they were caught, both would be gang-raped and sodomized; her breasts would be sliced off, as would his penis and testes. They would probably have their eyes gouged out, their ears, arms, and maybe even legs cut off, before finally being beheaded. They both had seen top secret photos of civilian contractors, usually retired Green Berets and Navy SEALs who had been hacked up this way on the roads in Pakistan, while searching for Osama bin Laden and Ayman al-Zawahiri. They always had signs hanging on them written in Pashtun or Arabic, warning that this would happen to any and all infidels who came looking for jihadists in the tribal areas.

Charlie and Fila lived in the real world. Fila had grown up in that seventh-century mind-set and laughed whenever she heard newscasters or the politically ultra liberals who felt that Americans, Europeans, or Israelis would be spared terrorist reprisal if they would simply be kind and loving toward any and all Muslims, ascribing Western morality and values to those jihadists who honestly believed they would go to Heaven and be richly rewarded if they killed an American, a Christian, or a Jew, and most especially if they first tortured the victim for the glory of Allah. They did not understand at all the concept of *Dar el Islam,* the "Nation of Islam," with no borders but simply world domination. They had no clue how those in al Qaeda and other terrorist groups like Dabdeh's, Hamas, the PLO, and similar, had totally bastardized the religion of Islam for their own selfish and savage ends.

They both knew they need not wear a unit badge, as they simply could not be captured. To that end, they also knew that, before leaving, they both would be given cyanide capsules. The United States of America, which they both had written a blank check to, payable up to and including the sacrifice of their own lives, had to be protected. If capture was imminent, both would quickly put the cyanide pills in their mouths, bite down, and swallow. In short order, they would begin breathing very deeply and then would go to short, rapid breaths, then convulsions, unconsciousness, and death. The alternative, which Fila did not know about, was that Charlie would shoot her behind the ear, killing her instantly, and then would jam the pistol up under his own chin, aiming toward the upper back part of his head, and pull the trigger. These were very grisly scenarios for both to consider, but it went with their jobs, and both took great pride in being the best in the world.

Weasel said, "Ladies and gents, this would be a good time to look at a successful Delta Force operation. It was Operation Just Cause in Panama in December of 1989. I was lucky enough to be involved. One major portion of the bigger operation revolved around Kurt Muse, a single American citizen who the bad guys thought was a CIA agent. Detachment-Delta had to mount a difficult operation to rescue him, and sometimes he made the rescue even more difficult.

"Muse served in the U.S. Army and spent time in Panama, and he liked it and the people, so he returned there. His wife worked as a schoolteacher. Kurt sold printing, copying, and graphic arts equipment throughout all of Central America, not just Panama. As he got more involved, and his wife taught more, he got really frustrated at the actions of General Manuel Noriega and the PDF, the Panamanian Defense Force, and their oppression of the Panamanians.

"Muse and a group of five Panamanians began broadcasting anti-Noriega messages, jamming Panama radio stations and overpowering the broadcasts with their own stronger signal. This got the attention of the people of Panama but also the folks at the CIA, 'cause they had all kinds of people in Panama at the time monitoring every-thing. We used to joke that you could tell CIA agents there, because they had brown suits, spoke fluent Spanish, wore spit-shined low quarters, and had flat-top haircuts."

Everyone in the room laughed at this, with a few shaking their heads picturing some they had known in specops who retired, went into intel, and just never made the transition.

Weasel continued, "The CIA thought the radio broadcasts were a great idea, and had planned to help Muse broadcast overtop of Noriega's major speech to the nation, when the most citizens would be watching and listening. They supplied him with the radio equipment to jam the signal or actually overpower it. This would be a major coup for our psyops and counterintelligence efforts.

"Muse waited until a key time in the introduction of President Manuel Noriega when it would cause the most impact, and he played a prerecorded propaganda speech.

"Wooey! Old Noriega was one pissed-off *El Presidente*. It went off so well, the Panamanian government and the PDF went nuts. They immediately blamed the United States, too."

Weasel took a large drink of coffee and continued. "Then Muse kept it up for a few more months, until they finally arrested him, tortured him, made him listen or watch others being tortured, and so on. They held him at the police headquarters downtown but finally moved him to the *Carcel Modelo* (Model Prison), an old prison that contained over a thousand inmates but was made to house maybe two hundred to two hundred fifty. Muse had an eight-by-twelve cell and adjoining bathroom, and he had one small window. The prison was not one building but was actually a small fort.

"Because of pressure by our government, we were finally able to get people in to see him a few times, and we then knew that in nine months he had lost over fifty pounds, so we had to get him out quickly, but we planned and prepared like we are doing now. We planned here and also at Eglin Air Force Base in Florida. We made models, mockups, you name it.

"We were working with the 160th Special Operations Aviation Group, and also had two Spectre AC-130 gunships from the 1st Special Operations Wing. The Little Birds were our lifeline on that mission, and the Blackhawk was our command and control ship. Some of us got bloodied up and even got shot down in our Little Bird with Muse after we rescued him, but the operation was really a success for 1st Special Forces Operational Detachment-Delta. We had to blow our way through the roof, but we took out the killer guard and some others, pulled off the operation, and got the hell out of Dodge. You can all read the after-action report on it.

"The important point is, we even made mock-up buildings to practice the operation, and we kept it small as far as inclusion of planning and tactical personnel, and as always on a need-to-know basis. Delta Force did it right that day. Colonel, the one point I want to make is, we know Poke and Booty will be on their own and thinking on their feet, but as far as my vote, I cannot tell you how important the Little Birds, Spectre, and Blackhawk were to the success of our operation. I personally feel we must have an effective QRF ready to come in if they yell for the cavalry," he said, referring to a quick reaction force, "and we have to have aircraft in the neighborhood to bail these two out if need be. The rescue of Kurt Muse was the very first big public success for Detachment-Delta, and this one will be a major victory, too, although this one has to stay out of the news."

Custer was ushered in with the rest of Charlie's team and they were introduced by nicknames, and it was stated they would be the QRF for Charlie and Booty if the pair got into serious trouble.

Now it had to be determined how the QRF could get in. Several scenarios were suggested.

Finally, Pops spoke out. "I think it is imperative that we move them into a staging area in the desert. We have to have them close enough to be able to strike quickly if needed, but out far enough to not be spotted."

Rozanski quickly spoke up, his jowls quivering with indignation. "That is preposterous! How can you possibly get aircraft into Iran undetected?"

Pops said, "The same way we already have plenty of times, General. We can take them into Iran by land or by air and can stage outside Tehran or other major cities undetected. We most definitely have that capability. How do you suppose we got pictures of Iranian nuclear facilities development in varying stages?"

The general stared at Pops a moment then said, "You mean Delta Force has gone into Iran to take reconnaissance photos?"

"Need-to-know, General Rozanski."

"How can you possibly get helicopters into Iran undetected, especially close to a place like Tehran?" Rozanski said a little indignantly.

"I am sorry, General." Pops grinned. "But again, that is on a need-to-know basis."

Now definitely indignant, Rozanski said, "Colonel, I have a need-to-know. I am part of the planning of this operation."

Pops said, "Excuse me there, Mr. Rozanski, but you have been part of the preop planning, and your expertise is the G2 capability, but you are not part of the execution of the operation phase. You need only be concerned with us planning to take aircraft in there. You do not have a need-to-know how we will do it."

"I do not appreciate being called Mr. Rozanski, Colonel. I am General Rozanski," the retired flag officer said angrily.

"No, if we are being technical, you are Major General Rozanski," Pops said, jaw jutting forward in his best imitation of former Steelers coach Bill Cowher, "but when I allow you around my command and in my facility, I expect you to conduct yourself like a flag officer and speak to me and to my people with respect and a sense of cooperation. You visit this facility at my pleasure, General. So let's say we try a do-over."

Charlie tapped Fila with his knee, and she tried to suppress a grin. Custer shot him a knowing glance across the big conference table and flashed him a hand sign as if grabbing his testes as he glanced at Pops. Charlie grinned. Then he heard Fila chortle almost aloud, and he and Custer realized she had seen the interchange.

Rozanski was speechless and gave Pops a half nod, and Pops embarrassed the man further by saying, "Good. I am glad we can get along and make things work."

The rest of the afternoon was spent briefing the quick reaction force for Operation Angry Godfather, which it was now called, a name created by Weasel for the famous movie.

A C-130J Super Hercules aircraft would be used to transport the backup team to a point in the desert where they would be hidden, capable of flying into Iran at several points, where technology had shown the aircraft could actually fly under the radar screen. This would be aided by an AWACS aircraft jamming Iranian security when the flight came in. The C-130J Super Hercules would transport the seven-man QRF team as well as three Little Bird specops helicopters, which would be off-loaded on the desert floor, and made flight-ready in fifteen minutes' time.

Additionally, a much larger quick reaction force of Army Rangers would be standing by at Fire Base Glory at Mosul Air Base in northern Iraq, from where all aircraft would fly out. It was decided that because there was so much air activity in Iraq, it would not be the likely place for the U.S. to strike Iran from. Additionally, Tactical Air flying missions over Iraq would be available for prioritized diversion if a major strike would need to be put in to support any problem arising out of Operation Angry Godfather. The government of Iran was constantly looking for Stealth-type jet strikes from the U.S. or Israel on their nuclear processing facilities, so they were watching for jets to come in over one of the sea areas, Dubai, or Kuwait, but believed they would be less likely coming from Iraq or Afghanistan.

Getting in and out undetected and having the quick reaction force deployable was critical, so having the three Little Birds standing by in the desert along with the quick reaction force was the only way the President would allow the operation to continue. If an international incident occurred, he said he would take the heat. He made it clear that he wanted this team to have the best aircraft and equipment available to accomplish the mission. Pops said that besides the C-130J Super Hercules, he also wanted an AC-130U Spooky "on station," flying just outside Iranian airspace, since it did not have the short jet-assisted takeoff capability of its less-armed brother, the C-130J Super Hercules.

Designed and built by Lockheed Martin, the Super Hercules is the world's most advanced tactical airlifter. It can be converted to any number of uses, from delivery of humanitarian supplies to air-to-air refueling to delivery of combat material. It can be used for deep covert penetration, combat rescue, and low-level night entry.

It has been purchased by air forces in Australia, Italy, the United Kingdom, Denmark, and, of course, the United States.

Then of the sister aircraft covering both Charlie and

Fila and the quick reaction force if need be, the Department of Defense said of the Spooky:

> The AC-130U is the most complex aircraft weapon system in the world today. It has more than 609,000 lines of software code in its mission computers and avionics systems. The newest addition to the command fleet, this heavily armed aircraft incorporates side-firing weapons integrated with sophisticated sensor, navigation and fire control systems to provide surgical firepower or area saturation during extended loiter periods, at night and in adverse weather. The sensor suite consists of an All Light Level Television system and an infrared detection set. A multi-mode strike radar provides extreme long-range target detection and identification. It is able to track 40mm and 105mm projectiles and return pinpoint impact locations to the crew for subsequent adjustment to the target. The fire control system offers a Dual Target Attack capability, whereby two targets up to one kilometer apart can be simultaneously engaged by two different sensors, using two different guns. No other air-ground attack platform in the world offers this capability. Navigational devices include the inertial navigation system (INS) and global positioning system (GPS). The aircraft is pressurized, enabling it to fly at higher altitudes, saving fuel and time, and allowing for greater range than the AC-130H. Defensive systems include a countermeasures dispensing system that releases chaff and flares to counter radar infrared-guided anti-aircraft missiles. Also infrared heat shields mounted underneath the engines disperse and hide engine heat sources from infrared-guided anti-aircraft missiles.

Having the most state-of-the-art aircraft available for this type of mission was going to be extremely critical for

mission success. So now they would actually fly in with
the quick reaction force on the Super Hercules. The larger
Ranger quick reaction force would sit on full-alert, ready
to board a C-130J Super Hercules at the U.S. airbase at
Mosul, Iraq.

Their expensive vehicle, a new BMW, would be purchased by a CIA agent in Ankara, Turkey, and would be
transported by him to Van, Turkey. From Van, an indige-
nous U.S.-sympathetic Iranian CIA agent handler would
pick it up and drive it to Tabriz, Iran. From Tabriz, it would
be transported to the desert location by two of the indige-
nous Iranian freedom fighters being advised and equipped
by a team from the 5th Special Forces Group out of Fort
Campbell, Kentucky. The 5th Group had long had a team
on the ground with Iranian resistance fighters waiting to
help with just such missions. The 5th Group team and its
Iranian counterparts would be tasked with locating the
best spot on the ground to locate the insertion point and
landing area for the C130J Super Hercules. That would not
be difficult in the vast Garmsar Desert south of Tehran.
Out of sight of their Iranian counterparts, two American
Special Forces team members would sweep the vehicle for
electronic surveillance devices just to be sure that no in-
digenous agents involved were moles.

Pops summoned the Detachment-Delta financial officer
and told him to take someone and drive to a BMW dealer-
ship in Fayetteville and buy a black loaded BMW with
tinted windows, which would be identical to the one they
would buy in Turkey. This would be used for Charlie and
Fila to get used to, so they would not look like greenhorn
car owners if Davood saw them in the car or if he rode
with them. Pops wanted to ensure that both of them looked
like they knew where everything was in the Beemer and
that Charlie knew how it handled. And, in case Charlie
was dead or wounded, he also wanted Fila to have plenty
of hours behind the wheel.

It was decided that the 5th Group team members would use simple expedient landing zone markers to mark a flat, even, solid strip where the C-130 Super Herc could set down and take off. When the plane was inbound in the daytime, they would mark the strip with fluorescent orange air panels, which they carried with them. Or at night, they would mark it by burning small cans of gasoline buried in the ground.

They would locate and prepare a *fara-kan*, or ravine or wash (called a wadi in Iraq), where they could hide the plane, Little Birds, personnel, and equipment, too far from any roads in the desert to spot. The team would fix the site up in a way only a Special Forces–led unit could do so, and the C-130 would also carry in desert camo netting to effectively hide the site from any and all aircraft flying overhead. Any small military or law enforcement patrols that might somehow stumble on the site would be immediately destroyed and buried.

If the quick reaction forces did get involved, the key for the success of the whole operation, even more than the C-130 and AC-130, would be the Little Birds. They were vital to mission success with 1st Special Forces Operational Detachment-Delta on most missions.

Technically, the Little Bird was known as the Hughes H-6 "Cayuse" helicopter. It is the U.S. Army's primary special operations light attack and cargo aircraft. The AH-6J attack variant can be equipped with two miniguns, or rockets. The MH-6J troop ship can handle everything from fast-rope insertions into jungle conditions to dropping off two operatives with motorcycles in better-developed areas.

It was decided to bring two Little Bird mechanics, volunteers with top secret security clearances, along on the C-130 Super Hercules, and they would also have an array of weapons to quickly convert one or two Little Birds from a slick version to a gunship if need be and also provide any needed maintenance.

Everybody was starting to think about Desert One and the fact that this was an operation going back into Iran and staging out of the desert, but there was one big difference. This was being totally controlled by Pops, the commanding officer of 1st Special Forces Operational Detachment-Delta. Desert One was comprised of Delta members, but there were too many cooks that spoiled the broth. Lessons had been learned. And this would be different. If the mission failed, it would be because of other causes. There would also be one set of planners constantly looking at the weather in the area, staging areas, and alert areas such as Mosul. The planning was just getting going, but it was being kept in-house as much as possible. Those at JSOC (Joint Special Operations Command) at Fort Bragg agreed and were in full support of Pops and his men, but even more important was his friendship with the CINC (commander in chief), who was a big supporter of Detachment-Delta.

Next, they would have to determine how Charlie and Fila would get in, affect the assassination, and get out safely with Davood Faraz Dabdeh's excessive security measures and layers of bodyguards.

Various alternatives were discussed around the table, which now had been cleared of all support personnel except for Kerri Rhodes, the national security advisor. The only ones remaining were Pops, Weasel, Poke, Booty, Custer, Bones, the tall lanky lieutenant colonel who was Pops's executive officer, and Kerri Rhodes. It was felt nobody else had a need-to-know and the fewer involved the better.

Pops liked to involve Bones in a lot of planning sessions in case anything ever happened to him. He was scheduled in two days to have a colonoscopy performed, and he wanted to ensure the command was covered just in case. He lectured all his men and women over forty years old to get colonoscopies on a regular basis, so he felt he had to set the example and did not want to cancel his appointment, a decision he had made six months earlier. He'd had his last colonoscopy five years earlier and there were no polyps or problems. He was not thrilled about having to take a laxative the night before, but remembered it really was not very bad at all.

Weasel said, "What about popping him with a Ruger Mark III pistol with a silencer in .22 Long Rifle? Eleven rounds, lightweight, quiet, easy maintenance."

Charlie said, "What's good enough for the Mossad is good enough for me, and Booty and I actually talked about the Ruger Mark III, but we will be searched, or at least I will be. We did talk about Booty carrying one in a thigh holster under her dress."

Pops said, "What if they use a metal detector on her?"

Fila laughed, saying, "Then we are dead."

Charlie said, "We have discussed this already. Women are so insignificant to him, we doubt he will want to check her out. On top of that, she will be wearing a level IIIA Kevlar vest under her dress. When we first see him, I am going to beat her back with a stick for whatever excuse we make up. She won't feel a thing but will scream and cry. We think that will help establish some early friendship, believe it or not."

Weasel grinned, saying, "Booty's tough. She earned a Silver Star in Afghanistan. Why not beat her without the body armor?"

Fila grinned back, saying, "You want to do that, Top?"

He laughed, putting his hands up and shaking his head.

Kerri Rhodes interjected, "You were awarded the Silver Star?"

Fila chuckled, saying, "Some general was trying to be politically correct, Ms. Rhodes."

"Horse manure!" Pops said. "You left off the Purple Heart you also earned when you got wounded saving soldiers under fire."

Kerri said, "I am very impressed, Sergeant Jannat."

"Thank you, Ms. Rhodes, and please call me Booty or Fila."

Kerri said, "Only if you will call me Kerri, please, all of you."

She shot a glance toward Charlie when she said that, which only Fila noticed. She felt her face redden a little and that embarrassed her even more. Now Fila was very upset, as she had always been in control. She had let her guard down and let Charlie cross that secret boundary that no man had ever stepped over. He had been one with her, and she thought about him continuously. She knew that she was in love, and it scared her.

Kerri Rhodes was one of the closest people in the world to the President of the United States of America. She was at White House dinners all the time and was very well educated and good-looking, beautiful actually. She had handsome popular Hollywood stars interested in her, business leaders, and some of America's most eligible successful bachelors. Fila thought about all of these things and wondered why the woman was so interested in Charlie. As a woman, she knew why, but it did not make her feel any more comfortable.

Charlie said, "The problem is that we do not know what city or setting we will meet him in. We don't know if we can even get in to see him, or if we will be able to breach his layers of security. The CIA reports we read on him state that he already has doubles, like Hussein and bin Laden."

"How are you going to even be able to speak to him?" Kerri asked. "If males and especially Dabdeh are so backward and chauvinistic, Fila can't be your spokesperson."

Fila said, "Yes, I can. Poke speaks Arabic at a level three or even four proficiency. He will wear hearing aids and will be an Iraqi businessman with an Iranian wife. I will translate for him, and we want to have an Iraqi and Iranian interpreter speaking to him through one of the hearing aids, in case he has trouble with saying the right words. If that is the case, he can say 'Huh?' in Arabic to stall for time, and through the hearing aids they can tell him what and how to say it."

Pops said, "That sounds like a fine idea. Top, make sure that we have the very best translators. We also need the hearing aids made right away."

More details were brought up and discussed, and at the end of the day, Pops called Charlie and Fila off to the side and said, "I'm having the new Beemer rigged with all the nice accoutrements that you would find on a 14 Company car in Great Britain. Two of our guys will do the rigging and then we will fly them with the materials to do the exact same thing to the Beemer over there."

Charlie said, "Awesome, Colonel. That could save our lives. Thank you."

Fila said, "Yes. Thank you very much."

Pops shrugged it off and said, "We will have it ready to go when you two get back, but right now, I want you both to pick a place to go and get outside the AO for one full week. Go together somewhere. It won't count against your leave time and you'll get TDY," he added, referring to temporary duty pay. "Just be sure you stay in the continental United States. We will have the car ready to train in when you get back."

Charlie said, "Oh gee, Pops, I don't know if we could make ourselves do such an assignment."

Pops laughed and said, "Can you guys think of a good place to go?"

Fila smiled, looked over at Charlie and back at the CO, and said, "I can."

CHAPTER THIRTEEN

Pre-deployment

FILA looked all around at the tiny modular-looking homes dotting the small neighborhood. Many of them had old abandoned cars sitting in backyards, weeds growing around them and out the windows in some cases. A couple of the houses had junk piles or rubbish piles in the backyard, and every other house had a propane tank covered with spray-painted gang graffiti.

They pulled up in front of one small house that was much tidier than the rest in the block, and there was a tiny flower garden running along the front of it from both sides of the concrete slab that served as a porch. Charlie approached the front of the house and the screen door flew open and a moderately heavyset woman with a wide smile and tears in her eyes ran out, her arms wide open.

"Charlie!" she shouted with glee. "You're home."

Charlie bent over and swooped her up in a careful bear hug, saying, "Hi, Mom. I've missed you."

She was very loving and kissed him on the cheek several times. He set her down, and she looked at the Iranian-American beauty.

"Young lady," she said, "you are beautiful. What tribe are you?"

Fila laughed and said, "The Persians, ma'am."

Charlie said, "Mom, this is Sergeant First Class Fila Jannat. She is my partner. Fila, this is my mom. Her name is Betty Walks Fast."

Betty said, "Fila, I am glad to meet you, but you call me Mom."

Fila's face reddened, and she said, "Gee, I am . . . I am at a loss for words."

Charlie said, "Mom! You just met her."

"Charlie!" Betty said sarcastically and laughing. "How many women have you ever brought here for me to meet?"

Now he felt his own face redden, and Fila looked at him, hands on hips.

She said, "Yeah, Charlie, which number am I?"

Charlie looked down and sheepishly said, "The first."

Now Fila's breath caught, and she did not know how to respond.

Betty said, "Charlie, your uncle Eddie had a vision."

Charlie interrupted while he looked in the oven and Betty slapped him with a towel. "Eddie Three Horses. He is what you would call a medicine man."

Betty continued, "Eddie saw you riding a painted horse with its tail tied."

Charlie explained, "When a horse's tail is tied, that means the rider is at war."

Betty said, "But I will tell you about that later. You are from Iran, Fila?"

"I am an American and a Christian, ma'am," Fila responded, "but I grew up in Iran, in a Muslim family, then moved to Iraq as a young girl, and when I got a little older, I moved to America, and I was adopted by a wonderful family. He was a full bird colonel and was the commanding officer of the 5th Special Forces Group at Fort Campbell, Kentucky."

"What are you cooking, Mom?"

"Antelope steaks, potatoes, carrots, peas, and salad," Betty answered. "And for dessert, apple pie a la mode."

Fila said, "Oh, I don't want to impose."

Charlie and Betty started laughing. Fila was puzzled.

"Mom did not know we were coming, right?"

Fila said, "Correct."

"I will bet you that she made enough for four people anyway," he explained. "Mom always senses when someone is coming and cooks enough for them. I can never surprise her."

Charlie had never realized that she did that for almost every meal and gave away the excess, with an admonition that they could never tell, to her church or dropped it off for the Tribal Police, who were actually called the Oglala Sioux Tribal Police Department. She wanted Charlie to know he could always come home and have a warm meal waiting. She also had many people who simply loved her and her cooking and often dropped in at dinnertime.

"Pour us some coffee, Charlie," his mom said, "and let's all go in the living room and talk. Dinner won't be ready for an hour."

She led the way into the living room, and Fila said, "Is there anything I can do to help, ma'am?"

Betty said, "Yes, Fila, I know you are an army sergeant, but please quit calling me ma'am and start calling me Mom."

"Okay, Mom," Fila said, grinning.

Betty said, "I am surprised you have not said anything yet about eating antelope."

Fila laughed and explained, "Mom, I grew up eating things like goat's eyes or *berryooni*, which is lamb lung, which we ate with kind of a bread called *nan-e-taftton*."

"Oh, I guess nothing I cook will bother you," Betty said. "Well, antelope and cougar are the two very best-tasting wild meats, in my opinion."

Charlie walked in and said, "Mom, whatever you fix tastes great."

"Wait until you two eat breakfast," she said.

He smiled. "We already have reservations at the Rapid City Rushmore Plaza Holiday Inn, Mom. Sorry, but we have some other places we have to go while we're here."

"Okay, baby," Betty said. "I know never to question what you do. You are both welcome to stay here, but anyhow, how long will you be in the area?"

"A week."

"Good, then I will enjoy whatever time you are here," his mom said. "You are getting ready to go into battle, aren't you?"

"Yes," he replied, never lying to his mother.

"I want to tell you about your uncle's dream, or better yet, you should go see him," Betty said. "We will eat a little late. The food will keep."

"That important, huh, Ma?"

"Yes."

They got up just like that, and he kissed his mom's cheek, saying, "See you for dinner in about an hour."

Fila stuck out her hand, and Betty took it and pulled her into a warm hug. Betty really liked this woman.

"I am so glad I got to meet, you m— uh, Mom," Fila said.

"We will see each other a lot more, I think," Betty said. "Don't stay too late. You know Uncle Eddie needs his sleep."

Eddie lived in a small house trailer with a ramshackle unpainted porch built on and matching carport, which housed Eddie's short, scruffy, gray horse. Fila noticed, though, that his carport-turned-into-stall was clean, the water tank was full of clean water, and the horse was eating green alfalfa that looked like it was in very good shape. Around the house were a half a dozen rusted-out cars, most on cinder blocks, and several goats grazed in the weeds around the treeless property.

Fila, Charlie, and Eddie sat on homemade chairs on the ramshackle porch. Eddie was pretty much what was called a traditionalist. He wore a ribbon shirt and very long shiny gray hair in pigtails, with beaded bands and strips of leather tied around the bottom of each. He also wore a single eagle feather hanging diagonally from the back of his hair.

"I was fasting on a vision quest on the mountain yonder," he said, assuming Charlie would know which mountain he meant.

"I fell into a deep sleep after a sweat," he said, which meant he had built a sweat lodge, and probably had smoked some peyote and tobacco both, Charlie thought.

"I saw you, but you were painted for war and rode a mighty painted horse," Eddie said.

"There was a warrior woman riding beside you and sometimes in front, and she said her name was Buffalo Calf Road Woman," he went on, making reference to the Cheyenne wife of Black Coyote, a dog soldier who fought alongside the Lakota against Lieutenant Colonel George Armstrong Custer at the Battle of the Little Big Horn.

"Both you, Wamble Uncha," he said, using Charlie's Lakota name, meaning "One Eagle," "and Buffalo Calf Road Woman had bullets in your arms and legs and blood flowed from your wounds." Eddie went on, "But when I yelled out to you in the battle that you were bleeding, you said your grandfather had given up fifty pieces of flesh.

"The Pawnee lay all around you on the prairie," he continued, "and the buzzards were eating on their flesh and so were the coyotes. Then an eagle came and sang a song above you, and he flew down and lifted you both up in his mighty talons and carried you towards the mountains."

Charlie had chills running down his spine and said, "Uncle, in your vision, did I sing my death song?"

"Yes, but the eagle took you away towards the mountains to fight more battles. You sang your death song, but death did not come. You stood before the tribal council and wore many eagle feathers," Eddie went on, "and Buffalo Calf Road Woman wore many eagle feathers, too, and she was allowed to sit with the council."

"What happened next?" Fila said, totally intrigued.

"That ended my vision," Eddie said, "but I must go now to Lakota Heaven."

He walked off his porch and headed toward his horse. Fila was horrified, almost crying.

She yelled, "Are you sick? Don't go!"

He raised his hand without looking at her and grabbed his saddle blanket.

Charlie started laughing and was holding his sides.

Fila turned, as angry as a bumblebee that had been stepped on.

"What is so damned funny, Charlie Strongheart?" she asked, fuming.

He said, "Honey, Lakota Heaven is reservation slang. It means Wal-Mart."

She looked at Charlie, then at Eddie, and suddenly started laughing at herself. She and Charlie just sat on the porch and laughed and laughed. They laughed for so long that by the time they finished, Eddie had gotten his horse saddled, mounted up, and ridden down the dirt road without even looking back.

Fila watched the last of him disappear from sight and, now serious, said, "He didn't even say good-bye. I didn't tell him good-bye."

Charlie said, "It is not his way. He probably did all that to look stoic but was emotional about me being in Delta. The vision was real, and it probably scared him for me."

"What did it all mean?" she asked.

He said, "Come on. I'll tell you on the way back."

On the way, he told her about Buffalo Calf Road Woman. "Buffalo Calf Road Woman was the wife of Black Coyote. Before the Battle of the Little Big Horn, General Crook and his men got into it with Crazy Horse. You have heard of him?"

Fila said, "Oh yes. I knew about Sitting Bull and Crazy Horse when I lived in Iraq."

Charlie said, "I will tell you in the words of my grandfather, since you like when I speak more traditionally."

"I love it, Charlie," she interjected.

He went on. "Sitting Bull saw the vision he had seen in his Sun Dance ceremony: the sight of many enemy Indians and earless white soldiers falling into the Lakota camp, bloody and dead. Just a week earlier, Crazy Horse had led some Oglalas against Gray Fox (General Crook) in a big fight on the Rosebud River, and he had soundly defeated the general and his troops. Sitting Bull thought about it and knew that this was not, however, the giant victory he had envisioned. When he did his Sun Dance ceremony, he cut fifty pieces of flesh from his arms, and that was what my uncle was seeing.

"Even so, when Crazy Horse defeated Crook on the Rosebud, a magnificent event took place, which the Cheyenne would recall for years to come. A tall Cheyenne chief, Comes-in-Sight, noted for his courage and fighting ability, charged into the fray to count coup on a group of Crow scouts and Crook. His horse was shot out from under him, and neither Crazy Horse's Oglalas nor their Cheyenne brothers could rush out to save him, such was the volume of gunfire being rained upon him. Then, the Crow scouts decided to charge the lone Cheyenne, ride him down, and count coup on him. He faced them and taunted them as they charged, while the helpless Sioux and Cheyenne watched from a hillside.

"I told you she was married to Black Coyote, but she was also closely related to Comes-in-Sight. She was his sister, and Buffalo Calf Road Woman was not prepared to let her brother die that easily. She jumped on a pony and charged out toward the advancing warriors. She rode right through their midst, swooping down on her brother under a hail of deadly gunfire and arrows. He swung up behind her on the war pony, and they darted out of there under the Crow fire and to the cheers of the Lakota and Cheyenne warriors, including Crazy Horse, who witnessed this event and could not believe the courage of the woman. The fight on the Rosebud against the Gray Fox was called, from that day forward, *Kse e Sewo Istaniwe Ititane,* meaning 'Where the Young Girl Saved Her Brother's Life.' "

"I assume you figure I am Buffalo Calf Road Woman in his vision?" she said.

"Naw," Charlie replied. "Our nation's beautiful national security advisor, Kerri Rhodes."

She playfully slapped him, saying, "You son of a bitch!"

She got embarrassed then and was mad at herself for letting him know she was jealous.

He laughed and said, "I only said that because I saw how she was treating me, and I saw a few of the looks you gave her."

Fila said, "You saw that?"

Charlie nodded.

She said, "Amazing! I have always felt men were totally oblivious to beautiful women putting the make on them."

"Putting the make on them?" He laughed. "Is that a Persian expression?"

She chuckled and said, "No, it was something my dad said several times in Fort Campbell. He teased my mom just like you do."

"Is that bad?" Charlie asked.

She said, "Oh no! I love my dad very much! He is

wonderful and so is Mom. You'll love them both. They will love you, too."

"Your dad won't," Charlie said. "I'm not a West Pointer."

She laughed. "Are you kidding? My dad isn't a West Pointer either, and he is SF through and through. He will love that you are SF, officer or NCO. That does not matter to him at all."

"Great!" Charlie replied.

They visited with Charlie's mom for a couple of hours and headed back toward Rapid City, a long drive. Fila truly did love the antelope meat and was amazed at how tender and delicious it was.

They got back to their hotel too late for a hot tub, so they went to their room. Although they had not been intimate, Fila suggested they share rooms and spend all their time together to pick up each other's nuances as a couple.

Charlie said, "What time will your mom and dad arrive?"

She said, "They were on a red-eye and checking in late. They are meeting us for breakfast tomorrow, if that is okay?"

"Of course," the tall warrior replied.

"The whole time we visited with your mom," Fila said, "not one time did she ever mention your hair being cut short. I really liked her."

"She liked you as soon as she met you," he said. "I can tell. She senses both good and bad things about people. She will never mention my hair, because she knows I am in Delta and would not cut it off unless there was a good reason."

"I can't wait to see Mom and Dad. It has been a long time," she said, "but right now, I want to think about you. Come here."

She wrapped her arms around him and kissed him.

CHAPTER FOURTEEN

Serpents

"SPANK me!" he commanded handing her his rolled up belt.

Her black hair was glistening already with perspiration from all the rough pre-sex rituals, and her dark complexion was shining in the dimly lit hotel room, but she wanted to oblige. She swung her arm down and lashed him across the buttocks, causing a big red welt.

He cried out in pain, then said, "Harder and tell me I'm a bad boy."

She shrugged her shoulders and swung even harder, and this time it went across the back of his legs. He screamed in pain and gritted his teeth. Tears welled up in his eyes.

He said, "Harder, bitch! And I told you to tell me I'm a bad boy!"

The session lasted for the full hour. Major General Rozanski got up and paid her the $500 fee and showed her to the motel room door.

I hate honky crackers, the prostitute thought to herself. *They are all wierdos. I should have stayed in Fayetteville tonight. I would have made more money and not had to work so damned hard.*

She said, "Hey, how do I get back to Fayetteville? Do you now what a cab costs from Southern Pines?"

He said, "You just got five hundred dollars from me. Work it out somewhere else."

He pushed her out the door amid some creative curses he had never heard before.

Rozanski went to the bathroom and put salve on his battered and bruised thighs and buttocks. He could not wait until his clandestine breakfast the next day.

He awakened, showered, and arrived at the twenty-four-hour breakfast restaurant as scheduled, for the agreed upon 8 A.M. appointment. He ordered coffee and saw a very slender man with red hair and muttonchop whiskers come in the doorway, and Rozanski signaled him over to his table. He was a reporter for a very liberal New York City newspaper. The two men introduced themselves, ordered their food, and started talking.

The reporter, Alan Homer, said, "General, may I use your name in the article?"

"Are you kidding me?" the general whispered. "I am giving you the biggest dirt you have ever gotten about the President of the United States, and you want to use my name? You have to be shitting me, young man."

Alan said, "Sorry. I have to ask. That is my job. We will keep you as a very anonymous source, General. Don't worry. Trust me."

General Rozanski leaned forward across the table and said, "How would you like to know about the President of the United States sending trained professional hit men into Iran to kill a businessman simply because they think he is tied to terrorists?"

"Holy cow!" the reporter said. "Are you positive?"

"Young man, I hold a high government position in intelligence," Rozanski said, fuming. "I am a retired general. I was there in the planning for the operation."

"Where?"

The nasty general replied, "In the Delta Force compound at Fort Bragg. I have been involved in the planning."

"Who are the trained professional hit men you were talking about?"

"There are two, a man and a woman. He is a master sergeant named Charlie Strongheart, a Cherokee or a Sioux or something. The woman is Sergeant First Class Fila Jannat, and she is a member of Delta Force, too. She is originally from Iran."

"You mean the President of the United States is using Delta Force to do political assassinations for him?" Alan asked, already picturing the Pulitzer Prize above his mantel.

"Damned right he is."

Alan said, "Just a woman being in Delta Force—that alone is a major story."

"Ha, there is a whole platoon of them," Rozanski said. "They call it the Funny Platoon."

"How can she be from Iran and become a member of Delta Force?" the reporter wondered.

"Because of who we have in the White House," Rozanski said. "How do we know where that Muslim woman's loyalties lie?"

CHARLIE and Fila walked into the sunny restaurant and a handsome couple stood up, smiling.

Fila whispered, "I'm nervous. I hope Dad likes you."

They got up to her parents and her mom and dad both hugged her warmly.

Then Fila was totally shocked as her father stepped forward and embraced Charlie in a big bear hug, laughing and saying, "Cochise! How in the hell are you?"

Fila said, "Dad, you know Charlie?"

"Know him? I'll tell you a great story about him," the man said.

"Well, I am shocked," Fila said. "Well, you know my dad. This is Mom."

Charlie stepped forward and kissed Fila's mom on the cheek and said, "Hi, Angela. You look even younger."

Angela looked at the colonel, saying, "He hasn't changed, Dave."

Fila slapped Charlie on the arm, saying, "Why didn't you tell me you knew my mom and dad?"

Charlie laughed, holding her chair, while Dave held Angela's, and saying, "You never asked me, honey."

"Honey?" Dave said, "So you two are more than teammates?"

Fila said, "How was your flight?"

Angela said, "It was okay. Dave, tell Fila how we know Charlie."

The silver-haired retired officer leaned forward, saying, "Punkin, Charlie and I were classmates in Ranger School. He broke his foot just about the first day that we were in Florida. Every morning he would go into the latrine and tape it up tightly with strips of adhesive tape and never told anybody but me."

She looked over at Charlie and shook her head.

Her dad said, "I know what you are going to say. Why didn't he go on sick call? I asked him, too."

She looked at Charlie and said, "Why?"

Charlie said, "They would have recycled me. I had a mission to accomplish, so I convinced your dad to promise to not tell anyone."

She said, "Did you both belong to the same group?"

Charlie said, "No, in fact in Ranger School we did not wear rank, unit patches, any identifying patches or symbols. He and I were partnered up a lot and the guys we were around called me Cochise."

"What did they call you, Dad?"

"Top," the colonel said. "They all thought I was a first sergeant or sergeant major. I was a major then. Charlie was a staff sergeant."

"Your dad never told them any different."

Dave said, "I was very honored to be thought of as an E8 or E9. Hey, you were an E6 then. What rank are you now?"

"Master sergeant," Charlie said. "I just lucked out and made the list for E9."

"That is great," Dave said. "When you were a staff sergeant, I told Angela you would be command sergeant major of Special Forces someday."

Charlie cleared his throat and said, "Coming from you, Colonel, that is a great compliment."

Dave said, "Charlie, I am a civilian and you are seeing my daughter. Please call me Dave."

Charlie smiled, saying, "I'll try."

Fila said, "So tell me the rest of the story."

Charlie said, "Oh, there is nothing to tell."

Dave said, "My butt! He had the broken foot, and we were running some small unit tactics and humping for miles wearing a loaded rucksack, weapons, and blank ammo. I did not know how he could handle it. We set up an L-shaped ambush in a swamp overlooking a trail along the higher ground. We all fell asleep on the ambush, they kept us so exhausted. I would shoot my men in combat for that just about, but we all zonked out."

"You've never known Dad to zonk out, have you, Punkin?" Angela said, a big smile on her face.

"Oh, Charlie," Fila said. "Football season. All he talks about is the Tennessee Titans. We would get home from church, eat lunch, and he is ready to watch football. The Titans! Mom or I would walk in the living room, and he would be asleep in his La-Z-Boy."

"Continuing on," Dave said, embarrassed. "While we were on the ambush, I had a critter crawl in my boot. It was either some kind of spider or a scorpion. Anyway, the next thing I knew I had a horrible reaction to the bite or sting, whatever it was. My foot and ankle swelled up to about triple its normal size and turned colors, too. It swelled up so bad, I had to take my boot off. I had never had anything like that happen.

"We were on our final FTX at Camp Ruddy," he went on, referring to a field training exercise, "you know, at Eglin Air Force Base in Florida, so we were near the end of a nine-week long Ranger School. I didn't want to get recycled either, and Cochise didn't want me to, so he picked me up in a fireman's carry across his shoulders and carried me for a couple miles, while he carried his ruck and carried mine on his chest. This young man was mighty strong back then, and looks even stronger now."

Fila excitedly said, "Oh, he is! His pec muscles are so large, and—"

She stopped and got very embarrassed as Angela and Dave started laughing.

"Anyway," Dave said, "that is the little story of Charlie's character, which really tells you volumes about the man."

Fila smiled and stared at him as he looked down, very embarrassed himself. Angela really noticed how Fila stared at Charlie, and she tapped Dave under the table with her knee and, using her eyes, indicated the glances. He grinned at his wife.

MAJOR General Damien Percy Rozanski grinned in an evil-looking twisted smile at Alan as the reporter lined up for his putt. He missed the cup by a full foot. Any other golfer would have told him to putt out. Using his pitching wedge, Rozanski had just chipped onto the green from the rough right next to a white sand trap. His ball was only five

feet from the cup, but he waited to walk over to his llama
to put away his wedge and grab his putter. They were playing Talamore Golf Club in Pinehurst, North Carolina, not
far from Fort Bragg, but far enough away that he did not
worry about any of Pop's friends spotting him with the reporter. This was a challenging course in the town where
the Professional Golf Hall of Fame was located, and they
actually used trained llamas as caddies to carry the bags of
golfers around.

Now, putter in hand, Rozanski had added more drama
to the scene, and Alan would be even more impressed
when the accomplished golfer sank his putt. He lined it up
and saw that the green broke slightly to the left. He aimed
for the right edge of the cup and tapped. The ball rolled
right at the cup, hit the edge, swirled around it like a bug
in a flushing toilet, and spun out two feet off to the left.
The story of Damien's life. When his putter spun through
the air like the spinning rotors of a Blackhawk, it whacked
against the edge of a bench by the next tee and with a loud
crack, the handle broke in half. The story of Damien's
life.

Alan thought to himself, *We are only on the second
hole. I wonder how many clubs he'll have left after nine
holes.*

Rozanski hated to get embarrassed, but it happened in
his life frequently. It never dawned on him that it was because he was a jerk, and what goes around, comes around.

Later, in the clubhouse over ice-cold beer, he started
filling Alan's ears and tape recorder even more. He let the
young man know everything that he could remember from
the planning meeting. The President would be plenty embarrassed, and politically hurt, when the exposé hit the
front page of a major NYC newspaper, Rozanski decided.
The great thing was that he would not be tied to the leak.
This young man had already gone through a trial in New

York City, because he refused to reveal his source on a major drug exposé of some bureaucrats in a New York state office. Several went to prison for trafficking in cocaine, and all because of the front-page exposé by Alan. And even facing a jail cell himself, he refused to divulge his source, which was the secretary for the principle perpetrator. Damien Percy Rozanski felt he would finally have great revenge, plus strike a major blow for his political party.

DAVE, Angela, Fila, and Betty, with Charlie driving the big black SUV, left Pine Ridge, South Dakota, two days later at six o'clock in the morning. The Detachment-Delta operator headed northwest and passed through Gillette and Sheridan, Wyoming, on the trek to Crow Agency, Montana, and the Little Big Horn Battlefield National Monument. They arrived shortly after noon.

Charlie said, "Back in the 1800s, the drive we made in six to seven hours would take a wagon train well over a month to make. We just traveled 392 miles. Many wagon trains would take forty days to make that trip."

They ate lunch and then entered the Little Big Horn National Monument.

As they drove up the little road from the base of the Grassy Ridge, Charlie pointed out the tree line along the Little Big Horn River and said, "See all that meadow on the flats on this side of the river? That is where the giant encampment was."

A half hour later, the group stood just below a series of small gravestones where Custer and some of his command's bodies were found. The others watched in fascination as Charlie pointed in the direction where Reno's command had been attacked and Benteen's command had been attacked. He pointed out Medicine Tail Coulee, where, he said, a distant cousin from long ago had actually

fatally wounded George Armstrong Custer as he charged
across the Little Big Horn. He had died by suicide at one of
the markers, with his brother Tom's company. The group
listened to this modern-day war hero tell what had been
passed on to him from father to son to son as the real version
of the famous battle. Charlie knew with his forefathers,
warriors had been encouraged to boast about battlefield
and hunting exploits, but to lie was unforgivable and was
actually one of the few grounds that the Lakota had to ban-
ish someone from their tribe. Even adultery was not treated
as harshly as lying. So Charlie always wondered why the
U.S. government did not utilize that and get the real facts
from the true survivors who were there.

The foursome were totally fascinated as they went over
the battlefield and Charlie recounted every detail. Fila was
especially fascinated, because she knew that this man was
essentially descended from royalty, and that this famous
historical battle defined Charlie. They looked at the long,
rippling green grass on the surrounding ridges and the
sparse patches of trees, and pictured the battlefield as he
described it in total detail.

Pointing, Charlie said, "Custer went down there from
this big ridge we are on and entered Medicine Tail Coulee.
He would attack the giant village by crossing the Little Big
Horn at a ford where the ravine ran into the pebble-bottomed
river. At that spot, to the left of those trees, the waterway
was about forty yards wide, but only knee-deep on the
horses. It still is. I crossed it before on a horse. Custer had
witnessed several warriors crossing the river there, so he
figured it would be a strategically sound place to attack,
while Reno was hitting the other end of the village.

"Just then, the point spotted five Sioux who had been
hiding in Medicine Tail Coulee. I think right about in that
area. The warriors rode in several circles, yelling and waving blankets in the air, then fled at a dead run down the
coulee toward the river.

"Mitch Bouyer, Custer's chief of scouts, turned to Curley, the youngest Crow scout, and handed him his field glasses.

"Mitch said, 'Curley, you are the youngest. You should live. Go to those bluffs yonder and watch. Those five Sioux are tricking Custer into chasing them. There will be thousands of Sioux waiting to kill us. You watch awhile, and if the Sioux are besting us, you ride as fast as you can and tell No-Hip-Bone'—that was what the Indians called General Terry—'that we have all been killed. Now go!'

"Mitch Bouyer and some of the Crow scouts rode up to Custer's side, and the lieutenant colonel turned to them and said, 'You have all done your job well. You are not to fight in this battle. Go back and save your lives.'

"Mitch Bouyer related this to the Crows, and they started to ride back toward the pack train, but stopped when Mitch remained where he was. Hairy Moccasin and Goes Ahead told Mitch he must go with them and join his Crow wife, Magpie Outside, back at the fort. They were cut off by a voice from across the river, in the trees.

"'The Lakota call someone?' Goes Ahead asked, in sign language.

"Bouyer tapped himself and listened as the voice said, 'Wica-nonpa! Two Bodies! Go back, or you die!'

"Bouyer said, 'The Sioux have not forgotten me. They tell me to go back, but I cannot.'

"He waved at the scouts, wheeled his horse, and took off down the coulee to rejoin Custer at his side.

"Over seven hundred warriors had charged off to fight against Reno, and they were not yet back. Only four men capable of fighting remained in the camp of the Cheyenne: Bobtail Horse, Roan Bear, White Cow Bull (the only Oglala), and Calf. Bobtail Horse looked across the river and saw the blue-clad soldiers charging at full gallop down Medicine Tail Coulee across the river, headed for the all-but-deserted Cheyenne camp, which was right there.

"For the umpteenth time that day, Bobtail Horse shouted the alarm, '*Nutskaveho!*' which meant, 'White soldiers are coming!'

"White Shield, another Cheyenne, had been fishing upstream, and he saw his four fellow villagers and the soldiers at the same time. Dropping his fish, he rode out of the river and disappeared into the trees with his bow and quiver full of arrows. The other four rode in and out among the trees, firing and yelling, trying to make the noise of a thousand warriors.

"So four Cheyenne warriors and one Oglala Sioux held off the two hundred and fifteen troopers of Custer's command at the ford. Custer just halted on the side of the river and waited, possibly expecting an ambush by the thousands of braves who were hidden in the trees.

"Finally, Custer turned and gave the command for the column to go ahead. He led out, with his horse Vic prancing and dancing in the knee-deep river at the ford. The Crows, who had left when Custer told them to, stopped on a bluff to watch. They saw hundreds of mounted Lakota and Cheyenne charging toward Custer through those cottonwoods along the river. A soldier near Custer toppled backward out of the saddle, but Mitch Bouyer and Custer both kept firing at the four village defenders, Custer with an octagonal-barreled Remington sporting rifle and twin English self-cocking Bulldog pistols.

"Just then White Cow Bull's rifle belched smoke, as did two other guns from the four defenders. The lead man crossing the Little Big Horn River, the one with the fringed buckskin jacket and the red sash around his waist, the one on the spirited, prancing, big red horse, that man flew backward out of the saddle, a big bloody spot on the middle of his chest.

"Suddenly, the charge stopped, and Mitch Bouyer and several soldiers jumped down into the water and grabbed Custer to keep him from going under. He wasn't dead, but close to it. The soldiers got him up on a horse and turned around and retreated while White Cow Bull, Bobtail Horse, Roan Bear, Calf, and White Shield jumped up and down in celebration.

"Hundreds of Sioux and Cheyenne alike took off after Custer's column. Up to this point, because Libbie had made her 'Autie' cut his hair short, the Indians still did not know that the man they were fighting was Long Hair Custer himself.

"The warriors kept arriving in droves from the Reno fight and charging after the fleeing cavalry. The troopers led their horses as they dismounted and, on foot, tried to make their way up here on that grassy knoll above Medicine Tail Coulee. They wanted to form a defensive perimeter and make a stand there. But it was like being attacked by a swarm of angry bees: The more they ran and the more they tried to fight back, the more Sioux and Cheyenne came on the scene to attack them.

"One of the bravest warriors in the fight was actually a Ute Indian named Yellow Nose. He had been captured by the northern Cheyenne down in Colorado when he was four years old and had grown up Cheyenne. He was the first brave to ride in and capture one of the cavalry company guidons. He even touched one of the cavalry soldiers with it as he rode away, counting coup on the man while a great cry went up among the assembled warriors.

"Custer was not a factor at all, and sometime during the battle, near death, he turned one of his English Bulldog pistols to his right temple and pulled the trigger. Tom Custer's company took charge of Long Hair's body, slinging it across the colonel's own saddle.

"Captain Myles Keogh took over the rest of the Custer command and led the men up the north edge of the ridgeline right over there, fighting inch by inch for more ground and hoping to form a defensive perimeter on the higher ground.

"By this time, Curley was already gone on his horse, heading after No-Hip-Bone to tell him of Custer's death.

"Crow King led Hunkpapas and Blackfeet up Medicine Tail Coulee to surround the troops heading that way from the east and probably rode right across where we are standing."

Charlie stopped and looked at everybody.

He said, "I apologize. Is this boring you all?"

Dave said, "My word, Charlie. I cannot speak for the rest, but I could listen to this all day. This is like getting a fascinating fresh view of history without political motivations in the telling of it."

Angela said, "Absolutely. This is kind of like watching *Roots* in person."

He looked at his mother and Fila, and both had tears in their eyes and smiled warmly at him.

Charlie continued, "Gall, leading more Hunkpapas, as well as Minniconjous and Sans Arcs, rode up out of the coulee and kept attacking the rear of the soldiers. Comes-in-Sight and Brave Wolf led a large group of northern Cheyenne along the left flank of the retreating soldiers over there on that part of the ridge.

"The bullets and arrows flew at an astounding rate, and numerous warriors started to charge in and out of the troopers' ranks, winning battle honors. The battle was so one-sided that many Indians were able to return to the village to get fresh horses and more arrows and bullets.

"Near the end of this part of the command, an entire group of troopers' horses got away from the dying soldiers and bolted up the hill at one time right across that strip. Some of the Indians thought that the troopers were trying to run away, so they charged and brought down even more soldiers.

"Suddenly, a whole group of foot soldiers, in sheer hysteria, charged down the hill toward the river, at the Lakota assembled there. The troopers screamed and fired blindly, but all were cut down by withering Sioux fire.

"At last, several leading warriors yelled, '*Hokahey! Hokahey!*'

"This was the signal for the assembled warriors to charge, and charge they did, eagle-bone whistles screaming over the gunfire. The horde of Sioux swept over the few remaining troopers, and they all went down in a hail of gunfire.

"Custer, along with most of his command, was dead. Barely believing their good fortune, braves went from soldier to soldier to collect scalps and battle honors. The severely wounded were quickly dispatched with head shots, then scalped. The L, I, F, and C companies were not in the group that went down. Keogh had kept most of the command in some sort of formation as they advanced up that hogback, but now one thousand more Brules and Oglalas were coming up from the river, right down there and there, where they had served as a blocking force. Crazy Horse led the thousand from the river, up a ravine, to emerge at the end of the hogback where the soldiers stood.

"Two Moons led another large force of Cheyennes up over the other hillside and struck the fleeing troopers there, so that now the balance of Custer's command was surrounded on all sides, unable to get away or to fight through in any direction. Most of the Indians now dismounted and started to pick off soldiers with carefully aimed shots. Some of them sneaked in closer and closer to the soldiers, using every bush and gully they could for cover. Some still charged in, counting coup and getting battle honors, but most hung back and picked the rest of Custer's command apart bit by bit.

"One of the things that happened in the midst of the battle was similar to what had happened in the Rosebud fight. A very pretty young Oglala woman named Walking Blanket Woman had lost her brother in the Rosebud fight and decided to avenge his death. Fila and I talked about it the other day. She dressed herself in full battle regalia and war paint, just like a brave, and charged into the midst of the battle carrying her brother's battle staff. The whole time Walking Blanket Woman fought, she sang in the Oglala language, 'Brothers, now your friend has come! Brave up! Brave up! Would you see me taken captive?'

"Rain-in-the-Face saw and heard her song and yelled to everyone within earshot, 'Behold! A brave young woman rides among us! Let no warrior hide behind her!'

"Some of the braves who won battle honors that day were talked about for a long time to come. Not the least was Sitting Bull's eldest nephew, White Bull, who was my great-great-great-uncle. He rode up to many cavalry troopers and struck them with a club, then yanked them from their horses. He was considered by all the Sioux and Cheyenne to be the bravest warrior in the entire battle, even besting Crazy Horse.

"On one of White Bull's courageous charges at the remaining troopers, a bullet toppled his pony. The brave ran forward and got into a hand-to-hand fight with the trooper he had been charging. The trooper grabbed White Bull's rifle, but the brave struck him across the face with his quirt and made him let go. Finally, the soldier grabbed White Bull by the hair, yanked him forward, and bit the warrior's nose, trying to bite it off. White Bull screamed for help and two warriors came, but finally White Bull broke free and butt-stroked the soldier in the face with his rifle.

"White Bull and a Cheyenne were side by side in a ravine by the hill, shooting at the ten soldiers there, and the troopers finally got up and charged White Bull's position. White Bull shot one of the two leaders of the charge, who was already severely wounded, and the Cheyenne shot the other. The other eight kept charging, which forced White Bull and the Cheyenne up over the edge of that ravine. But up above, White Bull stumbled and fell down. He had been hit by a ricocheting bullet, which numbed his leg and made it swell, but never broke the skin.

"The attack went on, with soldiers trying to mount up and break away. So terrorized were the troopers that, near the end of the battle, some of the soldiers started to shoot at each other. Finally, there were only four left in that group, and they all mounted up and made a mad dash for freedom. Three were overtaken easily and killed, but the fourth, Lieutenant Harrington of C Company, had a fast-moving horse. He outran the pursuing Cheyenne and made his way to and along the river right down there, running that way.

"They chased him for a distance and finally caught up with him. Instead of killing him, however, they rode up alongside and lashed his horse's rump with their quirts and bows. Several times they fired at him but missed. Finally, Harrington pulled out his gun. Instead of shooting at them, he stuck the barrel beneath his chin and pulled the trigger.

"The last survivors of Custer's command were from C and F Companies, and they tried to make their stand on the hillside there where you see the headstones. There they were to be cut down by long-range fire, their bodies falling onto those of their own dead buddies as they died off one by one.

"The very last one to go down was Sergeant Butler of L Company. He had been severely wounded earlier in the fight, but now stood up to face the thousands of warriors and fire in every direction, apparently wanting to die fighting. A number of warriors, genuinely respectful of this brave pony soldier, rushed forward, eager to count coup on an enemy so worthy. He repelled every attack with well-placed shots, and many warriors gathered around to watch, marveling at his courage. Several warriors mounted up, and had just started to make a charge when the sergeant was struck down by a long-range shot into his chest.

"In the great battle's aftermath, old men and young boys who'd only watched the fight rode down and killed off the soldiers who were critically wounded but still alive. Women came out from the encampment to strip and mutilate bodies, while warriors and young boys took scalps.

"As the final troopers died, Captain Myles Keogh seemed to rise from the dead. Braves were going from soldier to soldier shooting the troopers in the foreheads with their own pistols. As they approached the body of Captain Keogh, he suddenly sat up and leaned on one elbow. He was dazed and disoriented.

"Now, pistol in hand, the captain looked around wildly from Indian to Indian. A Lakota warrior finally ran forward, yanked the pistol from the commander's hand, and shot Keogh in the forehead with it. A number of Cheyennes then ran forward and stabbed and clubbed the captain's body over and over again. According to all the Indians who were there, he was the very last man of Custer's command seen alive. His horse, Comanche, was the only part of Custer's command that lived, aside from Curly and some of the other Crow scouts who left earlier.

"Rain-in-the-Face had sworn an oath against Custer's brother. He found the body of Captain Tom Custer over there and, true to his vow to someday cut out the Medal of Honor recipient's heart and eat it, he knelt down and cut the man's heart out of his chest. While others watched, Rain-in-the-Face mounted up and rode down to the camp, presumably to eat the heart.

"Many of the warriors now remembered Reno's command, which was still fortifying its position on a bluff farther down the river, around that bend. We'll drive over there in a minute. They left for that location. Others, battle-weary, returned to the camp, while still others remained on the battlefield, collecting 'trophies.' Custer's body was not touched or mutilated, for he had committed suicide and thereby dishonored himself.

"The only comment my several times great-grandfather

Sitting Bull later would make about the devastating defeat his forces exacted on the 7th Cavalry was, 'They compelled us to fight them.'

"Now he went out to meet with his people and count the friendly casualties. Altogether, with the Custer and Reno fights, only thirty-two warriors had been killed. The families of the thirty-two slain warriors met together to mourn, and Sitting Bull joined them.

"He spoke solemnly. 'My heart is sad for our fallen warriors—and for those white soldiers who fell before us. This night, we shall mourn alike for our own dead and for those brave white men lying up there.'

"I am very proud to be a Sioux and proud of my ancestor's words and attitude towards the white soldiers he fought against. I am extremely proud to be an American fighting man."

Fila, totally moved, walked over and kissed Charlie passionately, not caring that her smiling parents and his mom were watching. She stepped back and stared up into his dark eyes.

Dave said, "Wow! What a day!"

They drove on along the ridgeline and Charlie explained about the commands of Benteen and Reno, who were also attacked that day, and some of the interesting things that happened during their fights.

They got out and looked at the groves of trees they hid in, and Charlie explained how they were literally terrorized by the sounds of the Custer battle and then many of the Indians who participated in it.

Charlie said, "Oh, by the way, our people did not even know they killed Custer, who was very hated by the Lakota and Cheyenne, until the battle was over. Where I pointed things out back there, that is called Battle Ridge.

"My great-uncle I told you about, White Bull, unable to walk because of his wounded ankle, and a friend, Bad Soup, rode back to Battle Ridge, so that White Bull could

find the leggings and saddle he had stripped from himself
and his horse in mid-battle, for speed and freedom of
movement. He found them, and had Bad Soup help him
re-saddle while he put on his leggings. As he looked at the
naked, mutilated corpses, he found one with powder burns
at the temple. He remembered that wounded man with a
hole in the left side of his chest, who had shot at him twice
during the battle. The man had a leather jacket with brass
buttons and long fringe, so White Bull took it for himself.
After all, the man might not have committed suicide. Per-
haps he had been shot in the temple by a warrior dispatch-
ing all the soldiers at the end of the battle.

"White Bull reached into the pocket of the jacket and
pulled out several locks of long blond hair. He showed
them to Bad Soup. They stared at the corpse, realizing now
that this was Long Hair Custer.

"Not long after, Monahseetah, a Cheyenne woman, accompanied by her aunt Mahwissa and her little son Yellow
Bird, went to Battle Ridge. They went up to one mutilated
corpse and saw a brave hacking off the man's finger. The
man had not been scalped, because his hair was cut so
short.

"Monahseetah screamed, '*Ohohyaa!*'

"It meant 'Creeping Panther,' and was the nickname
given this man years ago, by her brother Black Kettle. He
had been given the name in a council meeting between the
Cheyenne and the *wasicun*, the white man, soldiers. She
remembered, too, when this same soldier chief had killed
her brother Black Kettle and many of the Southern Cheyenne on the Washita River so many years before. She also
remembered when this soldier chief had taken her in his
bed, raped her, and planted his seed in her. That seed had
become little Yellow Bird, her son, who stood next to her
right now.

"Monahseetah bent over the corpse with an awl in her
hand and poked the awl into each of his ears.

"She said, 'So that Long Hair, the Creeping Panther, will hear better in the Spirit Land. He must not have heard our chiefs when they warned him that if he broke his peace promise with them then everywhere Spirit would surely cause him to be killed.'"

Fila just stared at Charlie and thought about his family history and what a part his family and Charlie himself had played out in the history of her adopted country, which she loved and wanted desperately to raise children in.

Charlie drove back toward Battle Ridge. The entrance and the headquarters building, store, could be seen along the same ridge and down a little lower. He got out and held the door for Fila.

He said to Dave, "Colonel, uh, I mean, Dave, would you mind driving you three to the building down there, get some souvenirs, and ask any questions you have of the Rangers? I need to show Fila something. We will walk down."

"Sure," Dave said and walked around to the driver's seat.

Charlie took Fila by the hand and led her toward the top of the ridgeline. They looked out over the massive battle-field area. They sat in the tall grass, and she pulled a little flower out and smelled it.

"This place means much to you, doesn't it?" she asked.

Charlie smiled warmly and looked out across the sweeping grassy valley and down at the long green serpent that wound its way along the base of the ridgeline. It was a serpent of trees, mainly cottonwoods, which had swallowed the Little Big Horn River. Cars drove by and people got out and looked around at the various sites.

Charlie said, "This tells me where I am from and what I am about. I feel a connection with White Bull and Sitting Bull. My great-great-great-grandfather and great-great-great-uncle were both incredible men and tremendous warriors. They respected strength in their enemy, and it was one reason they survived and did so well.

"I brought you here today for a couple of very important reasons. I'll get to the main two in a few minutes, but I want to share a little more about that day. I showed you all where Reno and his men had attacked the camp in the south and got pinned down in the trees. He lost over half his men just getting to the trees.

"My point is that Custer had told him to attack the south end of the village, but after Major Reno left to follow orders, Custer changed his plan without telling Reno, and he rode paralleling this ridge. He was worried that my people would get scared and ride away. The main thing, though, is he left Reno out in the cold, and because he was arrogant he left Captain Benteen and a large store of ammunition behind. Back near where we were parked but down in the trees, Isaiah Dorman was hiding. He had lived with the Lakota for a year or so, and spoke their tongue, so he had gotten a job with the 7th Cavalry as an interpreter. Isaiah was black, and the Sioux called him 'the black white man.' In the timber, Dorman had been shot through the chest and was dying from the gaping wound.

"An old Hunkpapa woman came out to the battlefield to start collecting battle trophies, and discovered him lying in the woods.

"She pointed an old muzzle-loading rifle at his head, and was about to pull the trigger when he spoke in her tongue, saying, 'Don't shoot me, Auntie! I'll be dead soon enough anyway!'

"She said, 'You're a sneaking cur! Why did you bring the soldiers here?' "

Fila interrupted. "What does 'cur' mean?"

"I forgot. You speak so well, I forget you are from the Mideast sometimes," Charlie said, while smiling. "It means 'dog.'

"Dorman said to her, 'I only wanted to see this Western country once more before I died.'

"Several Hunkpapa warriors rode up to strip his body

and count coup. Dorman asked them not to, to let him die in peace.

"Sitting Bull himself then rode up and recognized Dorman from his times with the Sioux.

"Sitting Bull said, 'Don't kill that man! He is *On Azinpi*. He used to be a friend of our people.'

"'Sitting Bull,'" Dorman said weakly. 'It is good to see you, old friend. Can I have water?'

"Sitting Bull dismounted from his pony, and pulled from his parfleche his own polished buffalo horn drinking cup, and got Dorman water from the stream. Isaiah Dorman drank from Sitting Bull's drinking horn while the chief of all the Lakota held him up."

Again, Fila interrupted. "I am sorry, but what is a 'parfleche'?"

"Oh, sorry," Charlie replied. "It is a leather pouch. Kind of like a daypack."

"Oh."

He went on. "Dorman looked around at the beautiful country and up into Sitting Bull's eyes, saying, 'Sitting Bull, this is a good day to die.'

"That is a saying my people had when they were going into battle or facing danger.

"Sitting Bull said, 'This is a good day to die.'

"Isaiah Dorman died. Sitting Bull mounted up on his black horse and headed back, telling the camp police to round up villagers and return them to their lodges.

"The chief knew, however, that this had to be a diversionary attack, and the main attack would still be coming. He told everyone to be on the alert for more attacks.

"Sitting Bull ran into my great-uncle One Bull, who was in on the Reno fight, too, and he was covered with blood. Great-Grandpa told him to get his wounds treated. One Bull replied proudly that he was wearing the blood of others and had no wounds at all. Relieved, Sitting Bull ordered him to go back and protect the encampment. One Bull set off for the area around Medicine Tail Coulee, where I showed you guys Custer crossed trying to attack the camp. Or actually tried to cross but was shot off his big chestnut thoroughbred, Vic. He had another like it, named Dandy.

"Custer had come back out onto the ridgeline, and watched Reno's attack until the battalion had to pull back in the timber. Custer got down off his horse and knelt in front of the column and prayed. He then made some hero speeches to his scouts and troopers. Next, he got his scouts and led the column along the ridgeline. He kept looking across the valley at the encampment, but it was mostly obscured by cottonwoods and little ridges.

"Finally, Custer got to a point way down there, where he could make out rows of teepees beyond the tops of the cottonwoods. Beyond those, he saw part of one of the village circles and a couple of hundred lodges. There was no movement, as most of the Indians were either out on the battlefield or in their lodges.

"One Bull, riding along with Sitting Bull, spotted Custer and his column up on the high ridgeline across the river.

"One Bull spoke. 'More soldiers, Sitting Bull. Come, let us go fight them, too.'

"'No, nephew,' Sitting Bull said. 'Stay here and help protect the village. Everyone wants to ride out to fight, but some men must stay and protect our homes and families. There may be more soldiers today who will come and attack our women and children.'

"On the ridgeline, Custer grinned and slapped his thigh, while looking at the seemingly deserted village.

"'We've got them!' the boy general cried. 'We've caught them napping!'

"Turning and waving his hat at the rest of the troops, he yelled, 'Custer's luck, boys! We've got them! We'll finish them off, then go home to our station! Come on!'

"It was three o'clock then, and the troopers all gave a cheer.

"Many of the warriors who had routed Reno's column saw Custer's excited soldiers and moved in that direction to attack.

"Son of the Morning Star, that is what my people called him, looked below, where Reno was just advancing to the attack. Sweeping his hat in encouragement, Custer rejoined his command. He led his troops down there into Medicine Tail Coulee, which runs down to the river as you can see just sitting here.

"Custer summoned his bugler, John Martin, saying, 'Orderly, I want you to take a message to Captain Benteen. Ride as fast as you can and tell him to hurry. Tell him it's a giant village and I want him to be quick, and to bring the ammunition packs with him. Wait, I'll write it down.'

"Custer wrote it down and said, 'Ride as fast as you can by the same trail we came. If it's safe, return and join us, but if not, stay with Benteen.'

"As the bugler John Martin rode away, he turned and waved at the troopers, and many of them waved back. He was the last white man known to have seen George Armstrong Custer alive."

Charlie stood and helped her up, saying, "Let's walk slowly. Fila, you and I are both soldiers. I wanted you to know about this great battle, but I also wanted you to know how things can go wrong. Custer let his ego rule the day here, and others died for it. I really respect Pops, because he is like me. He believes in very thorough planning if you want to accomplish the mission and in a great victory. You and I live in the real world, and you know there is a good chance we both can be killed."

She smiled, saying, "I'm not afraid of death. I'll go to Heaven."

He said, "I will, too. I am a Christian also, but I am not in a big rush to get there, honey."

She laughed.

"Many things go wrong on operations," Charlie said.

"If I do get killed, I wanted one last visit here. But thinking the way we should always think, which is about winning and not getting zapped, we have to adapt and make split-second decisions. But I have one mind-set and that is to accomplish our mission, even if we have to be bailed out by the QRF. I will want to go right back and try again. I want to know for sure you are in total agreement. That is a lot to ask of a partner."

"Absolutely!" she said with definite finality. "I know it sounds corny and is a line from a movie, but I would follow you to hell and back."

He pulled her close and kissed her softly but passionately.

Then he led her to a lone tree near the road and stopped under it.

He said, "You know, the way we live our lives we both are always making split-second decisions. We analyze and look at things from every angle. Well, I have not needed a year or two years, or even five months to know something. That is that I am madly and deeply in love with you, Fila."

Her heart skipped a beat and tears welled up in her eyes.

He reached into his pocket and pulled out something shiny, saying, "This was my great-aunt's, the granddaughter of White Bull. I want to know if you will wear it, always?"

He dropped to one knee saying, "Fila, if we survive this operation, will you marry me, please?"

"Oh, Charlie," she said, helping him slip the simple antique diamond ring on her finger. "Yes! Yes! I love you, too. With all my heart!"

He stood up, grinning broadly, and lifted her into his massive arms. They kissed for all they were worth.

DAMIEN Percy Rozanski shook hands with Alan, saying, "Good-bye."

The reporter said, "Off the record, General. I take it you do not like the President or the head of Delta Force?"

"Or the operators. They are all arrogant and filled with themselves," Rozanski said, fuming. "And this President is ruining our country! I hate him!"

"I feel so deeply honored," Charlie said, as he and Fila almost skipped toward the headquarters building to tell their families the good news, and to let them know they were going on what was almost a suicide mission together overseas.

They wanted their loved ones to think very positively but also have their eyes fully opened. On their way back to Pine Ridge the next morning, they explained what they were allowed to, which was simply that they had a very dangerous assignment together in a foreign country. Obviously, Dave, Angela, and Betty were all very excited about the proposal and engagement, and none were in the least bit surprised.

Charlie got his mom a room at their hotel and left her with Fila's parents to visit and have dinner, as Fila said that she needed to speak with him privately.

She was in the bathroom in the hotel, and he sat at the desk in the room and hollered, "Hey, Fila, do you want to visit the Badlands National Monument?"

She came out of the room and said, "No, thank you."

Charlie looked up and Fila was wearing a short gown that looked like a super-long T-shirt. It was black, and on the front it had a large green beret with a dagger diagonally behind it, and above and below it the words "I only sleep with the very best . . . US Army Special Forces."

Fila walked over to Charlie, and he stood. She unbuttoned and removed his shirt, walked around him seductively, and ran her hands over his chest. Next, she dropped down on her knees in front of him and unbuckled his belt, unzipped his pants, and pulled them off, followed by his socks.

She stood and looked up into his eyes, saying in a husky voice, "Ever since you proposed, I have been feeling giddy, very giddy,"

Charlie remembered his words to her and swept her into his arms. He picked her up, as if she weighed nothing, and carried her to the bed. He knew he must be slow and patient and careful, but he wanted to anyway.

Charlie kissed her slowly and then looked into her eyes from inches away, saying, "Fila, I prayed for a woman I could spend my life with, have many children with, and love forever. It was right after that prayer that I met you. You are my Buffalo Calf Road Woman, but you are also my Cleopatra."

They kissed, and she whispered, "In the thirteenth century a Persian poet and mystic named Jalal ad-Din Muhammad Rumi said, 'The minute I heard my first love story I started looking for you, not knowing how blind that was. Lovers do not finally meet somewhere. They are in each other all along.' Charlie, I want you in me now."

The next day, they said good-bye to Dave and Angela, who Charlie thought would be awesome in-laws. Fila already loved Betty and vice versa.

They took her back home, dropped her off, and went to the convenience store, and then returned to say their good-byes to Betty before flying back to Raleigh and taking the shuttle to Fayetteville. They had decided the night before that they would make up for lost sleep on the plane.

When they pulled up in front of the house, there was a gang of young Lakotas standing by Charlie's mother's propane tank. All were in their late teens and early twenties, and they had a sneer found only on those who congregate in a gang for strength.

Charlie's mother was standing on her front stoop, and Charlie could see by the stressed look on her face that she must have just had words with the punks. He and Fila jumped out of the car and ran up to her as one of the gang-bangers made some smart remark and the group laughed. A Pine Ridge Tribal Police cruiser pulled up just then, as Betty had called on her cell phone when the punks started smarting off to her while they spray-painted her propane tank. The officer inside was also named Charlie, Sergeant Charlie Ten Horses. Charlie Strongheart recognized him and waved him off and the cruiser sped away. This bothered the gang members. Why would the cop leave, they wondered, and why was he laughing when he did?

Charlie and Fila escorted Betty inside, and she told them the gang members openly spray-painted the tank, and she came out to confront them and chase them off. Then one of them, the one in the red ribbon shirt, she said, had flipped her the middle finger and cursed her horribly. Next, the one in the baseball jersey threw an empty beer bottle at her, and it broke on the front of the house.

Charlie opened the front door and looked at the front of the house where the bottle had smashed and saw pieces of glass on the ground.

The one in the ribbon shirt was the gang leader, named Louie Horse.

He yelled, "Git your punk-ass back in the house, Holmes, or we'll shoot it."

At the same time, he spread his thumb and index finger out in almost a V-sign, a gang sign indicating he was armed. As the punks all laughed, Charlie stepped back into the house and closed the door, looking out through the curtains. The gang members were laughing and patting Louie on the back.

Fila walked up and looked out through the sheers, saying, "Formulating a plan?"

Charlie chuckled and said, "Of course."

She said, "Need me?"

He said, "No, honey. You stay with Mom. I just need to borrow your Glock."

She handed it to him and stuck two spare magazines in his left hip pocket, saying, "Try not to kill anybody."

He said, "I won't. Just going to educate them."

Charlie thought back to his childhood. He had always been puzzled by men like these in the gang. They felt the same fear he and every other man felt, but they succumbed to it. He wondered how they would be able to go the rest of their days knowing that they had sneaked away from their duties as a man like a thief in the night. Avoiding hard work, responsibility, and life as young men, he felt they copped out and banded together for mutual support.

Charlie grinned as he remembered a conversation with his uncle Eddie. The man had been an LRRP (long range reconnaissance patrol) member of some great repute in the 1st Cavalry Division in Vietnam. Until an AK-47-toting Viet Cong had missed his chest and put a bullet through the back of Eddie's right hand. His youth and his wild fighting days were over, so he decided to settle down and return to the rez.

The man and young Charlie were having a conversation about courage one day when the uncle said, "Young 'un, the difference between a coward and a hero is about one minute in time."

Charlie was perplexed by that statement, and it bothered him for a long time afterward, but he had finally gotten a handle on it. He got into a fight with two brothers whose family lived in another neighborhood on the reservation. Their family and his attended the same church, but the two brothers were about the furthest thing you could get from walking the Christian walk of life. They were troublemakers from the get-go.

The two bullies simply beat up everybody, and finally Charlie's turn came up. Everyone had backed down from the bullies because they were so tough and brutal. They would chase a person down and beat him senseless. When one of them started to pick on Charlie, he tried everything he could think of to avoid getting into a fight. When one of the two, however, made some disparaging remarks about a girl in Charlie's church whose father had been arrested for public drunkenness, Charlie finally had had it, thinking about his drunk of a father and all the pain and embarrassment he had caused Charlie. He was scared—the bullies' brutality had become legendary locally—but he was beyond caring at that point.

Charlie managed to seem so ferocious in his demeanor alone that the two bullies looked a little unsettled. The boy had heard somewhere that a man using his head had a much better chance in a fight than one who just used his muscle, so he tried to think his way out of trouble. When the first punch was thrown, it landed square on Charlie's temple and sent him reeling to the ground. His right hand closed around a smooth, egg-shaped rock lying on the ground, and he grabbed it without his adversaries noticing.

The two brothers ran up, and both kicked him in the rib cage, knocking the wind out of him and severely bruising his ribs. Most boys would have folded over and cried, but this simply made Charlie furious. He came off the ground with a fury and tore into both brothers. His fists were swinging so wildly and so quickly, nobody noticed the rock sticking out of the ends of his right fist. The faces of the bullies, however, showed signs of the rock. Within a minute, both brothers were lying on the ground unconscious, each sporting two black eyes and a broken nose. Charlie dropped the rock behind his back and nobody ever saw it.

He became the hero of the young girl he had defended, and of the whole community. His repute grew each year as he grew, as did the story of the fight with each telling. In actuality, part of the reason he went off to join the army was his worry that the two bullies might try to get retribution. It bothered him to leave like that, but as he grew and gained confidence, he realized how smart he had really been. One thing he never forgot was the butterflies he'd felt in his stomach when he'd had to face the two bullies, and the great fear that had clutched at him. It would have been so easy to start his life out as a coward back then; instead, Charlie Strongheart chose to act like a man. That decision made him a hero, which he had proven many times since.

He went out the door with his Glock 19 in his right hand behind his back and walked rapidly toward the gang-bangers. His rapid walk toward them and the look on his face unnerved them. His hand went to the back of his waistline, and Charlie knew he was going for a gun, so Charlie's right hand came out holding the Glock 19 as he went into his modified Weaver stance, his left arm up in front of his chest, fingers up and wrapping comfortably around the grip of his right hand.

Louie was wearing a large fake diamond earring in his left ear. While he raised his gun, Charlie smiled on purpose to scare them even more, and he said, "Nice earring, punk."

Flame belched from the gun with a loud bang, as they all ducked, and Louie screamed, dropping his cheap little .380 pistol on the ground, as he grabbed his left ear. The ring and the bottom part of his earlobe were gone. Blood oozed out between his fingers.

They all stood, and suddenly a second Glock, Fila's, appeared in Charlie's left hand.

"Oh, man, battle," Charlie said enthusiastically. "Come on, punks. You started the dance, and I love to fight, so let's rock and roll! This is cool! I have a hard-on! Come on, assholes. It's party time."

One of them who was fairly slender started vomiting, and his legs were visibly wobbly.

Charlie knew he was significantly outnumbered, so he

spoke in a very bold and gross manner in order to gain a psychological advantage. He pointed both guns from one gang member to the next and back.

Then he said, "You boys wanted to fight. I am not a sweet old lady, like my mom is in that house. I am a real warrior. Any pussy can throw beer bottles at little old ladies. Let's do battle. I am ready to kill. You want to go home and get your daddies? I'll do battle with them, too. You have to have more guns."

He paused to give his remarks greater affect.

"Speaking of that, each of you that has one or a knife, toss it in front of me. If I catch you with one on you, I will shoot you dead."

Two more guns were tossed out and three sheath knives and one Boy Scout pocketknife.

Charlie yelled, "Fila!"

The front door opened, and Charlie said, "Tell my mom to come out, and you come here, too!" Fila and Betty came out on the porch, but Fila walked out to Charlie and stood behind and to his left.

"Baseball jersey!" Charlie said. "Grab your baseball hat by the brim and throw it straight up in the air as high as you can!"

The young man complied and Charlie yelled, "Fila!"

Without looking at her, he tossed her Glock back to her with his left hand. She caught it in her own modified isosceles gunfighter's stance, and three shots rang out as the hat flew with each and sailed to the ground with three holes through it.

Charlie commanded, "Go pick it up and bring it here for your friends to see."

Betty yelled from the porch, "My son is a Green Beret and a mighty warrior. You little brats better not mess with me again!"

Charlie looked back to his mom, shaking his head, while wearing a big-toothed grin.

The baseball brat showed the hat with three neat holes through it. They all were amazed.

Charlie said, "You know, sometimes it is not very smart to make war on women. You never know what you might be getting yourself into."

He grabbed Louie by the bloody ear, squeezing what was left of it, and dragged him in pain, almost on his tiptoes, over to Betty.

Charlie yelled at the rest, "All of you, come here!"

While still wearing a big grin, Charlie said, "Mom, these gentlemen starting with Bloody Ear all want to apologize to you."

Charlie gave Louie's ear a squeeze, and he screamed in pain before saying, "Ma'am, I am very sorry. I am very, very sorry."

All the rest of them started apologizing profusely.

Charlie said, "Mom, you can call the PD and tell them to send Charlie back."

She went in and reappeared with her cell phone, speaking on it.

Charlie said, "What is your name, punk?"

"Louie Horse, sir."

"Well, Louie, first let me tell you all about my gang. If you want to belong to a tough gang and win every fight you ever get in, grow some balls and join my gang," Charlie said. "Our gang colors are forest green and digital camo, and it is the baddest, toughest gang in the history of the world. My gang is called the U.S. Army Special Forces. If you guys want to fight and want to belong and do some good, then join the U.S. Army and try to get into my gang, if any of you are tough enough, which you are not."

He tucked his Glock away in the folds of his clothes, and Fila followed suit.

"Now, Louie," Charlie said, "I am going off to war again, but I can come back anytime, or I can send a friend. I am making you head of security for my mom while I am gone. If someone throws a cigarette on her lawn, I will hold you responsible. If someone disses her at the grocery store, or if she even has to carry a bag of groceries again, I will hold you personally responsible. Do I make myself perfectly clear to all of you?"

"Yes, sir!" they said in unison, then Louis added, "Don't worry, sir, we have your mom's back. Nobody will ever screw with her."

The PD cruiser pulled up and the other Charlie got out and walked up.

Charlie Strongheart stuck his hand out and shook with the officer, saying, "Been a long time. Hi, Charlie."

"Hi, Charlie yourself," the cop said. "I heard you got killed in Iraq or was it Afghanistan?"

Charlie said, "Neither. I am still alive, bro. You are mistaken. It must have been another Charlie." He went on. "Officer, young Louie Horse here had an accident with his pistol laying over there and accidentally shot his earlobe off. Thinking weapons in the wrong hands can be a bad thing, all these gents decided to turn all their weapons in to you. They are laying there on the ground. They knew that they will be very busy anyway. They have decided to clean up around my mom's house and yard, and starting with Mom's, they decided to get some paint and paint over all the gang graffiti on all the propane tanks and buildings in the neighborhood. Didn't you, guys?"

"Yes, sir!" they all yelled enthusiastically.

Charlie Ten Horses said, "I am glad that somebody was finally able to talk sense into you guys. I tried to tell you all to take pride in being Sioux. Don't buy into the lame excuses reservation losers use to become failures."

Charlie went into the house with his mom and Fila and sat down.

Betty started laughing and Charlie asked what was so funny.

She said, "You two are getting married. I was just thinking what would happen if some burglar ever tried to break into your house."

All three started laughing.

An hour later, after some talk and good-byes, they went outside to leave, and Charlie grinned as he saw the entire gang walking up the street with a gargantuan Lakota man in the middle front. Several of them carried bags.

The man walked up to Charlie and said, "Are you Charlie Strongheart?"

Charlie nodded.

He pointed at Louie, who was wearing a large bandage on his ear and said, "Louie is my son." He stuck out his hand and said, "Thank you, sir. Thank you from the bottom of my heart."

The man turned and walked away. The gang members pulled brushes and cans of paint out of the bags and immediately started painting the propane tank. Two guys pulled out cleaning supplies and walked over to the house and started cleaning where the beer bottle had hit.

Charlie and Fila got in the car and pulled out, waving at Betty.

Little did Charlie know that within the next year, two of those boys would start back working on their GEDs, one would join the navy, and four, including Louie, would join the army.

CHAPTER FIFTEEN

Time to Go

WHEN they got back to Fort Bragg, the Quick Reaction Force Team under Custer, now referred to as Team Dog Soldier, in honor of Charlie, had practiced various rescue scenarios repeatedly and had made mock-ups of different Iranian buildings and houses.

Charlie and Fila immediately started practicing with the car and found all the devices located on it. It had been armor-plated and fitted with all kinds of neat devices, which had been learned from the super-secret British 14 company.

They stopped speaking in English and only spoke in Arabic and Persian. Charlie started wearing the specially made hearing aids and practiced all day long and part of the evenings with the team of linguist/translators provided for him by the Central Intelligence Agency and the Defense Intelligence Agency.

Davood was being watched day and night, and Detachment-Delta had a constant stream of reports every time he moved, which was very frequently. He had built a large compound southwest of Tehran and started training his operatives there. Many were assembled there now, being trained on all aspects of jihad.

Within three weeks, Charlie, Fila, and the entire team were on the ground in Mosul, awaiting the green light. They stayed in air-conditioned trailers that had been brought in, and which remained on the edge of the tarmac. The Rangers stayed there, too, and maintained a tight twenty-four-hour-per-day security perimeter for the Delta operators.

Finally, after a week, the message came in. An operative had delivered a message to one of Davood Dabdeh's lieutenants about a wealthy Iraqi businessman with an Iranian wife wanting to meet with him privately about conducting business. Charlie's character would hire Davood's trained terrorists to sabotage American offshore drilling rigs, and he would also use them to kidnap wives and family members of the American oil companies drilling at the new platforms because of the oil crisis, until he could start taking over each little oil company by intimidation and strong-arm tactics. Then the platforms would also be disguised as staging areas for hit-and-run attacks inside the United States.

Dabdeh loved the idea, but saw no reason in the world why he would need this Iraqi to carry out such a plan. That, he did not convey in his message. He sent word to meet him out in the desert off of Highway 5, which runs between Tehran and Qom, and is in fact called the Tehran-Qom Highway. It is a well-paved, well-maintained roadway which runs for seventy-four and a half miles between the two major cities, but in between is some of the most desolate desert one could possibly imagine. There were a couple major ridges along the way and many gullies and gulches.

It was in one of these where the Special Forces team went with members of the Free Iranian Freedom Fighters Party, which is called the Komala, and which had created the hideaway and landing zone. Oddly enough, this party was headquartered in the mountains in Kurdistan, much closer to where Charlie and Fila were staying in Mosul than to the guerilla base near Qom in the southern part of the vast desert area. Davood Faraz Dabdeh's compound was also located some miles off of the Tehran-Qom Highway, also out in the desert but very close to Tehran.

The Komala had become one of the strangest revolutionary organizations in the world, in that there were actually two different Komala organizations and both of them had a red flag as their symbol. Both had the same founder, and each Komala had a separate headquarters, and the headquarters were actually within sight of each other. They were not identical twins, though. One Komala Party, which had a team of Special Forces advisors working with it, referred to itself as a leftist party, but the other Komala was actually affiliated with the Communist Party.

Both originally opposed the United States and most European nations, and the opposition was mainly because the U.S. supported the Shah of Iran, who brought a great deal of death and suffering to the revolutionaries. After the shah was deposed, however, and the Ayatollah Khomeini took the reins of power in Tehran, it got much worse—much, much worse.

In the beginning there was only the original Komala, or the Association, which was called the Iranian Freedom Fighters Party by many outside of Iran. Then after the ayatollah ascended to power and the suppression got worse, one group, which did not like the Communist Party or its precepts, became the leftist Komala—but not the communist Komala. It kept the name and the flag, but was diametrically opposed to its communist twin, and conversely so was the United States. Its group started becoming known outside Iran as the Free Iranian Freedom Fighters Party.

Dave, Charlie's soon-to-be-hopefully father-in-law, had commanded the 5th Special Forces Group at Fort Campbell, and he knew from his friends still there that a small contingent from the 5th Group, working with the Free Komala, had gone with some of the Iranians they advised to a place in the desert about twenty miles or so from Qom, but that was all Dave's friends knew about it.

But knowing that Charlie and Fila were going on a very dangerous assignment, Dave also knew that they would have simply told him if that assignment was into Iraq or Afghanistan. They would not have told him what their mission was, but they certainly would have stated that they would be in Iraq or Afghanistan. He also knew that after he knew Charlie in Ranger School, when his haircut was "high and tight," and Charlie ended up with 1st Special Forces Operational Detachment-Delta, he had grown his hair out long and worn it in a traditional Native American style or a long ponytail. He was expecting that before he met Charlie again. When he saw that Charlie was working on a beard and had his haircut high and tight again, a buzz cut actually, he knew he had to be going on an assignment where he would be trying to blend in with a traditional Muslim environment. The clincher was knowing that his daughter, who he knew was in the Funny Platoon in Delta, spoke flawless Persian and Arabic, so chances were almost 100 percent that the pair was going into Iran on a very dangerous mission.

The entire mission was told to "saddle up." Charlie and Fila went into their trailer. As a precaution he changed the powerful batteries in his fake hearing aids, just so he would not have to worry about one of them dying out in the middle of the mission.

Fila helped him attach the beard which covered his face from sideburn to sideburn and had been specially made with great pride along with two backup beards, by one of the top makeup experts in Hollywood.

Fila put on her twin inner-thigh holsters and put a little

Glock Model 19 in each holster, as well as a good supply of ammunition. She had ample breasts, and a sheath holding her Yarborough knife hung upside down under them. Charlie wore boxer briefs under his tailored suit, and he'd had a little holster sewn into the right leg. He now placed a black tactical switchblade knife in the holster, where it would be safely stored right next to his penis. He assumed he would be patted down before meeting with Dabdeh, but he figured he would not be patted down so thoroughly that some bodyguard would get his hands that close to his groin. Because Fila was a woman, and they both understood the mind-set of the group they were dealing with, and because she was supposed to be Charlie's wife, they knew she would not be patted down or searched.

They finished getting ready, and Charlie took her outside the trailer and around behind it. They looked out beyond the buildings, and he pulled a cigar out of a pouch and lit it. Then he blew out smoke and waved it over their heads with his hands. He did this several times.

He said softly, "Bow your head, honey."

They both did, and he said, "Father God, I pray to you in the spirit and the manner of those who have gone before. You are the creator of Mother Earth on which we stand, and Brother Sun, and Your Son our Heavenly Savior, who the Jewish call Y'Shua ha M'Shia. We, my fellow warrior, the woman I love and I, now go into battle. Shield our bodies from the spears and lances of our enemy. Protect our fellow warriors, and help us to strike down the evil ones for your sake and honor. Help us to count many coup and earn many eagle feathers. Grant us wisdom, discernment, and courage. Heavenly Father, grant us your righteous flaming arrows to shoot from our bows. Help us to sanctify your power and glory with the sacrificial blood of your enemies on our blades, those who destroy your greater glory and legacy by trying to destroy all who carry the Good News and those who are called Your Chosen People.

Help us to return victorious and then be blessed with a wonderful life and many children, to be raised in your eyes and under your guidance. In Jesus' name we pray. Amen."

Fila kissed him.

Charlie said, "It's time to go to the office, darling," and grinning, they walked around the corner of the building and toward the Super Hercules and an uncertain fate.

CHARLIE and Fila blinked at the vast expanse of light sand desert before them. The QRF team, Komala, and the three-man 5th Group team were putting up the camouflaged cargo netting over the C-130 Super Hercules. The Little Birds were assembled and were warming up.

The report came in on the commo man's satlink laptop that the caravan of white Mercedes sedans had left the training compound and were heading south on Highway 5. Davood Dabdeh was in the third of five vehicles. Charlie and Fila shook hands all around, got in their BMW, and headed out toward the highway. If the calculations were correct, they should arrive at the rendezvous spot along the highway about ten minutes or so ahead of the caravan of bad guys.

Custer personally went to each man and asked when he had cleaned his weapons. He checked personally to make sure the Little Birds were filled with fuel and loaded with ammo. He would not stop, between now and when the mission was accomplished or they were called into action, double and triple checking anything that could go wrong.

Something was about to. The one factor that had been overlooked was the coldness and sheer cunning and outright meanness of Davood Faraz Dabdeh.

When he was young, he was essentially raised by his uncle, who was an imam and who also liked to molest little boys. That is how Dabdeh developed his own penchant for homosexual behavior. He was his uncle's favorite victim.

Davood also raped and beat his two younger sisters when he was a teenager. His father scolded him and whacked him with a rod. Then he made him go and watch each time as the neighborhood zealots, and those who were simply followers out of fear and intimidation, stoned his sisters to death as honor killings for forsaking his family honor.

His father was also very, very wealthy, as he had been basically the guardian of the deep secrets for Ayatollah Khomeini. His pockets got lined, and he was brought in on many oil and other deals.

Davood inherited the estate because he was the sole surviving son when his father and mother both died in a Mercedes rollover. The young man who'd helped Davood bludgeon them into unconsciousness and then stage the accident on one of the winding mountain roads northwest of Tehran was now his chief bodyguard and frequent spokesman.

His name was Yaghoub Ardeshir, and was in the lead Mercedes, speaking to Davood when needed, using an earpiece and mike.

Yaghoub was Davood's friend, his only friend ever. Their joys were drugs, raping and terrorizing women, and killing people sadistically. Yaghoub was most interested, though, in being close to Davood because he knew the man's drive would make him a world leader in jihad.

He knew that he personally was a brutal killer, but he killed Muslims, too, not just infidels. He was very worried about ever getting into Paradise and did want the honor and glory someday of giving his life in the taking of many infidel lives. He was, however, not into dying just yet. He also believed he was a major disciple to Davood Faraz Dabdeh, who he was sure had the blessings of Allah.

The translators were very puzzled when Charlie and Fila pulled off the highway and stopped the car.

They heard Fila say to him, "Charlie, this is a good day to die."

Then they were even more puzzled when he responded, "Yes, Fila, it is a good day to die."

They had no clue the two had just spoken the words all true Lakota warriors said before going into battle.

The next seven minutes were like an eternity, and the pair mainly stared into each other's eyes and smiled warmly while holding hands. They finally spotted the caravan of black Mercedes.

Charlie said, "Brave up, warrior. Here come the white eyes. *Hokahey!*"

That struck Fila's funny bone and she started laughing. She had to control herself, though, as she handed the stick to Charlie and got out of the car, cowering on the passenger side. He started whacking her on the back, and as he felt the blow hit her Kevlar, she pretended to wince and scream in pain.

Now, the translators listening really thought the pair was crazy.

Charlie pointed his finger angrily at Fila and said, "There, woman. That is a hint of what you will get when we get married if you do not have breakfast and the newspaper ready for me each morning."

She bowed in mock subservience and said in a low tone, "In your dreams, Buster."

She put the stick in the car and walked forward meekly as the other cars pulled up. The occupants were close enough to have seen the mock beatings.

The problem Charlie and Fila would soon face, though, was that Davood Faraz Dabdeh did not think rationally, and that would prove to be the shortcoming in all the extensive planning and rehearsals of the Detachment-Delta members.

Charlie did not wear sunglasses, as he wanted total clarity. He was a handsome Iraqi with his massive build and rugged good looks, and his Italian-tailored suit, the ends of his turban flowing softly with the desert breeze.

Fila's beauty was hidden from view as she bowed her head and her clothes hid her great figure.

The Iranians had not left their cars yet, and Charlie whispered, "You know what I never asked. What does Fila Jannat mean in Farsi?"

She grinned to herself thinking about him asking such a question right now facing this danger, and it calmed her.

Acting like a ventriloquist, with her lips not moving, she said, "You are amazing, Sergeant Strongheart. Fila means 'lover' and Jannat means 'paradise.'"

Charlie turned and looked at her, winking with his head away from the Iranians and saying, "That sure fits you. If anything happens to me, you survive and accomplish the mission. Love of country and freedom is what is most important now, not of each other."

She bowed as if receiving an order and said, "You are preaching to the choir, Sergeant. And by the way, I love you."

Just then he heard the car doors open as Yaghoub Ardeshir and three henchmen, all armed with automatic weapons, got out of the lead Mercedes. Charlie knew Yaghoub by his size alone, as he was six foot five, slightly taller than Charlie, and weighed 251 pounds.

Not knowing that the exchange he and Fila just had had been listened to by Pops, Kerri Rhodes, and the President of the United States, who all smiled and shook their heads, Charlie whispered to Fila and into his mike, while smiling, "The big guy is Yaghoub Ardeshir, and there are three more with AK-47s. Ardeshir is carrying . . . It looks like a Soviet high-caliber pistol. Can't talk."

They approached and Charlie stepped forward, palms up, saying, "*Asalamalakum*," the traditional Arabic greeting, meaning "Welcome, peace be upon you."

Yaghoub said, "*Salam,*" the simple Farsi word for "Hello."

They grabbed each other by the upper arms and kissed

next to each other's cheeks three times in the typical greeting.

Then Yaghoub indicated that Charlie should put his arms up and allow himself to be frisked. Charlie complied.

Charlie spoke to him in Arabic, and his "wife" translated, "My wife is Persian, and I am Iraqi from Tal Afar. She must translate for me."

Yaghoub put his finger up to his ear and spoke, apparently to Davood Dabdeh, saying, "He has no weapons. His wife is Persian and translates. He speaks Arabic only. He is from Tal Afar. He is hard of hearing, too. He wears hearing aids in his ears."

"Shoot the Iraqi dog. We don't need him. I like his idea, but we can do it," Davood said into the earpiece. "Bring the woman. We will have fun. Leave his body here in the sand. The desert can be his new friend."

Yaghoub grinned and, in Farsi of course, said, "You want her in your car or mine?"

This was the only warning that Charlie and Fila received.

Samireh Ahoo was a very devout Muslim who grew up in Detroit, Michigan. After September 11, 2001, her two brothers enlisted in the Marines and fought in both Iraq and Afghanistan. Since her mother was Iraqi and father Persian, she was multilingual, in Arabic and Farsi. She was also a very patriotic American and wanted to contribute on the GWOT; she was working as a translator/interpreter for the Central Intelligence Agency within six months of the attacks.

She was very alert on this day and quickly said into the earpiece, "Look out, he wants to take Fila to the car."

At the same time, Fila's mind flashed methodically and immediately through her choices. Should she break character and go for a gun, or should she remain in character and warn Charlie in Arabic?

As soon as Davood Dabdeh had responded, Yaghoub

raised his gun toward Charlie, an evil grin on his face. The CIA translator was issuing her warning, and Fila did not have to think but react. Her hands went down under the front of her dress. Her right hand gripped the handle of one Glock just as Yaghoub's gun flashed and blood flew from the face of Charlie Strongheart, who fell to the ground face-first in a lifeless heap.

A hard thump hit her in the center of her chest, knocking her backward, and she saw that the jihadist closest to Yaghoub with his AK-47 in his hand had just shot her in the center of her chest, hitting her heart plate at an angle. She fell backward but aimed with a two-handed grip and put two bullets into the forehead of that terrorist.

She swung the gun toward Yaghoub, the man who had just murdered the man she loved, Charlie Strongheart, who was now lying facedown in a pool of his own blood.

His words, "Brave up," were in her mind as she fired at Yaghoub's forehead, but a split second before she fired, something slammed into the back of her head and her bullet hit Yaghoub in the left shoulder. Darkness enveloped her. She saw her true love dead in front of her and wanted to cry, but she could not. As Fila slipped into unconsciousness, she felt hands roughly grab her and drag her.

The terrorist behind her had butt-stroked her in the back of the head with his AK-47. Now he and the other remaining terrorist dragged her to the lead Mercedes and tossed her in the backseat.

When Charlie was in the 3rd Special Forces Group at Fort Bragg, besides running and weight lifting three days a week he drove to a boxing club in Fayetteville, put on wrist wraps, and trained and worked out boxing and kickboxing. When he did that, he would work out with several boxers sparring but controlling their punches and wearing sixteen-ounce boxing gloves. Two things happened during those sessions; one of those was that Charlie learned from an undefeated professional boxer that all he had to do most often was barely slip punches and let them graze his cheek or jaw, as he barely moved his head out of the way. That would save a great deal of wasted energy. The man explained that too many boxers wasted time moving an arm to knock a punch away, while the best boxers practiced economy of movement all the time. He urged Charlie to allow punches to be thrown at his face and simply move enough to avoid letting anything other than the boxing glove graze his face as it went by. Then, he said, was often the best time to counterpunch, as many boxers would throw such a punch and then be out of position, off-balance, or drop their guard. Charlie started doing this in practice and with time learned to really relax fighting and not swing an arm up defensively every time the opponent moved. He also noticed he was not biting on feints all the time, like he had earlier. He was amazed at how much better he was as a fighter and how much more endurance he had when he learned to relax and use this technique.

The other important lesson he learned at the time came indirectly from former World Heavyweight Champion and boxing legend, Muhammad Ali of all people. This boxer actually had been a sparring partner of Ali's back in the day. He told Charlie how generous Ali was to his partners.

Everybody called him Champ, and he said that Champ used to have three sparring partners he worked out with at once—a guy his upcoming opponent's size, then a real big, strong heavyweight, and then someone smaller and much faster. He said that Champ would allow his opponents to hit him, and they would really tee off on him since he was the Champ. He would do the rope-a-dope and taunt them and even put his hands down and let them hit him sometimes.

He said after one of those sessions he said to Ali, "Champ, why do you let the other guys and me hit you full power like that?"

The boxer said Muhammad Ali grinned at him and

said, " 'Cause I don't want it to be no surprise in the ring in a real fight."

The friend then went on to explain to Charlie that it was important to let himself get hit and keep sparring nonstop in the ring. He did this, too, in practice and really learned to take a punch. This helped him win several boxing smokers at Fort Bragg. His mind-set was to work through the maze if he got his bells rung, and keep fighting.

These two factors came into play on this day, as well as the warning from the translator.

The Little Bird helicopters whizzed along the highway at top speed, and dust blew all over Charlie as the first set down and Custer jumped off and ran to him.

He rolled Charlie over on his back, and Charlie, barely able to speak, said softly, "Medic, quick, smelling salts."

There was a horrible gash under his right eye and the cheek was torn open, leaving his chipped and cracked cheekbone exposed.

Charlie thought he heard Custer yell, "Medic!" and he suddenly was smelling that old horrible smell of ammonia. He had always wondered why they called them smelling salts and not "horrible ammonia or bleach smell that wakes you up quickly."

Charlie sat up and shook his head, blood flying all over the Delta medic and Custer.

Things now flooded into his mind, and he yelled, "Fila?"

Custer said, "They took her, Charlie, but we will get her, I promise you we will!"

"Bullshit!" Charlie said, trying to stand but falling back. "I am still in charge! Doc, quick patch me up fast. Give me a shot of adrenaline. Stop the bleeding. I need weapons."

The medic gave Charlie a shot of adrenaline and said, "Poke, you have lost lots of blood, have a concussion, a broken cheekbone . . ."

Charlie said, "Screw that! We are SF! Delta Force, not the Kindergarten Whammies football team! Get me on my feet! Let's go!"

His head started clearing as they roared off in the three Little Birds.

The medic held on to Charlie's arm as they roared along, paralleling the highway at treetop level, if there had been any trees. He somehow patched the bloody cheek and got a bandage over it. Charlie's hair and shoulder were drenched in blood. He did not care.

Custer said, "I called for the Spooky."

Charlie said, "Negative! Our mission is to affect the job without making international news headlines. Any major air strikes will end up on the evening news back home. They are headed towards his compound, and I have a target to take out, and we have an operator in enemy hands. We can handle this by just doing what we practice over and over."

While they flew, Charlie was handed an M4A1 fully automatic rifle with an A203 grenade launcher mounted underneath. He was also handed a Glock 17 and several magazines. He tossed off his suit coat and put a tactical vest on, and he made sure he had ammo.

Charlie asked Custer, "Was Booty shot?"

"No," Custer said, "The vid cam on the UAV showed the guy behind her butt-smashing her in the back of the head. Like you, she is going to have a nasty headache, Poke."

Charlie was reminded how bad his cheekbone was hurting and his head was aching. His eyes went out of focus every few minutes, and he had nausea a few times. He knew he had a concussion. That did not matter right now.

Custer touched his arm and said, "Don't worry, Charlie. We'll get her back."

Charlie looked straight ahead, saying, "Damned right we will!"

Several minutes later, Custer said, "HQ reports that a UAV has them pulling into the road to the compound."

Charlie gave him a thumbs-up.

He said, "Are you translators still there?"

Samireh said, "Yes, sir, we are."

The President, Kerri, and Pops were all still monitoring his powerful microphone transmissions.

Charlie said, "Who warned me about him taking Fila?"

"That was me, sir."

Charlie said, "Ma'am, you saved my life. I got shot in the face, but your warning gave me enough time to keep it from being through my head. God bless you, ma'am. If I survive this, my fiancée and I are taking you out for a big steak dinner. How's that?"

"Sounds great!"

He said to Custer, "What's our ETA?"

Custer said, "That is the compound coming up on the horizon."

Charlie gritted his teeth and whispered to himself, forgetting that he was being listened to, "Stay alive, sweetheart."

FILA opened her eyes. She was in the backseat of the Mercedes, between two men and slumped over, lying head down toward the floor. The man behind her was moving around, and she did not know it was Yaghoub bandaging his shoulder. The one to her right was the one she was facing more directly. She would take him out first. Carefully, she slid her right hand up her thigh and discovered that both guns were gone. She slid her hand up farther and gripped the Yarborough knife. The car passed through a gate and was stopping. Her hand came out and up, and the blade went up into the base of the man's chin and drove straight into his brain. Both his legs straightened out, and he started convulsing violently.

Yaghoub's massive right arm wrapped around her neck from behind smashing and bloodying her lips and nose. Fila bit down on his forearm with all her might, and he screamed in pain, but she kept biting. He tried to use his left arm, but it would not work. She switched the knife in her hand and let go of her bite, pivoting at the hips and ramming the blade into his torso, just below the right rib cage. She twisted the knife as hard as she could, and he screamed in paralyzing pain. This totally unnerved the ji-hadist driving, who started yelling himself in panic. He knew he was next. The car was now stopped.

Fila's immediate concern was the monster next to her, who had killed her fiancé, or so she thought. She spun around and reversed the knife again, into an underhand hold, and struck forward, plunging it accidentally into his right bicep. He was genuinely scared to death for the first time in years, and he had the deer-in-the-headlights look. He screamed in pain again, and Fila turned the knife up-ward and thrust straight up with all her energy, and it went up into his sinus cavity. Blood spilled out his nose and down his throat. His eyes were opened wider than she had ever seen on anybody.

Staring into those panicked eyes, she pulled the knife out and in English said, "Yes, I am a woman and an Amer-ican soldier and this is for Charlie, you piece of trash."

She cut sideways, and his throat was slashed open all the way to his spine. Blood gushed out, and she heard him gurgling and drowning in it, as his massive body went limp and he voided his bowels and bladder. The door slammed, and she realized she was surrounded by crazed trained killers, all pointing guns at her. She jumped into the front seat and started the ignition, then she spotted Davood Faraz Dabdeh aiming an AK-47 at her. She looked around for a weapon and, finding none, stuck out her jaw defiantly and flipped him the middle finger. He opened fire and so did his men.

Fila waited for death but was amazed. The car was armor-plated. Hundreds of bullets bounced off the vehicle, even the windows. She saw the gate they had just come in, but she had a mission and that was to kill Dabdeh. She spun the wheel, slammed it into gear, and headed right toward the psycho killer. More bullets peppered her car, but she was intent on killing him. Fila reached down and grabbed her cyanide pill. She would not be taken prisoner again, nor would she ever be raped again. Those were certainties. She put it between her lips, but not her teeth.

She was upon her target, and a shoulder-fired rocket hit the rear of the car, just as she was about to run him over. The right front fender sent him flying off to the side as her rear end slid around, but he rolled to his feet, bloody and limping, but alive. Fila saw a man with a rocket tube on his shoulder. Then she saw a chance—a window in the stone wall, so the wall would not be as strong there. She floored it, stomping down on the accelerator. She might get killed, but Charlie was gone anyway, she thought. More bullets hit her car, thousands now, as trainees and cadre alike shot at her. Men jumped out of the way as the Mercedes sped across the courtyard. Right before she hit the wall, Fila spit out the cyanide pill.

She screamed as loud as she could, "Ahhhhhhhhhhhh-hhhhh!" and the heavy white car crashed through the wall, hitting so hard on the desert floor it knocked the wind out of the courageous sergeant and bounced several times, but she kept the pedal down, wondering why the air bag did not deploy. The bags had apparently been disabled.

A Mercedes came through the gate of the compound and sped toward Fila. She saw it in her rearview and slammed her brakes on, spun the wheel to the left, and floored it, spinning around 180 degrees.

"Screw this running!" she said boldly, stomping on the accelerator.

Just as she had crashed through the wall, the three Little Birds topped out over the rise and were heading right at the compound. They were now witnessing her acts of boldness and sheer courage, and Charlie got a lump in his throat.

Again, forgetting he was miked, he whispered with great relief, "Fila!"

They watched her car bear down head-on with the other white Mercedes, and the two cars roared at each other. It was a test of wills, and she made up her mind. She was going straight in.

Custer slapped Charlie's arm and yelled, "Look at that! She has brass balls, man!"

Charlie gave him a sidelong glance.

Custer laughed. "I don't mean literally."

Charlie held his breath. The windows came down in the other car, and men leaned out firing. The third Little Bird zoomed up, flying almost sideways and *whirrrr, brrraappp*. The 3,000-rounds-per-minute mini-gun opened with every fifth round a tracer, and Fila's heart raced as she saw the ribbon of flame over her roof tear into the approaching Mercedes, which now disappeared in a cloud of dust and sand. She was on it and still would not stop. The driver swerved at the last second, and it went sideways and did twelve rolls through the sand sideways. The Little Bird lit it up while it rolled, shredding the tires, and one tracer finally made its way into the gas tank.

Charlie looked at the medic by him and yelled, "Gotta move, Doc!" He crawled off the bench into the chopper, and it set down while the other two hovered and covered. The dust settled, and Fila, blood streaming from her lips and nose, ran from the car and stopped short seeing Charlie running at her, bandage on the side of his very bloody head. She could not help herself, tears streaking down her cheeks.

"Charlie!"

They flew into each other's arms, and ran to the Little Bird, where they jumped side by side on the bench. Custer slapped her arm with a thumbs-up.

Charlie yelled, "Doc!"

The medic was right there, swabbing her face with gauze. She smiled and took it.

She said, "Bloody lips and bloody nose! You should see the other guy! The one who shot you."

"Shoot him?"

"No," she yelled as the Little Birds lifted up amid a hail of gunfire from the compound. "Got him and one more with my Yarborough knife!"

Charlie put his hand on her shoulder

He yelled to Custer, "Call it in that the number two man is dead. Yaghoub Ardeshir." He grinned at Custer and said, "Booty killed him with her Yarborough knife!"

Custer grinned broadly and gave her a thumbs-up.

"I need weapons!" she said.

Custer yelled, "Booty needs weapons."

She was handed an M1911 Colt .45 automatic, four magazines, and an M-14 7.62-millimeter rifle.

She reached up under her dress and got her Yarborough knife sheath out and attached it to the belt she was handed. That knife would never leave her side the rest of her life. The father of the modern Green Berets had reached out from the grave and saved another life, she thought. *God bless General Yarborough. Heaven must be safer.*

Booty leaned over and yelled into Custer's mike above the rotor noise, "Dabdeh is wearing a light tan suit and tie, sunglasses, and no turban." She looked at Charlie and winked, "And he is limping."

He laughed.

She said, "Just missed him."

The armed Little Bird came up sideways again as the three aircraft went up and over the wall of the compound.

The mini-gun went to work, and automatics cracked in a steady staccato from all the Delta members. Bloody bad guys fell all over the compound, and Custer winced as a 7.62 bullet slammed into his forearm, shattering the radius.

Charlie yelled, "Doc!"

He immediately put an army pressure bandage over the wound, and Custer jumped down, yelling, "Thanks!"

When they first came up over the wall, Charlie and Fila saw Davood Faraz Dabdeh ducking into a door at the far end of the courtyard, and they fought their way there.

Custer and two others were right behind them firing in all directions. There were many more trainees, but none with the experience and training of the men, and now one woman, of Detachment-Delta, who established fire superiority. They made it to the door, and Charlie looked at each to ensure they were locked and loaded and ready to rock and roll. He went through first with a crash, with Custer right behind him. Charlie covered the center of the room with his weapon, while Custer moved to the right along the wall and took that side, and Fila moved in and immediately swept the left side of the room. Custer and Fila both made out gunmen in their respective corners and fired simultaneously, hitting each terrorist with two bullets center mass in the face. Something flew into the room and thunked on the floor,

Charlie yelled, "Grenade!"

The others went out the door, diving into the courtyard, but Charlie went headfirst into the room where the grenade was thrown from. This caught Davood completely off-guard. He was not expecting such a bold action by anybody. The grenade went off and he went into the next room and spun around, AK-47 in his hands ready to open up. The others came into the room Charlie was in, and all had been untouched by the grenade.

Charlie worked his way over to the door and looked in.

He gave the medic a hand signal for a flash bang grenade. The man reached in his tactical vest and pulled one out, tossing it to Charlie. Charlie caught it, as the group tightened up behind him. He pulled the pin, mouthed the words, "One, two, three," and tossed it in the other room.

The army describes the XM84 stun grenade in this way:

> The XM84 Stun Grenade is a non-fragmentation, non-lethal "Flash and Bang" stun grenade that is intended to provide a reliable, effective non-lethal means of neutralizing & disorienting enemy personnel.
>
> The M84 non-lethal Stun Grenade is a non-lethal, low hazard, non-shrapnel-producing explosive device intended to confuse, disorient or momentarily distract potential threat personnel. The device produces a temporary incapacitation to threat personnel or innocent bystanders. This device will be used by military personnel in hostage rescue situations and in the capture of criminals, terrorists or other adversaries. It provides commanders a non-lethal capability to increase the flexibility in the application of force during military operations.
>
> Detonating the M84 Stun Grenade in the presence of natural gas, gasoline, or other highly flammable fumes or materials may cause a serious secondary explosion or fire, resulting in death or severe injury to friendly forces or unintended victims, as well as serious property damage. The operator must wear proper hearing protection when employing the M84. Injury to personnel could result if the grenade functions prior to being deployed.

Davood Faraz Dabdeh had stopped long enough in the next room to kick over the can of gas and drag the box of blasting caps next to it. He was hoping they would use a hand grenade, or even a tracer round that might ignite the gas. The explosion sent all flying backward, totally stunned as part of the walls around them collapsed and the group was covered with debris. Charlie got the concussion the worst, because he was the only one not wearing a Kevlar vest. Fortunately, he had put on his K-pot, or Kevlar helmet, preventing him from worsening his concussion and fractured eye socket and cheekbone. Blood did pour from his bandage again. All were stunned and their guns had gone flying.

Davood Faraz Dabdeh limped forward. Fila had broken his right foot and cracked his shinbone with the car. He also had bruised ribs from landing on his rifle stock. He was amazed and amused as he walked forward slowly that this stupid infidel in the suit was reaching into his pants to grab his manhood at a time like this. He walked forward menacingly, slowly relishing the moment. He felt he was going to get away. He always had, his whole life, so he was not filled with wide-eyed panic like all his trainees. He was now ten feet away and felt that would be close enough to start shooting this infidel in various limbs so he could watch him scream. The man still was playing or protecting his manhood. Davood grinned, and that was when Charlie's hand came out of his boxer shorts and suit pants, and the switchblade whipped open with a click that could be heard above the outside gunfire and explosions. It flew from Charlie's underhand throw and stuck deeply into Dabdeh's right shoulder, and he dropped his AK-47, gritting his teeth in pain. He bent to grab it, and this was the split second Fila was hoping for. She lunged for the Colt M1911 .45 pistol lying five feet out of her reach and opened fire on Dabdeh, who took a round in the same spot as the switchblade. Charlie got to his feet swaying and picked up his M4A1 and his Glock.

He said, "Tend to them and their wounds, Fila."

He headed toward the door.

She said, "No, you need backup."

Charlie cut her off and said, "That was not a request, Sergeant."

She said, "Sorry," and moved immediately over to Doc to check on him so hopefully he could help give aid to the rest.

Charlie did not even look back. He felt bad about snapping at Fila, but this was combat, and he was the commander on the ground. He was doing exactly what he would have done with a team of men who were working with him for the first time. Two were functioning and the others were all wounded and needed care immediately. He had to chase his target and take him down. That was his mission, but he also wanted his men taken care of, especially if they could get up and keep fighting and rejoin him. That would be his best force-multiplier. If Fila could not handle what he had done, she would have to transfer out to another unit. He knew he was correct.

Fila was treating Doc, who was thankfully just stunned, and he and she worked on Custer, who had a concussion himself now and a fractured collarbone. Doc lifted his arm and had Fila hold it against Custer's tactical vest. Doc then produced a roll of adhesive tape and started wrapping it around Custer's chest and upper arm, immobilizing the arm up against the chest, his palm facing in. Custer was in a daze looking around, a blank stare on his face.

Fila took Custer's headset and radio and put it on. She asked about the other half of the team as the withering fire was now just occasional bursts. The other team member was unconscious. Fila told them their situation and said they could use help when they could spare it.

Charlie was quickly and none too carefully breaching each room looking for Davood Faraz Dabdeh, his target. Dabdeh was losing blood and knew it. He started thinking about how he could get excellent medical treatment if he simply surrendered. There was a noise, and he looked up and there was Charlie with an M4 pointed at him. Dabdeh was caught flat-footed and stared into Charlie's cold eyes.

He said, "I surrender, American. I need medical care,"

and he dropped his AK-47 and raised his one working arm.

Charlie had forgotten that Dabdeh could speak a little English and even had a little bit of a British accent.

Charlie raised the M4 up to look through the holographic sight. He put the red dot on the center of Dabdeh's chest.

Davood gulped nervously, "I surrender. You do not want your CNN to say you are a murderer, now, do you?"

The President, Pops, and Kerri all listened, as did the remaining translator Samireh.

Charlie said, "I am Master Sergeant Charlie Strongheart, a dog soldier of the Lakota Nation, descendant of Chief Sitting Bull and great-nephew of White Bull. I am with the 1st Special Forces Operational Detachment-Delta, and we do not perform for the news media. We operate in the shadows. I am a warrior, not a murderer, and I am here to kill you. I am not here on a mercy mission. You know the rules of the game. Now die."

He squeezed the trigger, and Davood Faraz Dabdeh stopped smiling, as his heart exploded from all the bullets that tore into it. He slammed against the wall and slid into a sitting position, eyes opened wide in horror at death. Charlie took out his cell phone and started snapping pictures.

The President of the United States called Pops, and the colonel answered.

The President identified himself and said, "Are you on a secure line?"

Pops said, "Yes, Mr. President."

The commander in chief said, "We will have to do a citation about her carrying troops to safety and giving them medical care under fire in Afghanistan or Iraq. Americans don't want their pretty young daughters getting shot and killing bad guys. We will have to make up a fake battle in one of those countries, but if I do not get anything else through Congress before I leave office, those two are going to be awarded the Medal of Honor. Everybody else on that mission better be getting nothing lower than the Silver Star. We will have a talk with the translators. Now I have something else to attend to right away. Get them home safe, pal."

"We will, Mr. President."

The three Little Birds buzzed back toward the desert base camp and soon spotted an Iranian Elite Republican Guard patrol on Highway 5 around the BMW. They were checking it out and had picked up the body of the terrorist Fila had shot dead. Charlie pulled out a small box, waited until a civilian car had driven safely past and beyond it, and pushed the enter button. The car exploded just as some of the soldiers noticed the Little Birds skimming over the desert floor.

The Detachment-Delta team had no deaths but a number of wounded. They still had to get out of Iran, though. The president of Iran was being rushed to an underground bunker, as were several high ayatollahs, imams, and government officials. The official alarm had just gone off that Tehran was under attack by Israel and the United States. Jet fighters had been scrambled, but several of them hearing the alert suddenly had trouble getting their jets started.

THE President turned to Kerri Rhodes. "Kerri, I want you to personally go to the CIA and speak to those translators."

She left and the President stood in front of his desk.

He called for his secretary, and he said, "Send in that reporter, please."

The young man entered the room, and they introduced themselves.

The President said, "Have a seat, Alan. Please."

They sat down, the President in a chair and Alan in a small love seat right in front of the center rug, individually designed by each new president.

The chief executive said, "Well, Alan, I promised you an exclusive interview, and you are going to get it. But first, off the record, why did you come to us instead of your editor with this outlandish story by this Major General Rozanski? I would think, even though it was not true, it could have gotten you plenty of accolades and awards for your paper."

"Well," Alan said, "Mr. President, I did not like the general when we met, but I do not allow that to interfere with how I write a news story. But I wondered how a man could make a living fighting for this country and wearing a uniform and then betray his chain of command. My father earned a Silver Star in Vietnam in the U.S. Navy. He was a Seabee, and I saw how the press treated him and other Vietnam veterans."

"Good for your father," the commander in chief said.

Alan went on. "Then during the course of the interview, the major kept getting angry, sir, and he called you a damned queer."

The President laughed and said, "I certainly have been called a lot worse, young man."

"That was not it, Mr. President," Alan said. "I am gay, sir, and my boyfriend, who I loved very much, was a New York City firefighter. He gave his life saving others in World Trade Center Building Number One on September 11, 2001. It is more important to me to preserve truth, and Thomas's legacy, than to build my journalism career on some self-centered egomaniac's political ambitions."

The President said, "Why aren't there more journalists like you around? I thought they all died."

He went to his desk and got a notebook, and returned, and started looking at his notes.

First, he looked at the reporter and said, "Alan, first of all, I want to express my deepest condolences on your loss of Thomas. You should always be very proud of him. Secondly, I did some checking on the names Major General Rozanski accused of this. Master Sergeant Charlie Strongheart is not in Delta Force. He is a Green Beret serving at Fort Bragg. That Sergeant First Class Fila Jannat he mentioned is an intelligence specialist and is a member of an intelligence group that is attached to Special Forces at Fort Bragg, also. She has a desk job and this loon tries to claim there are women in Delta Force? Working closely at Bragg is where I am told that she and Sergeant Strongheart met and fell in love. His group is deployed to Afghanistan, and she has been deployed there, too. We just got word today that their complex was attacked and both of them and many others were severely wounded, but from the report I got they were in the mountainous area along the Pakistani border and came under attack because they were developing solid leads about al Qaeda leadership hiding in that area just across the border. They are both in a hospital in Germany, and Sergeant Strongheart is undergoing surgery right now.

"The report I got was that either al Qaeda or Taliban or both attacked their compound and both of them were wounded, and Sergeant Jannat continuously exposed herself to enemy fire to save wounded soldiers from her office and dragged and carried some to safety under fire, and Sergeant Strongheart also distinguished himself by leading repeated attacks against the enemy, killing many, despite his own wounds. I will give you the exclusive news break on it as soon as our Public Affairs Office gives us the release. I will tell you this. I spoke to the overall task force commander there and both his and her commanding officers, and both of them have been submitted for the Medal of Honor, our nation's highest honor, and this trash-talking desk jockey general wants to slander two of our nation's bravest and finest. Rozanski knows about the investigations going on about his own moral character and shady dealings, so he is simply trying to divert attention."

"He is being investigated?" Alan said.

The President said, "You didn't know that? I'll have to ask the FBI director and secretary of the army what I can tell you, but we will definitely give you the exclusive on Major General Damien Rozanski. Give me a few days to talk to those people and find out what we can say right now, but you can be there when he is arrested if you want."

The President asked Alan if he wanted tea or coffee and started thinking about how he would teach Damien Percy Rozanski about playing politics with the big boys.

EPILOGUE

THE Crow Indians scouted for Custer, and it was odd and kind of neat that it was Crows who allowed Charlie and Fila's wedding to be held on their land, below the National Monument, on the very ground where part of the giant encampment had stood. It was nice for the guests to see the couple in U.S. Army dress blues, like half the wedding party, with the other half in white buckskins. After the Special Forces chaplain pronounced them husband and wife, it was also neat to see them mount up on two beautiful white Arabian geldings with eagle feathers tied in their manes and tails and ride where Charlie's ancestors rode.

While the attendees watched, they cantered along the Little Big Horn River, by the cottonwood groves, and the two geldings sensed they were showing off. They tossed their heads around, their long manes flying from side to side, and lifted their tails up in the air, curling off to one side. Charlie and Fila rode around imagining the circles of teepees and thousands of happy people surrounding them. Fila looked at the Arabian horses and thought about the beautiful horses like these she had seen in Iran.

Pops leaned over to Weasel and Custer and said, "Did you two hear about Major General Percy Rozanski today on the news riding over here?"

Custer said, "No, sir. What happened?"

Pops said, "The son of a bitch got arrested today, because of that big exposé in the big New York City newspaper. They say he dipped into his unit fund for thousands he spent on hookers and Internet porn."

Weasel said, "Couldn't have happened to a nicer guy, Boss."

At the reception, Kerri Rhodes presented the couple with a large engraved silver bowl from the President and First Lady.

She looked at Fila and said, "Okay, now since nothing is ever going to happen between us, can I give the groom a kiss?"

"Sure," Fila said, and was glad that worry had disappeared.

A young lady approached the couple. She was shy and backward, a little overweight, wore glasses and braces, but her smile was a mile wide, as she meekly spoke to them.

She said, "Sergeant Strongheart and, uh, Sergeant Strongheart. I am so very honored to be here. I did not want to bother either of you, but I wanted to thank you both so much for buying my airline ticket here, and taking care of my hotel room and meals. This is so wonderful and what a romantic wedding."

Fila said, "Samireh Ahoo?"

"Yes, ma'am."

Fila swept her up in a nice warm hug and said, "You saved my husband's life. I will never forget you, Samireh."

Samireh had tears in her eyes and said, "I will never forget you. You both saved my mother country and our world from another madman. There are many there who love Americans, but they must hide it."

Fila had tears in her eyes, too.

She smiled warmly and said, "Samireh, I know. It is my mother country, too, but now I have a new country that I love so much more than any place I could ever live."

Samireh said, "Oh, I know. I love it so much here in America. I want my children and grandchildren to grow up here. If I ever find a man."

Fila said, "Just be patient. Good men are hard to find, and good men who are also real men are even harder to find, but they are there."

Charlie, who had gotten Fila a glass of punch, handed it to her with a kiss, turned, and said, "Samireh, will you do me the honor of dancing with me? I think peace in the world begins with music, dancing, and lots of smiles."